AF278750

Terror West

Book Five

Mother Trucker Book Series

Terror West

Copyright ©2017 by CRLE Publishing

Mitchell, Robyn

This is a work of fiction. All names, characters, places, and incidents are the products of the author's imagination or are used fictitiously. Any resemblance to current or local events or to living persons is entirely coincidental.

Library of Congress Cataloging-in –Publication Data

p. cm

ISBN: 978-0-9972129-6-9   PCN: 2017937616

I. Truckers—Fiction II. Trucking Industry—Fiction III. Adventure Fiction
Fic MitPS 3606.A775M46

Editor-in-Chief: Mindy Reed, The Authors' Assistant
Interior Designed by Danielle H. Acee, The Authors' Assistant
Cover Design by Douglas Brown, Album Artist

Printed in the United States

TERROR WEST

ROBYN MITCHELL

PUBLISHING

Odessa, TX

For my husband, C.L.

Thank you for your patience and unquestioning support throughout the process of bringing this story to fruition. Without you, there would be no book.

CHAPTER ONE

"OH, MY GOD!" Shelby shouted. She dove under the sleeper portion of her truck, belly down. Her hands covered her head, and her nose was against the cement as shots rang out around her. Then, there was a sudden silence.

She slowly lifted her face and peered through the space between the two front steer tires. Fire and smoke rose in the air. The mangled metal of several eighteen wheel trucks and bodies—a lot of bodies—were strewn all over the parking lot where the Dallas truck stop once stood.

"Shelby, Shelby!" a voice rang out. Angelica slid out from under her truck, where she had taken refuge and crawled toward Shelby. "Shelby, are you okay?"

The ringing in her ears was so intense that Shelby could barely recognize her best friend's voice.

"Angelica, it's Shield Sheik. They're attacking us; I know it's them."

The DEA agent, still stunned, stood up and held out her hand, encouraging Shelby to emerge from under her truck.

"I agree with you that Shield Sheik has something to do with this." Angelica pointed toward the fire and carnage. "Two Shield Sheik trucks, or at least what's left of them, are parked right over there next to the store."

"I told you they were planning to do something awful!" Shelby was yelling because she was still unable to hear clearly. She took in the devastation around her. "We just came out of that café…All those people in there…Oh, Angelica, this is worse than I could have ever imagined."

Angelica looked at the parking lot and turned her thoughts to triage. "Right now, we have to go help as many of those people over there as we can." She looked at her shaken partner. "Are you hurt?"

Shelby brushed at the dirt from her clothes. She was still in shock, which kept her from feeling any pain. As her head cleared, she surveyed the bodies, the store—now a pile of smoldering wood and broken bricks—and the fuel island. It was ablaze with flames that seemed to reach toward heaven. "I'm fine. Come on!"

◊◊◊

"Oh, Angelica, she's the cutest little girl I've ever seen."

Angelica swelled with pride at the sight of her child. Angelica, her husband Rex, Jack, and Shelby, with little Harley Amber Brighten cradled in her arms, were enjoying a morning of breakfast, coffee, and conversation at the FJ Truck Stop.

"She's been a really good baby," Angelica replied. She pointed with her fork toward Rex, "Harley started sleeping all night at about three weeks, and Rex appreciates the extra sleep."

Rex sipped his coffee. "I sure do. Believe me, that little girl has some lungs on her when she's hungry! As long as I make sure her butt's dry and her tummy is full, she's content to just play and coo all day."

Rex gently bumped Angelica with his arm and looked with fondness at his wife. "Kind of reminds me of her mother: make sure she has a full tank of gas in a big truck, a bad guy to hunt down, and she'll play all day long on the road."

Jack laughed and pushed his plate to the center of the table. He picked up his mug and gulped the last of his coffee. "I know what you mean, Rex. Since Shelby graduated from the academy, she's been chomping at the bit to get back into a rig."

Shelby put the baby closer to Jack so he could take hold of a tiny hand. "Doesn't this make you want to have one of our own, Jack? You know I've always wanted a little girl."

Jack quickly pulled his hand back. He raised his cup in the air so the waitress could see he wanted more coffee. "No."

Shelby cuddled Harley. "Oh, come on, Jack. You can't tell me that having a little girl in the family wouldn't be fun. The boys would love her, and she would have three big brothers to protect her."

"No," Jack said emphatically, waiting impatiently for the waitress the fill his cup. "Enjoy holding her and spoiling her from time to time Shelby, because we are not having any more kids. Who do you think is going to take care of that little girl while you're out saving the world? Not me. I just don't have the time, especially now that I've been promoted to Corporate VP. I barely have time for you these days."

Shelby sighed and continued cuddling the infant. "I know, but she's so beautiful."

Harley began to whimper, and Angelica handed Shelby a baby bottle. "I tell you what, Shelby, now that the agency has moved us to Dallas, and we are partners, you can come get her whenever you like and keep her for a few days."

"That would be awesome." Shelby put the bottle in Harley's mouth and cradled the little girl.

Jack smiled and touched the baby's hand again. "That's what I'm talking about; you can come stay with Aunt Shelby every once in a while." Jack looked at Rex. "She's wonderful, Rex, but I sure don't envy you. I love my boys and wouldn't trade them for the world. I even like having the grand-kids around once in a while, but I'm glad that the 'raising kids' part of my life is over."

"I hear you, brother, but I really love taking care of Harley when Angelica is away. I think we are going to have one more and that will be it for us." Rex looked at his wife.

Angelica laughed. "Not right away, mister. Maybe in a couple of years we can think about having another one. I just lost the baby fat and got cleared for duty. I'm not giving up all my hard work for another baby right now."

Rex put his arm around his wife's shoulders and pulled her close to him. "Not right now, silly."

"Good. I was thinking I was going to have to hit you over the head with that breakfast skillet to help you think more clearly."

Rex moved in for a kiss, but Angelica's cell phone rang. She looked at the screen, nodded at Shelby, and motioned for Rex to move out of the way so she could slide out of the booth. "Here we go; it's Cody."

Rex sat back in the booth after Angelica removed herself. Shelby handed Harley to Rex, and then she motioned for Jack to let her out. "I'd better go use the little girl's room; looks like we just got orders."

As Angelica moved toward the front door, she listened to her new handler's instructions over the phone.

Shelby met up with her in the parking lot. Angelica filled Shelby in as they quickly made their way to their trucks. "That son-of-a-bitch Shades somehow slipped away from the agents in Alabama."

"Seriously? The bastard got away again? How?" Shelby was dumbfounded.

"We got a tip that someone may have him spotted in Atlanta," Angelica replied. "Cody wants us to truck our way to Georgia. We aren't exactly assigned to finding Shades. Our assignment is to track down Glacier Transports Associates."

"Who is Glacier Transports Associates?" Shelby asked.

"It's actually an international holding company that's not really in our jurisdiction. They've got outlets in the U.S., and that is our main area of investigation, but Cody knows how much I want to catch that prick, Shades, so he's keeping me up on that investigation, as well," Angelica explained. "The truck ring that's supposedly smuggling coke and other drugs around the country has two trucks currently headed down The 20, possibly toward Georgia. Cody wants us to follow them and keep an eye on all their stops and contacts. Since we'll be in the Atlanta area, he says we can also unofficially conduct our own surveillance on Shades."

"I really want to catch that monster."

"Me too, Shelby."

The women reached their respective trucks. "I'll be down on channel 22; we can talk more about this when we get on the road," Angelica said. "I want to at least find those trucks and make it to Birmingham before nightfall."

Shelby nodded at her DEA partner. "I got it—channel 22, Birmingham, Alabama before nightfall." She reached into her jean pocket and pulled out the keys to her truck. Before she could get her door open, she suddenly felt a tap on her shoulder. She turned with a start and then smiled when she realized it was only Jack.

Jack lifted up her purse and held it out for her to take. "I think you forgot something in the restaurant."

Shelby took the purse and threw her arms around her husband's neck. "Thanks, Jack, you've always got my back. I was having so much fun with baby Harley, I forgot all about it." She gave him a deep kiss. "Are you sure you don't want to try to have a little baby girl? It would be so fun making one."

Jack returned the passionate kiss and then stepped back. "You know I've got your back, and I would absolutely take you right now in the back of this big truck, but we are not having, adopting, or fostering any little girl or boy. I love you, Shelby Mathews, but I do not want any more kids."

"I know, but it was worth a second try." Shelby pulled away to open her driver's door.

Jack wrapped his arms around her waist and kissed her neck. "We've been through a lot over our years together, and I wasn't thrilled with you becoming a trucker, nor am I thrilled that you've decided to join the DEA, but you know you're my girl. I love you. I will support you."

Shelby turned and gave her husband a deep kiss. Then she opened her door and climbed the stairs. "I know, baby. You're my man." She threw her purse into the passenger seat and sat in the driver's seat.

Shelby started her truck while Jack stood on the steps for one more goodbye. "Please be careful, Shelby. Some really terrible stuff is taking place around the world, and they say it could be coming here."

Shelby gently stroked her husband's face. "Always and forever. Remember, Jack, always and forever."

With that, Jack kissed Shelby one last time and stepped down off her truck. He walked around the front of the big rig and waved.

Angelica and Shelby pulled their trucks out of the truck stop, and Shelby keyed her CB mic. "You know it's going to be hard making Birmingham before dark."

Angelica responded over the CB, "I know that, rookie, but I wanted to make sure you knew I was in a hurry. You take too long saying goodbye to that old man of yours."

Shelby laughed. "Yes, ma'am, boss lady. You know it's funny, these last few times I've changed companies you've been my trainer."

"Welcome to the DEA, Mrs. Mathews. Remember, we are here to keep the people of America safe from the drug dealers and their cronies."

"Protect and serve."

"I just wanted to say that I'm really sorry that you couldn't put the 'Barbie Car' out here on the road with you. I know you wanted to drive her, but she's too distinctive and unique for this undercover stuff we do."

"It's all good. I hired a cute little blonde female driver to keep her running for me in the oil patch."

"Like Barbie's little sister, Skipper?"

"Yep, she's turning out to be a good sand hauler."

"That's great."

"Yeah, I'm still making money with my truck while being an undercover agent. Jack likes that the truck's not just sitting at the house."

"Good. Let's get down this highway as far as we can before our eleven hours of driving time expires. Shades was in Alabama about two days ago, from the last intel Cody had on him. Apparently, he is back with Dante in Atlanta, and Dante is protecting him."

"Why would he be doing that? Didn't Shades cause Dante a lot of trouble?"

"Cody seems to think Dante is making deals with some new trucking company out of the Middle East. So, things could get really interesting."

"What's the name of the company?"

"Shield Sheik, or something like that. It's owned by some rich Middle Eastern guys, but they've got subsidiaries here in the U.S. They mostly hire and do business with American citizens of Middle Eastern decent."

"I've never heard of Shield Sheik. It must be a fairly new company or still small-time when I was long hauling. Most of the international drivers were very private. Most of them had family, or at least their wives with them, but they kept to themselves. They were very much about doing their jobs and sticking to business. I wonder why Dante is trying to use them? Better yet, why would Shield Sheik want to mess with Dante?"

"At this point, we have no idea if Shield Sheik is actually doing business with Dante. He's originally from Louisiana and his family is Cajun, but I suspect it has something to do with the money. Cody says the company is growing by leaps and bounds, with several new trucks. They are constantly hiring new drivers."

"Didn't the DEA take out most of his distribution?"

"We did, but somehow Dante avoided prosecution. He needs trucks to distribute his products, but he knows we are keeping a close eye on him. This company is so private that Cody has had a lot of trouble tracking down their terminals and their load information. The company hauls just about everything, and doesn't ask too many questions of the businesses that they haul for, which is a benefit for Dante. Somehow they are able to stay under the radar."

"That doesn't make sense if the people who own Shield Sheik are Muslim, Cover Girl. Doesn't Islam forbid drugs and alcohol? Do they even know what they are carrying?" Shelby asked.

"We all know of situations where followers have disobeyed their faith. Heck, I know people in my own congregation who are hypocrites," Angelica replied. "I can't even say for sure if this company has anything that has to do with Islam or if the owners or employees are Muslims. I never really thought about it. All I know for sure is that they are headquartered in the Middle East, but if they're in business with Dante, they're involved in something illegal. Their drivers might not ask too many questions about their loads, but the upper management of that company knows very well what they are hauling. Right now, we need to find those trucks Cody asked us to track. The last he knew, they were located around Tyler."

"How do we know they are still in that area?" Shelby asked.

"We don't. Most of the information we are getting is from truckers, working as informants for some of our agents in the area. They've been paying close attention to their routines and behaviors. There is plenty of reason to suspect they are transporting drugs. They may even be into human trafficking, and if that's the case, the FBI will want to get their share of the takedown."

"That doesn't seem fair; if we bust them for human trafficking, that bust should be ours," Shelby objected.

"I hear ya, Barbie. Of course, they'll wait for us to do all the leg work before they come in and take over, but our job is to take out the kingpins, dealers, and mules who are distributing drugs across this country. We leave the rapists, kidnappers, and scumbags that sell other people for profit to other agencies."

"What's the plan if we can't locate them in Tyler?"

"Well, the company name on the side of the trucks is, 'Glacier Transportation.' Checks on the legitimacy of that company's name have turned up nothing. We haven't had anyone close enough to the trucks yet to get a DOT number. So, that will be one of our first jobs when we locate these guys. Our informants are supposed to let us know when they move, if they can. Hopefully, they will stay put until we can get there."

"Are we going to take them down as soon as we come in contact with them?"

"No, we will get as much information off their trucks as possible. Then we will follow them as far as they go. We need to track their movements, find out who they are meeting, and if possible, what cargo they have in their trailers. We can get permission to bring some trusted truckers into the operation if their assistance helps take down some of the nefarious local connections. I plan to make as many busts as I can. I want Dante to squirm and know that I'm back and coming for him and his little drug smuggling operation."

"I see. This is kind of like what Pig was doing, just with different people."

"Exactly, Shelby. The problem with Pig's takedown by the FBI and DEA was that they didn't shut down the whole operation. I'm pretty sure a lot of the people who we are tracking had some type of connection with Pig before he got busted. I'd also bet that the Mexican cartel that kidnapped you is still moving their product the same way, just with different players."

"Wow! That's got to be a lot of folks. How are we going to shut them all down? It's like playing Whack-a-Mole—we get one group down and two more pop up."

"That's about the size of it, but we just have to keep chipping away at these organizations. When we take them down and confiscate their stuff, we get them where it hurts the most—their pocketbooks. This outfit we are tracking might be under the radar, but this could possibly be one of the biggest takedowns ever. The intelligence shows that this cartel is pretty brazen; they've been using a lot of their own family members to distribute their stuff."

"You mean people in their immediate families?"

"Yep. And extended family, too. People they know will be really loyal. "

"That sickens me. How can they live with themselves, knowing that they are putting their own family members at risk of going to jail or getting killed by other dealers, or even by us? Any number of things could happen to them, especially the women."

"They don't care, Barbie. Most of these cartels are family-run businesses like the Mafia. The only thing important to them is the money. Remember what they taught you at the academy: keep your emotions in check, your instincts on high alert, and always question everyone's motives. Sometimes your instincts will be correct and sometimes they won't, but never underestimate a perp or a possible perp. Don't trust, always verify," Angelica instructed.

Shelby reviewed the instruction in her head and then recited, "Take everything someone says as a lie, until you verify what they say is truth. Take unexpected movements as flight or aggression, until they comply with your verbal requests. Use lethal force only when you feel that your life or someone else's life is in imminent danger."

"Those rules will keep you from getting your ass in a jam out here, and your body off a slab in a morgue." The warning was clear in Angelica's voice.

"I will do my best, partner. I know I have a lot to learn, but they gave me the best trainer out there."

"Just watch my back."

"You got it. Hey, we are almost to Tyler?"

"Yeah, I just got a text from Cody. The trucks we're tracking appear to be preparing to leave. I'll send you into the truck stop when we get up here. I want you to check out the parking lot to see if they are still parked or if they've already left. It will take us a few minutes to get to that exit. I'm not sure if we will need to hold back and wait for them or haul ass to catch them."

"I got it, Cover Girl."

"I will let you know in a few minutes. You should back off a little, that way if they aren't coming out on the ramp, you can take the exit; then I'll back the truck down to a slow cruise until you let me know whether they are coming out of the truck stop or if they have already hopped onto the big road."

"Okay." Shelby backed her truck down and waited for Angelica's instructions.

Angelica's calm voice came across the CB. "Forget the exit, Shelby. Our two rigs are on the ramp right now. Come on up here and put your nose in my back door. We'll slow cruise for a while and give them time to pass us. I want to get a look at those DOT numbers."

"I'm almost at your back door." Shelby observed the two blue Petes pulling white box trailers with enormous pictures of sun-drenched mountains on each side. "Wow, they went all out for a fictional company logo, didn't they?"

"That's common, most of these cartels will go to great lengths to appear legit."

"I see two male drivers; one might be Hispanic. I couldn't get a really good look at the driver of the truck in the back." Shelby shared.

"Good job, Barbie. Way to be observant. We'll get a better look at both of them when they pass us up. Back your truck down to sixty-five, they'll pass us for sure at that speed. You stay here on our channel. I'm going down to 19 and channel eight to see if they are communicating."

"Okay, but channel eight?" Shelby was confused.

Angelica spoke quickly and quietly, "I'll explain later."

As soon as Angelica went over on the other channels, Shelby felt a quiet envelop her in her truck. She turned on the radio to listen to the news for a while. "The final year of this administration is coming to a close..." Shelby pushed the button on the screen in her dash to locate another station. She wasn't in the mood for politics. "It is predicted that terror attacks will increase this year in America," a voice from the next station announced. Shelby pushed another button.

"Who wants to hear about all the things that might happen? I want to know about what is happening right now." She pushed one more button and finally located a country music station. The song playing brightened her mood. "That's more like it." She hummed along to the tune and began singing to herself.

She was suddenly interrupted by her partner's voice on the CB radio. "How about you, Barbie?"

Shelby keyed the mic to her CB. "You got Barbie. What's happening, Cover Girl?"

"Barbie, I overheard them talking on channel eight. They're headed to Birmingham to make a small pickup before heading to Georgia in the morning. That will be perfect for us; we can check out their trucks and maybe even find out who they are making contact within Birmingham for that pick up. They're conversing in Spanish, so I'm pretty sure they are involved with at least one of the Mexican cartels." Angelica was energized. "I'm going to continue to monitor channel eight for a while just in case they might have any change of plans."

"Okay, do you want me to move to channel eight, too?"

"No, stay down here on this one. Most of the language spoken on eight is Spanish, anyway. I can understand most of what they are saying, but I need a safe channel where I can talk with you when I get more information."

"Channel eight is a Spanish channel?"

"Yeah, I'm surprised you didn't know that. It's been that way for a long time, especially in West Texas."

"I suppose I should have known, but I never had cause to change from channel 19 unless I was in a sand or pick-up yard. Most everyone I ran with used 19. You go ahead and take the Spanish channel, I'm not fluent enough to know exactly what they are saying."

"You might want to start studying up. It will help you be a better DEA agent since we deal with so many Spanish-speaking people. Besides that, it's a beautiful language everyone should know; I'd be happy to teach it to you."

"That would be awesome. Like I said, I know some words, but being able to speak and understand all of it would be terrific."

"Cool, we will start working on that tonight. Hey, look out your window; here come those two trucks. I knew if we held back on the speed for a while they would go around us. Listen up, I want them a few truck lengths ahead of us so we will fall in behind them and follow them all the way to Birmingham."

"Sounds great, Cover Girl, but I need to find a little girl's room real soon."

"Okay, no problem. Just before we cross the line into Shreveport, there's a roadside park. You get off and get back on the big road as fast as you can, and I will stay with our boys until you catch up. They aren't hauling butt, so it shouldn't be too hard."

"Sounds good, Cover Girl. I have the plan in my pocket. Now it's time for you to get back to your Spanish channel and me to get back to my country music!"

Angelica caught Shelby's attempt at a joke. "Funny, Barbie. Talk at you soon."

CHAPTER TWO

It was dark when Shelby and Angelica rolled into Birmingham behind the two trucks they followed all the way from Tyler, Texas. The nearly eleven-hour trip was broken up by only two stops: the rest area outside of Shreveport for Shelby, and in Jackson, Mississippi, where the two trucks they were following briefly pulled into a truck stop.

"Wow, Cover Girl, that was some trucking." Shelby sounded exhausted. "I'm ready for a nap. It's been a while since I've put in a full eleven hours of driving."

"I hear ya, Barbie. Unfortunately, we still have to maintain surveillance on these two yahoos. I will take the first five hours, and you can take the last. We need to make sure they don't leave without us. Let's park these babies and get some dinner. I'm starved."

As Shelby maneuvered her truck backwards into an open parking space, she said, "I'm all for that, Cover Girl, but are you sure you want me to take the last five hours? I don't mind taking the first five."

"No, I'm good. I want to Skype with Rex and Harley anyway." Angelica was backing up into a spot next to Shelby in the parking lot. "I miss my little girl and hubby so much right now. I love my job, but it's going to take me some time to get used to being away from those two."

"I understand, Cover Girl." Shelby had parked her truck and was gathering her things. "Let's get inside and have some food. I'm bringing my stuff for a shower."

Angelica parked and grabbed her shower bag. "I'm ready for that myself. Meet you at the front of the trucks."

Angelica sent a quick text and waited while Shelby locked her truck. "Just sent a text to Cody letting him know we are in Birmingham." She pointed to the two trucks they were following. "They did us a favor parking there; we have full view of their activities from the cabs of our trucks. I saw them both just a few seconds ago; they went into the restaurant. While we're eating, we need to keep our eyes peeled. If they don't meet with anyone inside, then it's likely that someone will meet them in the parking lot. It's also possible that this whole delivery-pickup thing is going to happen off this lot. If that's the case, and they move those trucks to make their contact, we are going to need to follow them—pronto."

They walked to the restaurant and Shelby opened the door for Angelica. "We can't follow them with our big rigs, they'll notice."

"Exactly, that's why my box trailer contains a small car, a motorcycle, and all the fire power we might need."

"Cool." They selected a booth and Shelby slid in on the right side. "I see you have everything under control." She looked around and spotted the two men seated at a table near their booth. Soon the waitress arrived and put a menu in front of her.

"What can I get you ladies to drink?" The waitress asked, pen and order pad ready.

Shelby spoke out first. "I'll have water with lemon."

"Me, too," Angelica said.

"Okay, do you know what you what to eat? We have the buffet and salad bar for ten ninety-nine tonight." The waitress sounded bored from a day of repeating the same information.

They responded in unison: "I'll have that."

After the waitress took the menus and left, Shelby leaned over and whispered to Angelica, "I think I spotted our subjects over there next to the window."

Angelica was staring at her cell phone, retrieving the text messages and emails she had missed while rolling down the highway. "Yeah, I noticed them when we sat down. I have my back to them, so be sure and let me know if they get any visitors."

Shelby slid out of her seat, paused, and stretched. "I will. I'm headed to the salad bar."

Angelica finished up with her phone. "I'm coming, too." She placed her phone in her front pocket and followed Shelby.

"Yummy." Shelby starred at all the vegetables on the bar. "Now, this is what I'm talking about."

Angelica laughed as she piled her plate with pea and potato salad. "You are a nutcase, Shelby Mathews. I've never seen a woman so in love with fresh vegetables."

Nibbling at a raw piece of carrot, Shelby smiled. "I can't help myself; I love anything that is fresh. Especially a fresh, clean man."

Angelica laughed out loud. "I know you're right on that one, Shelby girl."

Shelby looked at Angelica's plate. "Now that stuff probably tastes good, and I'm proud of my bestie for trying to get some good old veggies in her tummy, but I really doubt those peas and potatoes are going to be good for those beautiful hips of yours."

Angelica rolled her eyes. "Leave my hips out of this, Little Miss Rabbit. You eat all that 'good for you' crap, and I'll take care of this yummy stuff."

Shelby smiled and tapped her hip against Angelica's hip as she chomped on a piece of celery. "I'm just saying…."

"Shut up, Barbie." Angelica laughed.

Just as the women were about to return to their table, a man tapped Shelby on the shoulder. "Barbie?"

Shelby turned with a start. "Damian!" She put down her plate and hugged the young man who stood in front of her. "Damn it, boy. How are you?" She pushed him a way slightly and then gave him another hug.

"Angelica, look who's here." Shelby turned her attention to Angelica who had put her plate down and was waiting to hug the young man.

Shelby let Damian go so that Angelica could embrace him. "How the hell are ya, kiddo? It's been a long time since we've seen you."

Shelby hadn't seen Damian for a while. He had aged some, and even had a well-groomed beard, but his big blue eyes were impossible to forget.

"I'm doing pretty good, ladies. I'm still hauling cargo off the broker boards, keeping my head above water at least. What the hell are y'all doing out this way?"

"Come sit with us," Shelby suggested. They picked up their plates, and he followed them to their table. Shelby slid to the far side of the booth and made room for Damian.

"So are you hauling?" Damian asked Shelby.

"Yes. Angelica and I are hauling for Road Riders Trucking."

"Road Riders Trucking?" Damian said, confused, "I ain't never heard of that company before. What do you haul?"

Instead of responding, Shelby and Angelica focused on their plates and started shoveling food into their mouths.

"Oh, I understand," he murmured.

Angelica looked up from her plate and smiled. "Oh, we haul just about everything you can think of, all across the country: cars, motorcycles, bullets..."

Damian smiled back. "So, where are you headed?"

"Georgia. Atlanta, to be specific." Angelica smiled again and winked.

Damian now understood that Shelby and Angelica's trucking work was a cover. "So, do you think you'll have trouble with your delivery in Atlanta? I might be able to help you with some directions."

"Really?" Shelby stopped eating and looked at Damian in the eyes. "I don't think we'll have any problems, but if you have some better directions, we're all ears. Why don't you meet us at our trucks in a little while? I have a map out there to show you. Unless you're getting ready to take off."

"No, I have a friend who's an owner-op; she lives here in Birmingham. We are supposed to take off in the morning again after we finish out our restart. I can come by your trucks. Where are you parked?"

Shelby pointed in the direction of their two trucks. "Down the west side, front line, about half-way down. Can't miss them two simple white babies with the black logos on the doors."

Shelby put her salad plate in the middle of the table and raised an eyebrow. "*Friend* who lives in Birmingham?"

"Just friends." Damian laughed a bit, adjusted his ball cap, and waved his hands in protest. "I swear. She's at her house right now, and I'm here. I just ain't ready to go down that road again yet. I still miss Amber too much. I don't think I'll be ready until that bastard Shades is either dead or locked up. It's just not over for me yet. You know what I mean? I can't go on to something else until it is."

Shelby nodded and sat back. She sipped at her water. "We know, Damian. It isn't finished for us, either." She put down her glass. "Let me out for a minute, Damian, so I can go get some of that roasted chicken. I think they have steamed broccoli, Angelica, That's really good for your skin."

Angelica rolled her eyes, picked up her water, and took a big drink. "I think I'll stick with the mashed potatoes, gravy, and corn."

"Yuck. Carb alert," Shelby sassed her friend.

Damian moved out so Shelby could get to the food bar. "I'll come by the trucks in a little while. I think my shower will be ready by now."

Shelby hugged Damian before heading to the buffet. Angelica touched his arm and then got out of the booth, too. "We will see you in a little while. Shelby needs a bath as well."

Shelby shot Angelica a look.

Angelica laughed. "We both do. We should be out there in an hour or so."

Damian headed toward the cash register. "That'll work."

After retrieving her chicken from the buffet, Shelby sat back down in the booth. Before Angelica could sit, however, Shelby noticed that one of the men they had been watching stood up. Another man approached their table, and they all shook hands and introduced themselves.

"Some man just joined those two men at their table," Shelby whispered to Angelica and sat back down.

"I think I need to go back to the buffet for bread. You need anything?" Angelica asked.

"I'll take more veggies off the salad bar." Shelby knew that if Angelica made a pretense of getting food from the salad bar, she would be in position to hear some of the men's conversation.

"Sure, be right back." Angelica picked up a plate from the side of the salad bar and positioned herself so that she could hear as much from the men as possible. She made a mental note of the accents. The two original men spoke Spanish and were most likely from Mexico's interior. While of similar complexion, the man who had joined them was not Hispanic. He attempted to speak in broken Spanish, but his accent and the English words he reverted to led Angelica to believe his native language was either Farsi or Arabic. She knew she'd need to get a picture of the guy to send to Rex.

Unable to communicate in Spanish, the three lowered their voices and continued in English.

"We will be your new distributor for your product," the newcomer said. "We know that you are having to transport a lot of your product yourselves, and we understand how dangerous it is to involve your families. We have a large operation working here in the United States, with several thousand trucks. We are constantly recruiting new drivers."

"I think we can work something out with you," the older of the two Hispanic men said. "I have to talk to some of my connections in Atlanta to find out what will work for them. Besides money, what is it your people want from us? How do I know that I can trust you?"

His response came quickly, and the first two words were in Arabic. He switched to English. "You can trust us. We have similar interests. We have already had extensive discussions with some very important people involved in your business. They are supportive of our interests. They recommended that I introduce myself to you so you would know who your contact is when the deal is completed."

Angelica was so focused on what she overheard that she dropped some food from her plate onto the foot of the diner in line behind her.

"Hey!" the woman scolded when the broccoli crown bounced off her toe. "Pay attention to what you're doing."

Startled, Angelica's entire plate lurched from her hand and hit the floor.

The men stopped talking when they heard the woman's protest.

Angelica seized the moment. "Sorry," she said. She quickly bent down and positioned herself so that she was able to pull the cell phone from her pocket and snap a picture of the men while making moves to clean up the mess she had created.

A waitress carrying a towel came to assist.

"Oh, thank you so much. I'm such a klutz." She snatched the towel from the waitress and draped it over her hand to conceal her cell phone.

Angelica stood up and backed her way into the men's table, while the waitress helped to clean up the area and calm the other diner. Angelica bumped their table with her butt, which caused a glass of tea on the men's table to tip over. The waitress looked up and sighed.

Tilting the phone under the towel, which now hung near her waist, she snapped some more photos and said back to the waitress in a loud voice, "See, I told you I was a klutz." She pretended to wipe her hand on her hip as she turned toward the men. She was actually slipping the phone back into her pocket. The towel fell to the floor, but she ignored it. The flustered waitress was headed her way. "I'm so sorry," she said to the obviously perturbed men.

The men were not interested in her apology. The man who had joined the original two at the table stood and said in broken Spanish, "Stupid American woman. I will be in touch with you in Atlanta when you make contact with Dante."

Angelica stood there with a blank stare as the man stormed off. She batted her eyelashes at the other two men and smiled. They were amused by her playful flirtation and laughed.

"Sorry, didn't mean to make your friend mad," Angelica said.

"No," the younger of the two men said in heavily accented English. "It was rude of him to be so rude to such a beautiful woman. Would you like to join us?"

"I'd better get back to my friend."

When Angelica made it back to their table without any food, Shelby frowned and then burst out laughing. "Way to go, Agent Brighten; that was some pretty good acting."

Angelica laughed, too. She sat down and looked over at the two men she had just spoken to. Their heads were lowered, and they were talking in hushed tones to one another. Confident they were no longer paying attention to her, she pulled her phone out of her pocket. "All the shenanigans will have been worth it if, I got some good pictures of those guys. Wait 'til I tell you what they were talking about."

"Let's get our showers and then we can talk at the trucks," Shelby suggested.

"Good point, Agent Mathews. We'll have more privacy in our trucks. You take your shower first. I'll keep an eye on those two. We need to know if they are just shutting down for the night or making a delivery."

◊◊◊

After their showers, Angelica and Shelby met back at their trucks. The Glacier Transport drivers did not leave the parking lot. Shelby had finished dressing for bed and was sitting in Angelica's passenger seat. "Doesn't look like those guys are going anywhere tonight. They've got their curtains drawn and everything."

Angelica came out from behind her sleeper curtain, brushing her wet hair. "Yeah, but they might have someone meeting them here later tonight."

"Or they might be making a delivery in the morning. "

Damian knocked on Angelica's driver's side door.

"Possible." Angelica leaned down and opened her driver's side door. "Get in here, you young hunk of a man. Be careful, though; you are entering the Cougar Zone." Angelica pointed toward Shelby while Damian sat in Angelica's driver's seat. "One a little older than the other of course."

Shelby laughed. "Only by 12 years."

"Well, if I'm in danger, what a way to go!" Damian smiled.

"You always say the sweetest things." Angelica touched Damian's face. "So, young man, what you been up to these last few years? I haven't heard a thing from you."

Damian stared out the windshield. "Oh, just trucking around the country while trying to find that snake, Shades. I hooked up with some new truckers—like Skyler, my female trucker friend. She and I truck together a lot."

Shelby raised an eyebrow. "Tell us more."

"Like I said before, she's from here *and* we're just friends."

"Well, it's good you've got some new friends, but don't forget about your old ones."

"Never. You guys have been on my mind a lot lately. In fact, after I found out where Shades was last week, I was going to call you guys and let you know. I thought I had Shelby's number in my cell phone, but it must have disappeared when I changed carriers. I called that trucking company you used to work for, but they said you quit."

"Yeah, I went to school and became a DEA agent. Angelica and I are partners."

"Really? Wow, that's cool. Quite a change from being a trucker, I'll bet."

"Well, I don't have to make delivery times. I'm not being scrutinized by DOT on hours or breaks. I still get to truck around the country without all the stress and B.S., and I get to do it with my best friend. They let me carry a loaded gun, and I get to hunt down bad guys. Who could ask for more?" She sounded almost giddy.

"True. We let her carry a gun, we just haven't let her use it yet." Angelica laughed.

Damian laughed, too. "Guess I have two friends in high places now."

"Well, I don't know about high places, but we are definitely your friends." Angelica sat on her sleeper bed. "Now, tell us what you know about Shades. We have some intel on him as well, but we can always use more."

"I tracked him down at Dante's estate two days ago, but I had to make my load delivery and couldn't stay to watch his movements. Dante is definitely protecting him. Shades and Dante are working with several trucking companies now. I guess they figure if they use several companies, it will be harder to tell where the drugs are. One is called 'Glacier' something. I've never seen their logo out on the road before, so I'm guessing they're new. I only observed one truck at the estate while I was watching it. The other companies I saw at the estate are Dover Trucking Company, Prince Island Trucking Company, and another one with an unusual name, 'Shield Shams,' or something like that. To be honest, I didn't really pay that much attention because I'm more interested in taking down Shades than the other stuff Dante has going on. Not that I approve of any of it.

"I asked Skyler if she knew about this Shield Sham outfit. Word is their corporate headquarters in somewhere in the Middle East—maybe Iran or Iraq. They never put any loads on the broker boards. They only hire people from the Middle East, too. Saudi Arabia and Syria, I think that's what she said. Hell, they're all Arabs to me."

Angelica didn't have time to give Damian lessons in geography or political correctness. She realized that different people had wildly ranging opinions on the situation in the Middle East. She got enough in her line of work. There were plenty of agencies tasked with trying to discern who was friend or foe of The United States. She and Shelby were tasked with drug enforcement, and that had to be their focus. "That's all very helpful information, Damian," Angelica said. "Does Skyler have any idea what they're hauling?"

"She doesn't know much about them, but I can tell you, they've got a bunch of trucks. If you pay attention, you see them everywhere. Skyler has her suspicions about them. All the drivers stay to themselves, and they almost never speak English. It's obvious to her that they don't approve of women drivers. She's pretty sure some of them have called her 'whore' under their breath. I think she's being paranoid. But...they don't seem to be taking away too much business off the broker boards, especially with all the trucks they own."

"Are you sure about the name?" Angelica asked. "Could it be Shield Sheik by any chance?"

"Yeah, I think that's it. If I don't see one of their trucks in this parking lot soon, I'll give Skyler a call and ask her. A few years ago, no one ever saw them on the road, but now they are everywhere. If you gals are looking into them, is it possible that Skyler's suspicions about them are valid?"

"I wouldn't go that far. The feds still have a pretty good handle on threats coming into this country. I'm sure if there was a terrorist organization building up a sleeper cell in the trucking industry, Homeland Security would be all over it."

Shelby reached for a pad of paper that was on the dashboard and wrote down Angelica's and her phone numbers and handed the slip of paper to Damian. "Here, put these in your phone so you won't lose them."

"We're on our way to Atlanta tomorrow," Angelica said. "We've got a lead on some drug traffickers; that's our main assignment. But no matter what, Shelby and I are determined to hunt down Shades. He's not getting away with what he did to Amber—we promise you that."

"The information you've given is a big help," Shelby assured him.

"I hope so. But DEA agents or not, I'm telling you that I'm never going to stop until I see that bastard buried six feet under for killing Amber. He has to pay for what he did."

"I understand, Damian, and we can use your help, but we don't want you hurt. Shades is a mean son-of-a-bitch. He doesn't care about anyone or anything, only himself and his empire," Angelica said. "We are on this. I promise we will get him. And we don't want you becoming a vigilante. You're the one who could go to jail if you try to take the law into your own hands."

"I know, but I want to help. There isn't a day that goes by I don't think about Amber."

Shelby touched Damian's arm. "We know. We just don't want to see you hurt, arrested, or killed."

"So what if he does kill me? If he does, then I get to be with Amber."

"That's not what Amber would want for you," Shelby said.

"Anyway," Damian continued, "I'm heading back to Atlanta with Skyler after she finishes her break at home. I'll catch up with you there." Damian moved to open the door. "I need to go get some rest."

Damian's sudden change in attitude did not escape Angelica's observation. He seemed in a hurry to leave. She studied his face and noticed a tear forming in the corner of his eye. "Okay, Damian, we will talk at you in Atlanta. Be sure and call me later. I need the confirmation on the name of that trucking company."

Damian stepped out of Angelica's truck. "Sure will."

After Damian left, Shelby looked at Angelica who was now seated in her driver's seat. "What was that all about?"

"Oh, just a young buck not wanting to show his true emotions."

"I thought I saw that in his eyes," Shelby confirmed.

◊◊◊

"Shelby, wake up," Angelica yelled over the CB.

Startled, Shelby jumped from her sleeper bed and grabbed the mic on her CB. "Yeah, I'm up. I'm up! I'm ready to take my turn at watch. What time is it? My alarm didn't go off."

"Never mind that, Shelby, look out the windshield. I told you they would do something during the night."

Shelby pulled her sleep curtain back slightly and looked across the parking lot. There they were, out in the open, loading cargo out of their trucks into a van. "Where is security on this lot?"

"They don't have any. I'm looking at the van's license plate through my binoculars, but I can't make out the complete tag number. Probably a rental. I'm going to get out and go get a cup of coffee. I might be able to get a better look at the plate as I walk across the lot. You keep your eyes on them. I'll be back."

"Be careful, Angelica. They might notice you looking at them."

When Shelby did not get a reply, she knew that Angelica was already out of her truck.

Shelby watched as several men took cargo boxes from the two Glacier Transport trucks and put the cargo into the white van. She saw Angelica talking on her cell phone and walking toward the trucks. Suddenly, Damian appeared from out of nowhere and joined Angelica in the middle of the parking lot. They hugged and appeared to be having a conversation. Shelby admired Angelica's brilliance. The seasoned operative always seemed to know what to do to get what she wanted, without letting anyone know what she was actually doing.

Shelby continued to watch. Damian appeared and she saw him write something down on a piece of paper and hand it to Angelica. Then the two hugged and Damian walked with Angelica toward the coffee shop. The men who were unloading the trucks looked at the couple for just a few seconds and continued with their work.

"Mission accomplished! Way to go, boss lady."

CHAPTER THREE

"Angelica! Get up, Angelica! The trucks are moving toward the fuel islands. I'm heading that way now." Shelby let go of her mic and released the air brakes on her truck. She moved her truck in behind the Glacier trucks waiting for an open fuel spot.

"Yeah, okay. I'm awake." Angelica keyed her mic. She hurriedly brushed her hair and threw on some jeans and a t-shirt. After pulling her truck into a fuel line, she keyed her mic again. "I'm in line, but I need coffee. You stick with them, Barbie. I'll catch up with you on the big road if I can't make it out of here at the same time as you do."

"You got it, boss lady. We only have about two and a half hours to Atlanta. I'm going to call you on your cell phone."

"10-4. Let me put my Bluetooth in my ear." Angelica yawned, and then her phone rang. "What's up, Barbie Doll?"

"Well, I was just wondering what the plans were when we get into Atlanta. Since I'm getting out of my truck here in a few minutes to fuel, I thought using my cell phone would be smart. I'm also right next to one of the Glacier Transport trucks, and I wrote down the DOT number for Cody."

"Way to go, Barbie. I'll make an agent out of you yet." Angelica laughed at her own joke. "Just give it to Cody today when you make your daily call-in report. He'll run it through the computer database and see if it's legitimate."

"What if it's not legit, are we going to bust them?"

"No, not right away. We'll contact DOT and give them a heads up on our investigation; that way they'll know to leave them alone for a while. Once we complete our investigation, and take down a good chunk of their distribution empire, then we'll bust them. Right now, those numbers are our tracking devices into Dante's world."

"Okay. I'm finished fueling. I'm going in for a fuel ticket and some coffee. Those two drivers are in the truck stop right now, so I'd better hurry. I don't want them leaving without me."

"I'm fueling right now. I won't be too far behind you."

"Sounds good."

◊◊◊

The two hours on the freeway to Atlanta went by quickly. Shelby was getting back into the swing of things after being off the road for three years. She had talked to Jack on the phone last night, and things were good at home. He was enjoying his new position at work, and the boys were doing great with their families. Mark and his wife just had a little girl, and Steven and his girlfriend had gotten married two years earlier. Jack Jr. was always busy with something new—golf, or planting a garden, or even trying his hand at raising chickens on his twenty-acre piece of land near the Pecos River. Shelby was content with her empty nest family, but she couldn't help wishing that she and Jack had had a little girl. She had two little granddaughters, but the new one lived in Ohio. Shelby loved spoiling all her little grandbabies, but the girls were special to her.

"Barbie, the trucks are taking the next exit. If they head north after they make the exit, then most likely they're headed toward Dante's estate. Let's go on down to the truck stop and park these rigs. I'll pull out my service unit from the trailer—we can use it for surveillance tonight."

"I'm right behind ya, Cover Girl."

"I need to call Cody and get the exact address on Dante's estate. If those trucks don't show up there, then we'll be on the hunt for them. I'm sure they'll be around the estate, in any event."

"I can follow them if you want." Shelby offered.

"No, our trucks are too conspicuous. I don't like the idea of having to hunt them down, but if we have to, then I don't want them to know that someone is tailing them. Besides, Cody has a local unmarked unit keeping an eye on Dante's place."

"24/7?"

"He doesn't have them on constant surveillance yet, but he patrols the area on a regular basis. He'll probably be able to tell us where they could be headed if they don't show up at the estate."

"Sounds good. I just hope Shades is there. I'd love to get him in my rifle scope."

"Hey, remember what we told Damian? This isn't the Wild West where gunslingers settle the score. We have no warrant to get on Dante's property and good luck getting a visual on that bastard Shades from the wall that surrounds his property. We can't even use drone or helicopter surveillance legally over his property without a court order."

"Doesn't it seem odd to you that criminals have more rights than law-abiding citizens?"

"Yep, it's true, but laws have to be imposed equally, or the rights that law-abiding citizens have will be totally trampled. It's not a perfect system, but it works most of the time. I do agree that criminals get away with way too much. But then again, we're law enforcement, so it's natural to feel that way."

"You're right. It just makes me so angry. He's a murderer and a drug dealer. He deserves to be taken out for all the terrible things he has done—and not only to Amber."

"Hang tough, little lady. We'll take him down all in good time. In fact, this call coming in on my phone may be what we need."

Although Shelby made it through her DEA training with high marks, the one thing she hadn't learned to control was her impatience. By the time Angelica came back on the radio, almost ten minutes later, Shelby's fingernails were chewed to the quick.

"We're taking the next exit so we can put these rigs to bed," Angelica instructed.

"What's up?" Shelby asked

"Damian arrived in town a couple of hours before us this morning. He's on his motorcycle now and will meet us near Dante's. I'll tell you the rest after we get these trucks parked."

"Okay."

"Look to your left. See those two open spaces on the back line? We'll take them and unload my car."

"Got it."

◊◊◊

"Look, Dante, I know things are hot right now, and we have to be careful, but this new trucking company Shield Sheik will help us get our product out quickly and more efficiently with all the trucks they have. All they want is for us to help them get access to some of the more difficult loading facilities in the country. All of this new legislation is making it difficult for foreign-owned hauling companies to get access." Shades explained.

"Things are only hot around here because of you, Shades, and your poor judgment. You never let things go. Whores are whores and money is money, but money trumps a whore—any whore every time."

Dante berated Shades from his custom-made leather office chair. "This new trucking company…I don't like their prices, and I don't like doing business with foreigners. Now you've gotten us involved with them, and we desperately need transportation, so that leaves us with no choice but to do business with Shield Sheik." He pointed his finger at Shades across the large solid oak desk. "But you listen to me, Shades, I do not want to meet with their higher-ups. In fact, I don't want anything to do with this. My name is not to be associated with them in any way. You get my drugs from the cartels, you get them to my distributors, and you bring me my money. Got that? Now, where is Chrystal?"

"I'm not sure; she might be sitting out near the pool." Shades pointed toward the window. *Why is Dante asking about Chrystal?* Shades wondered.

Dante got up out of his chair and went to the window. "She's going to be mine now, Shades. I like her. Thanks for the gift. I deserve something from you for protecting you from the DEA."

Shades face turned red, and he stumbled over his words. "She's not a whore, Dante, she's my woman."

Dante stared at Chrystal as she lay sunning herself near the pool. "She is mine now. You owe me. Make it happen. And make sure to keep the Sheik Shield folks away from me."

Shades was furious, but Dante had him over a barrel. "Fine. I'll send her to you tonight."

Dante smiled. "No, that won't be necessary. I want to pursue her. I want her moved into her own room. I don't want you to touch her again…ever. I want her all to myself. She is the price you must pay for your blunders."

Shades hands balled into fists at his sides; his body shook with anger, but there was nothing he could do. He turned away from Dante. "I need to go take care of those trucks that just came in. You take care of Chrystal. She's your problem now." Shades left his boss' office.

"Bastard. I will kill you, the first chance I get. I promise I will kill you," he murmured from the other side of the closed door.

◊◊◊

Shelby and Angelica drove down a boulevard that ran parallel to Dante's estate. Shelby surveyed the vast property on the other side of the chain-link fence. "This estate reminds me of Pig's place. It's not as big, but it sure is more fortified. It's amazing how well drug lords live. This Dante, is he as crazy as Pig was?"

"Dante is ten times worse than Pig. Dante is a pervert, and there are reports that he's into masochistic sexual behaviors. He's been linked to several prostitutes who have gone missing. I'm sure if we get a chance to search his property we'll find their graves or possibly find them confined as sex slaves. Hell, with his connections to the cartels, it's possible they have been traded to Mexico as sex slaves there. Who knows?"

"Wow, he really is some piece of work." Shelby became pensive. "You know, when I was kidnapped in Mexico, I was so afraid I was going to be forced into the sex trade. That's why I took the chance and escaped. I think I would have rather have been shot and killed for escaping than suffer through something like being a sex slave."

"I hear you, Shelby. When I found out what Pig had done with you, I knew we had to get to you before it was too late. You were one brave cookie taking off like you did across that country, not knowing who to trust or where to go. I would like to think I would have done the same, but I'm not sure I'd have been that brave."

Shelby smiled at her friend. "I know you would have done that exact thing. Besides, with your Mexican heritage, you would have been able to communicate so much easier."

"Maybe. Look over there." Angelica pointed at a man on a side street near the estate. He was leaning up against a motorcycle. "It's Damian. He told me where we could find him."

Angelica pulled her black Charger behind Damian's bike. The women exited the vehicle and shook hands with him. "I see you found my second home." Damian pointed to several of the fancy looking homes around the beautifully manicured neighborhood. "Thought about buying one of these babies, but they are a bit out of my trucker price range. Not sure they would appreciate me parking my rig on the street in front of my house, either."

The three friends laughed. "Well, some agents' pay is much less than trucker pay," Shelby said. "So we won't be moving here anytime soon, either. Have you seen those Glacier trucks go into Dante's estate?"

"Yeah, they went in there via the service road about an hour and a half ago. I also noticed a couple of Shield Sheik trucks leave a couple of Dover trucks." Damian pointed down the road to the west. "About fifteen miles down that road there is a warehouse building just off the freeway. It's pretty well hidden by the trees, but it's enormous, and I've followed lots of trucks to that facility. They are definitely loading and unloading out of that place. I have no idea exactly what they're hauling, but chances are, it's drugs."

Angelica agreed. "We've had this place under surveillance with local law enforcement. We haven't been able to get enough evidence to get a warrant so we can bust him. Even if we do take him down, we need folks who will turn on him and testify against him in court, which is unlikely. That warehouse is on his property and very well fortified. Our plan is to tail the trucks coming in and out of his place. If we can bust his distributor, it will cause him so much pain financially that he'll have to come out of his spider hole."

Shelby spoke up. "Perhaps he'll get so irritated that he'll send Shades out to investigate. That way we can nail him too."

"Oh, you can be sure he will send Shades out to be his fall guy." Angelica acknowledged. "So, how long you going to sit here, Detective Damian?"

Angelica poked Damian with her elbow. "Why don't you give it up for the night and take two beautiful women to dinner?"

Just as she finished chiding him, the two Glacier trucks that she and Shelby were following passed them and turned onto the feeder road. Shelby and Angelica moved toward the Charger. "Looks like they are headed to unload at the warehouse. Let's take a spin down that way and see where they go afterward. So, you want to take us to dinner tonight or what?" Angelica yelled toward Damian as the two women got into their vehicle.

Damian waved them off with his hand. "Yeah. What truck stop are you parked at?"

"We're at Fairburn off 85. I hear it's the best in the Atlanta area."

"That's where my truck is, too. I'll be over there later tonight, and we'll have dinner. I know a great little place."

Shelby and Angelica waved at Damian as they drove away to check out the warehouse.

◊◊◊

The three sat at around a table, drinking sweet tea and eating burgers. The food was good, but to Shelby, it was really a guy's place. Shelby was only able to finish half of her double-decker cheeseburger. "I was full after the salad, Damian. Do you want the rest of my burger?"

Damian took the half-eaten burger and placed it on his plate still piled high with fries.

"How can you eat so much? I'm about to burst," Shelby said.

Angelica had done a little better on her burger, but she finally had to push away from the table. "I can't eat another bite. It was good, though." She rubbed her belly and sat back in her chair. She looked at Shelby. "You and I should have ordered one and shared."

"Amen."

"Oh, come on, ladies. I told you this was a fantastic place to eat. If you would have shared a burger, then I wouldn't have gotten to finish your leftovers. I would have had to order another burger to go just for a midnight snack." Damian smiled and then took another bite of his burger and washed it down with tea. "Yum, nothing like a greasy spoon burger and a cold glass of tea."

Shelby shook her head, amused. Damian was so much like her sons.

"We need to talk about tomorrow," Angelica said. "Let's review. The Glacier, Shield Sheik, and Dover trucks all took on cargo after they dropped what they were carrying at the warehouse. They picked up some of it at another warehouse. Several of the trucks went back to Dante's estate, and I'm pretty sure they didn't leave empty. Most of the trucks are parked out on the 20, and I think they are going to hit the road tomorrow. I haven't cleared this with Cody yet, and I'm sure I'll get my ass reamed for this, but I want to know what those Shield Sheik trucks are up to. I just have a bad feeling about this company, and I want to know what they're about."

"What do you have in mind?" Shelby asked.

"Tomorrow I'm going to track a couple of the Glacier trucks; I'll follow them as far as I can and take out as many of the connections as possible in Dante and Shades' traffic line. Shelby, I want you to find some of the Shield Sheik trucks that came out of Dante's place earlier. They were parked at that truck stop off 20. I just want you to follow them; don't make contact. Just take notes of all of their activities."

"I can do that. But why don't you want me to investigate? I could probably find out a whole lot more about them if you would let me do a little P.I. work. I won't do anything dangerous, just snoop a little." Shelby insisted.

"You're still a rookie. If anything happens to you, it will be my ass," Angelica said. "But I guess if you think you can do it without getting yourself into trouble, you can investigate a little. We sure could use the information."

"What about me; what do you want me to do?" Damian asked.

Angelica looked at Damian. "You're a civilian; I would lose my badge if I put you on an assignment."

Damian continued eating. "So, don't give me an assignment."

He pointed to Shelby with a french fry before putting it into his mouth. "Tell Shelby what you would have another agent do if you had one available to help out. I'm just a civilian listening to your conversation. I have no idea what the hell you two women do for a living. I have lots of time on my hands and lots of money in my pocket. I have a grudge to settle with a man who killed my wife and child. I have no idea what I'll do with the information that I overhear between you two crazy gals."

Angelica looked at her tea, then at Damian, then at Shelby. "Well…if Cody were to give me another DEA agent to work this case, Shelby, I would put him behind those Dover trucks. They don't run more than a two-hundred-mile radius around this city, and Dante owns them all. I would really like to know where they go and what they do. I would also like to keep a close eye on Dante's estate to find out when he or Shades leaves, where they go, when they return, and who visits them. The locals just don't have the resources to get me that deep of intelligence. But if I had another agent just assigned to those two activities, I could probably take Dante and Shades down a lot quicker."

"I totally agree with you, boss lady. But you know Cody, he won't go against the higher-ups at the agency. He's a 'yes man,'" Shelby mocked.

"Yes, he is, Agent Mathews. I sure could use some more eyes on this case." Angelica looked at Damian who had devoured not only his huge hamburger but the rest of Shelby's and Angelica's burgers as well. He had managed to eat every last fry that had been piled high on his plate. Angelica prodded her friend, "So, Damian, how was your meal?"

Damian gulped another drink of tea. "It was delicious." He sat back in his seat. "I need to get to my truck and take a nap. I don't know about you ladies, but I have a bunch of things to do tomorrow."

Angelica knew that Damian had heard every word that she had said to Shelby and that he would accomplish everything that she wanted him to accomplish. "I totally agree. It is time to get to our trucks for some good sleep. We all have busy days tomorrow."

CHAPTER FOUR

"Look, Cody..." Angelica's sentence was interrupted by her handler's angry voice.

"No, you look, Angelica, the whole reason for her being out there with you on this case is for you to keep an eye on her and train her. That's why we call you her trainer."

"I know, Cody, but there are several trucking companies involved in Dante's empire now, and Shield Sheik employs a strange bunch of characters. She's just going to be following them. She knows not to make contact or do anything. All she is going to do is track their activities. Those guys are up to no good. I know they are somehow associated with Shades and Dante."

Cody was not pleased. "So, what you are proposing is that we let this fresh-out-of-school rookie fly alone? Are you freaking out of your mind? I already checked those clowns out, and I can't find anything out of the ordinary on Shield Sheik. They appear to be a legitimate, fast-growing trucking outfit. I think you're paranoid. Listen to me. Do not let Shelby out on her own yet."

"Okay, then I want you to look deeper into Shield Sheik. If they are so on the up and up, then why are they doing business with a known drug trafficker? Something just isn't kosher. Damian told me that he sees them everywhere, but they aren't hauling jobs on the broker boards at all. They are hauling loads, but no one seems to know what they're hauling or who they're hauling for."

"I will dig deeper and check with Homeland Security, but Shelby needs to stay with you for her six weeks of training. And keep Damian out of this! He's a civilian and not even a registered informant," Cody ordered.

"It's too late, Cody. She left two hours before me this morning and when she called me an hour ago, they appeared to be heading to Memphis."

"Oh, that's just wonderful, Angelica. The brass is going to have both our asses on this one. You just want to see me lose my job, don't you? And to make matters worse, she headed into the mega hub of eight ball distribution. I know you've lost your mind now!" Cody yelled.

"No, Cody, I don't want you to lose your job." Angelica remained calm. She did not want to argue; she just wanted to get Cody to see her side of things. "I'm close to her, but I need her keeping track of that trucking company for me. If I'm going to strip Dante and Shades down to their underwear, I need to catch them with their pants down. I think Sheik is hiding in the pocket. I need to shake them out, and she's not going to get anywhere near the eight ball dealers. Hell, she probably won't even enter West Memphis. You have to trust me."

"I do trust you, but you're still going to get both of us fired if anything happens with Shelby and you're not there." Cody sounded more frustrated than angry. "Not enter West Memphis? Really? We're talking drug traffickers and dealers here, Angelica. That's a trophy spot. If they don't stop there, I'd really be surprised."

"See? You do think that Sheik is involved in Dante's ring, or you wouldn't be so pissed about Shelby following them into Memphis. She's not going to do anything but watch them. I promise," Angelica said with her fingers crossed.

Cody conceded, reluctantly. "Make sure that's all she does…and I mean it. If she starts wanting to get too close, I want her pulled out immediately. Do you hear me?"

"You got it, Cody, you have my word. She'll just track them."

"Yeah, we'll see. She's too much like you, and I know how you are."

"Well, that's a compliment coming from you, Cody. I'm glad you have noticed what a great agent I am in the limited amount of time we have been working together," Angelica replied, deflecting Cody's sarcasm.

Cody laughed. "Rex has told me all about you, Angelica, and your reputation around the agency is that of a gun-slinging, round 'em up cowgirl. Just make sure that cowgirl number two doesn't fall off her horse."

"Funny. We were just talking about the Wild West, Mr. Texas Ranger," Angelica joked.

"I'm from Detroit, Angelica. We don't even understand why you people in Texas have Rangers anymore."

"Well, I didn't grow up in Texas, but I sure like it there. Oh, and Rangers are more than historical novelty. They are a legitimate arm of the Texas Department of Public Safety. They do a lot of crime investigation in Texas."

"All I know about is the baseball team—who I hope the Tigers beat. Now get off my phone, I've got work to do."

"Okie, dokie." Angelica pushed the button on her Bluetooth and immediately called Shelby.

"Hey, girl, what's happening?" Shelby answered.

"Well, I just got off the phone with Cody."

"Was he pissed?"

"Oh, for a little while. I convinced him to let you continue tracking Shield Sheik, but you need to be really careful not to do much more than follow them. Cody will have both of our butts if you start investigating them."

"I'll do my best to just follow them and take notes of their activities, I promise."

"Okay. That will save both our asses. So, are you in Memphis yet?"

"About an hour out, I think. These truckers are some load movers. They stopped for thirty minutes once. Boy, was I glad for that stop, too! I really had to pee. But they haven't stopped for anything else."

"Try not to lose them, please. Because if you do, you know you'll be rollin' along behind me, and I am a hell of a lot worse on the bladder than those guys. Plus, we'll lose all that intelligence on Shield Sheik. We really need to know what those bozos are up too."

"Gotcha."

"The four trucks I was following split off in K Town. I followed two of them to a warehouse on the north side where they unloaded some cargo out of one truck and put some cargo into another truck. I couldn't get close enough to see what it was that they were distributing, but since it's Glacier, I'm pretty sure we know. I'm currently crossing the state line into Kentucky, and I haven't seen hide nor hair of those other two trucks. I sure wish I knew where they went. Now you see how easy it can be to lose a tail."

"I'll be a good little trucker agent, boss lady. I won't let you down."

"Good. Make sure you stay out of the West Memphis truck stops. I don't want you in there by yourself."

"I hear ya. I was there some years back, and even then it was a sewer hole for junkies and dealers. If they go into West Memphis, I'll be careful and not hang out at the stops."

"I'm so glad you have experience in the trucking industry. That means I can concentrate on your agent training."

"I think I could probably teach you a few things about the trucking industry, little lady."

"I'm sure you could. That's what makes us a good team. Okay, get back to your driving and keep me informed. I've got a call from Rex coming in."

"Oh, tell him I said 'hi,' and to be sure to give little Harley a kiss from Auntie Shelby."

"I will." Angelica pushed her button on her Bluetooth and connected with Rex.

◊◊◊

Once she arrived in Memphis, Shelby followed the designated trucks to an industrial area full of warehouses. She stayed as far back as possible so the drivers wouldn't see her while at the same time not losing sight of them. She noticed the trucks had turned into an old abandoned building. Shelby parked her truck in a parking lot not far from the building and walked toward the dilapidated chain link fence choked with weeds that encircled the facility. A large dying tree stood outside the fence. Shelby hid behind the tree and watched as several men inside the fence busied themselves by spotting the trucks and guiding them backwards into the old cracked and broken down cement dock. Two forklifts appeared from inside the ramshackle building and removed several palettes stacked with plastic-wrapped cardboard boxes.

"Oh, no." Shelby ducked behind a clump of bushes to hide.

Before she knew what was happening, the gate was flung open. The view from the bushes obstructed her view, but she heard the roar of an eighteen-wheel truck coming to the gate. She popped her head out just enough to see another Shield Sheik truck enter the facility. Shelby noticed that the trailer of one of the trucks she had been following was now closed. The man on the ground in front of the truck was directing the truck to an open area on the other side of the building where several trailers without trucks had been placed. The man Shelby had been observing moved his truck away from the dock and backed it into an open space near the parked trailers. He got out of the truck, lowered his landing gear, and disengaged the fifth wheel. Then he returned to his truck and pulled his tractor out from under the trailer. He maneuvered his truck into position under another trailer and locked the fifth wheel into position before raising his landing gear. The Shield Sheik truck that had just driven through the gate was then directed backwards into the dock.

The other truck Shelby was observing was then directed to the same area as the first truck and conducted all the same maneuvers as the first driver.

Shelby stayed hidden for almost an hour. During that time, she observed eight more Shield Sheik trucks come in, dump their load, and perform the trailer change out as the original two drivers had done. From what she could see from her hiding spot, the same type of pallets had been removed from all of the trucks. She longed to know exactly what the contents of the boxes on the pallets contained, but it was impossible. The only way she could find out would be to move from her hiding spot. *I'll just have to document the location and let other agents check out the property,* she concluded.

After all the trucks entered the yard, and the man in charge of the gate had secured the mess of stretched chicken wire back into place, Shelby decided that now was her best chance to get back to her own truck. Once inside her truck, she wrote down everything she could remember including street names and even some of the truck and trailer numbers. She wrote down descriptions of several of the men she saw, particularly the gate attendant.

Before she had a chance to complete her report, the two trucks that she was following passed her on the street. She wanted to talk with Angelica, but that was going to have to wait. She pushed in on her air brake button and turned her truck and trailer down the street behind the trucks. After all, she had promised Angelica that she would not lose them.

◊◊◊

Angelica's phone rang just as she was backing into her parking place at the Road Ranger truck stop in Lexington, Kentucky. She pressed her Bluetooth button. "Hey, Barbie, what's up?"

"Well, I followed the two trucks to a rundown warehouse in Memphis where they dumped their cargo and picked up new trailers. I also got the truck and trailer numbers off eight other Sheik trucks I saw delivering to the same place." Shelby said excitedly.

"Wow, that's terrific! How did you do that without them seeing you in your truck?" Angelica already knew the answer. "Shelby! You didn't get out of your truck and follow them on foot, did you?"

"I had to, Angelica. I couldn't have obtained the information we needed without it."

"Agent Mathews, you disobeyed my direct orders. Do you want me to pull you off your first assignment and babysit you?" Angelica was obviously pissed off. "Come on, Shelby, if something happens to you, not only will I hate myself, lose my best friend, and lose my job, but your husband will kill me."

"Nothing is going to happen to me, Angelica. I got this, and I'm good at it." She spoke reassuringly, "I swear to you, I won't do anything stupid, but I'm going to have to get out of this truck from time to time to check things out. The truck is too big to use for surveillance. Please give me a chance. You trust me enough to be your partner and watch your back, don't you?"

Angelica begrudgingly agreed. "Yes."

"Well, then trust me enough to know how to get the information that we can really use. I will be extra careful. I just wish I had a small car or a motorcycle that I could use to track these guys without being seen."

"I can't believe you actually just said that."

"Why?"

"When you stop for the night, have a look in the back of your trailer," Angelica said. "Your trailer contains the same, or pretty much the same equipment that mine does."

"Why are you just telling me this now?"

"I didn't want to tell you at first because I didn't want you doing things without my supervision. But since you're already performing like an agent, you might as well make use of the equipment you need to do your job."

"Wow, you mean there's a car and a motorcycle and firepower in the back of my truck too? Awesome!"

"Hold on to your panties, missy. I didn't tell you it was there for you to go nuts. Use your head and the training you've had; don't go Rambo or 007 on me. Be smart, Shelby, and don't get us both kicked off the force because you want to impress someone."

"You know me better than that, Angelica. I'm very level headed. I would never put you or your job at risk. I just think it's great they supplied me with the same stuff they gave you. You have my word that I will use it only when I need it, and I'll use it properly. These guys are long haulers, and the longest stop has been their drop. I'm hoping they stop pretty soon so that I can get some more fuel and food. I have no idea where these trucks are headed, but we're headed east on I-55."

"Glacier Transport isn't like that; they like stopping. In fact, I think we just stopped for food here in Lexington." Angelica paused. "Damn it, here comes those two trucks I lost back in K Town. Those bastards are parking right next to me. How convenient, a powwow at the Roadie. Hey, you be careful out there. I need to get inside and listen to what these guys are planning to do next."

"I promise, partner. You be careful, too." Shelby disconnected. She looked at the trucks she was following and spoke to them as if they could hear her. "Where to now, boys?"

Angelica got out of her truck and headed to the restaurant. Once inside, she looked around for the two Glacier drivers she was following. She spotted them sitting with two other men at a table. One of the men reminded her of one of the drivers that she had seen in Birmingham, but she didn't recognize any of the others. She found a booth near the group and ordered a cup of coffee. She looked at the menu while eavesdropping on the table of men. The entire table was speaking Spanish.

"I'm going on to Dearborn tonight. You bitches can hang back in Cincinnati after we make delivery if you want," one of the new drivers said.

"Fine, but Juan and I are staying in Cincinnati and waiting for orders like the boss told us." The man Angelica recognized was speaking. "I don't know what your hurry is to get to Dearborn. We can't pick up those loads from Shield Sheik until late tomorrow afternoon."

The man who sat closest to the window said, "I don't like hauling for those guys. There is something suspicious about them, and the only reason they are hauling our stuff for us is because the DEA has been watching us like hawks."

The man that Angelica knew spoke up again. "I'm with Hector on this one. That Shield Sheik company is strange. I don't know what they are doing with all those chemicals. I know we haul stuff that is illegal on both sides of the border, but those wackos are really up to something crazy."

"Sanchez and I are going on to Dearborn. I want to get this shit off my truck at their terminal, pick up my load of dope, and get the hell out of there. I don't mind hauling our stuff, but the stuff they are moving around seems dangerous," Hector interjected.

"What about Mendoza? What is he going to say if we don't do what he wants done how he wants it done? What about the drop in Toledo?" The man Angelica knew was reminding the others of their orders.

"Oh shit, I forgot about that Ohio load. Wait, we can transfer those two palettes of stuff to Juan and you, Rodriguez. It will only take us an hour to transfer, and then you can make the stop in Toledo tomorrow for all of us," Hector suggested.

"You just don't want to do your job. Have you got some pro waiting to screw you in Dearborn or something?" All the men at the table laughed. "No. Juan and I will not be taking your loads to Toledo. Lazy bastards!" Rodriguez chided both Hector and Sanchez.

"Come on, Rodriguez. It won't hurt you to do this one favor for us," Hector begged.

"No. We are not your bitches and besides, Mendoza will be pissed if we do." Rodriguez shook his head vehemently. "You make your own loads. Go on to Toledo tonight if you want, but Juan and I are staying in Cincinnati just like we were told to."

Hector wasn't laughing now. "Fine, wait until you want me to do you a favor, bitch."

"That will never happen. I don't do favors or ask for favors." Rodriguez picked up his tea. He was done talking.

As Angelica listened to the argument, she nibbled on her BLT sandwich. Being fluent in Spanish helped her tremendously in her line of work. The information that she had gotten from this one conversation was better than she could have hoped when she entered the restaurant. Besides being bilingual, Angelica had a condition that allowed her to recall everything she heard or experienced in great detail. She had heard some part of each of the drivers' names as well as the cargo they were hauling. They were hauling Shield Sheik's cargo, and Sheik was transporting some of their cargo—that's how Shield Sheik was keeping it off the boards. She now had some idea of where they were headed, and she also learned that Glacier Transport had an important guy in their organization named Mendoza. This was a goldmine of information, and Angelica hoped that the men would continue with their conversation. Unfortunately, their food arrived, and they all stopped talking.

Angelica couldn't wait to tell Shelby and Cody. Then it hit her: *Oh no! Shelby is following trucks carrying drugs.* She considered getting up and calling her friend. *No, wait. They dropped off their loads in Memphis, so the drugs might be at that abandoned warehouse she was telling me about. So, what is on those trucks now?* Angelica knew this investigation was going to get crazy. Her head was spinning with all the possible places the drugs could be by now. She was going to have to reach out to Cody and have him log all the information into his computer and give her a possible projection of distribution. *What a mess*, she thought as she ate her sandwich.

◊◊◊

Shelby was relieved when the two trucks she'd been trailing all day finally pulled into the fuel island of a truck stop off I-70. She was tired, hungry, and wanted a bath. She hoped that the trucks would be staying the night in the stop. Relief came when she noticed that the trucks both found parking spots on the lot. "Yes. They are staying here for the night." She ran quickly into the store while she waited her turn to fuel.

After getting her fuel, Shelby found a parking spot across from the two trucks she was surveilling. She got her truck into place and then sat in the driver's seat filling out her log. She watched as the drivers in question helped a woman out of each of their trucks. Each woman carried a shower type bag and a small laundry bag. The women walked together into the truck stop. The men, however, stayed behind and lifted the hood of one of the trucks. They appeared to be checking on the truck's engine.

Shelby put her log aside and grabbed her shower bag. She gathered what laundry she had, although it wasn't much, along with her small bottle of laundry soap. She decided she'd wash what she had just so she could get close to those women.

When she entered the laundry room, the women were not there. *I guess they must be taking their showers first. I'll just hang around in here and wait,* she thought.

Not having any quarters to wash her clothes, she went to the cashier and got some change. She then put her clothes in one of the washing machines and started it. She sat down on one of the vinyl chairs and picked up a magazine to read. Just as her clothes were completing the final cycle, the two women she had been waiting for entered the room. Shelby got up from her seat. "It's almost finished with the rinse cycle. You can have this machine in just a minute," Shelby told one of the women.

"Thank you," one of the young women said in broken English. Shelby couldn't place the accent. It definitely wasn't Spanish. She looked at the woman's scarf. It barely sat on the back of her head and draped around her neck. Shelby assumed she was Muslim since she was covering her head. Shelby had seen pictures of women wearing hijabs and other veils. The traditional clothing varied in modesty, from simple head scarves to full body coverings.

Angelica had explained to Shelby that Middle Easterners included Arabs, Persians, Africans, and Semites, and they all had different customs.

Shelby's load soon finished, and she removed her load from the washing machine and placed her clothes into the dryer. "I didn't have a lot this time, but I like to keep up with it," Shelby said, trying to encourage a conversation.

"I know what you mean. My husband and I travel together in his truck, and it gets too crowded sometimes if the laundry piles up," the younger women responded. Her older friend gave the young woman a disapproving look. The younger woman didn't seem to care what the older one thought because she sat down next to Shelby. "Don't mind her; she's from our home in Syria, and we aren't supposed to be as friendly with strangers as I am. My husband, Amar Rajah," the young woman pointed to her friend, "and Abal's husband, Sumrah Nagi are truck drivers for Abal's uncle's new company, Shield Sheik."

Shelby held out her hand to her new friend. "My name is Jessica North," Shelby lied. It was not the agency's protocol to give anyone, especially people they were investigating, their real names.

The woman shook Shelby's hand but let go quickly when the older woman, who was still putting her clothes in the wash, shot her an even more disparaging look. "Hi, I'm Husha. So, do you drive trucks with your husband?"

Shelby laughed. "No, I drive my truck, alone. My husband is at home working. We don't work together. I like taking him with me sometimes, but I think if we were stuck in that truck together too much we might get on each other's nerves."

"You drive all alone out here, by yourself? Your husband must not like that too much. My husband would never let me be out here alone. But I do go with him from time to time to keep him company. I also think it would be hard to be with him all the time, though. I would miss my children too much."

"Oh, you have children?" Shelby asked. "Are they back in Syria?"

"No, no, we live in Salina, Kansas. My husband and I have been here for several years now. Abal and her husband just came here last year." Abal continued to give Husha angry looks, but Husha didn't notice, or pretended not to, and just kept on talking to Shelby. "I have a little boy and a little girl."

"Oh, that's awesome. I have three boys, but they are grown, and now I have a few grandchildren."

"You don't look old enough to have grandchildren."

"Thank you, but I do. So, when will you get to see your children again?" Shelby probed.

"I will get to see them in two days. We have to go on into Kansas City, and then on to York, Nebraska. After we make that delivery, my husband has promised that we will be going home for a few days," Husha said excitedly.

"That's great. Who takes care of your children for you when you're out here with your husband?" Shelby questioned.

But before Husha could answer, the women's husbands came into the room. Shelby could tell from the expressions on the women's faces that their husbands did not approve of them conversing with strangers. Shelby heard the ringer on her dryer go off. "Well, I'd better get my clothes and go take my shower."

Husha got to her feet. She pointed at her husband and the other man standing there. "This is my husband, Amar Rajah, and his friend, Sumrah Nagi."

Shelby placed her clothes from the dryer into her shower bag without folding them.

"Nice to meet you." Out of habit, she stuck her hand out to shake the two men's hands. Neither man put his hand out to accept the friendly gesture. Shelby quickly put down her hand and looked at Husha.

Husha looked embarrassed by the men's rudeness, but she didn't utter a word.

"Well, it was nice to meet you, Husha," Shelby said. "Perhaps we will meet each other again out here on the highways."

Husha nodded her head.

Shelby left the laundry room and went to the counter to purchase a shower room ticket.

CHAPTER FIVE

"**I** can't talk with you right now, Cody. The trucks are pulling into a small strip mall parking lot here in Toledo." Angelica hung up.

"Damn it, Angelica." Cody hung up just as Shelby was calling in her daily report. "Yes, Agent Mathews; I hope you have good news for me."

"Well, I don't know if it's good, but I met two of the Shield Sheik drivers and their wives last night in the truck stop laundry…," Shelby was abruptly interrupted.

"You made contact with the people you have under surveillance? I knew it! Angelica promised that you would only be tracking them." Cody made no attempt to hide his anger.

"Wait, Cody. I didn't make contact with them on purpose, I was just in the laundry room and they came in." Shelby stretched the truth, hoping to eliminate the consequences she felt might be coming if he knew the truth. "Husha introduced herself and started talking with me. I was minding my own business."

"Right, and I have a tropical island off the Alaskan coast I'll sell you. Shelby, I have no way of protecting you if you get yourself into a serious life-threatening predicament," Cody explained.

"I'm not putting myself in any life-threatening predicaments. I simply had a light conversation with a nice young mother. She wanted to make a new friend and I was there. She doesn't know my real name; I told her I'm Jessica North. She doesn't know anything about me except that I drive a truck, and she doesn't even know which one. You need to chill out and give me a break. I might be new at this agent stuff, but I'm not an idiot. I didn't plan to make contact or gather information from them, it just happened."

Cody calmed down. "You're right, I'm sorry. It's just frustrating because you shouldn't be out there on your own yet, and I'm responsible for you."

"I understand, but have a little confidence in me, please," Shelby insisted. "Now, do you want the information that I gathered or not?"

"Yes. Tell me everything you learned, and give me all the information you have on these Shield Sheik trucks."

"Okay." Shelby took several minutes explaining to Cody the route she had used to follow the trucks, the stops they'd made, truck numbers, and the number of people involved. She told them what Husha said about coming from Syria, where they lived in the U.S., and the names of her children, the older woman, and the two men. She explained to Cody exactly what the women had told her about the family connections to Shield Sheik and their home country.

"Oh! I almost forgot. I also observed one of the men leave his truck last night around two a.m.," Shelby said. "I only noticed because I got up to get a drink of water. I pulled back my curtain a little, just to make sure that they hadn't left during the night. He was carrying a backpack and walking into the store at the truck stop. I'm sure he was just going to take a shower. I didn't follow him because I was instructed not to, so I'm not sure if her went anywhere else."

"Wow, you really fell into a nest of intel, didn't you?" Cody conceded.

"I sure did. But something is really strange with these people. I'm not sure what it is, but I just have a feeling about them, and it's not good. I plan to stay with these two trucks unless they disconnect from the circuit altogether. These people are up to something, but I'm not so sure it has anything to do with drugs. I think they are transporting the drugs for Dante on the side, but I don't think that is their main haul or their reason for being out here. Something is really weird with these people, and it has nothing to do with the way they dress or sound."

"This was in St. Louis, right? Last night?"

"Yeah? Why?"

Cody responded while loading information into his computer. "Yeah, I'm beginning to think the same thing, but I can't find anything wrong with the company. Everything is coming back as legitimate. Homeland Security hasn't gotten back with me yet either, but you can be sure that if Shield Sheik was on their radar, the company would be on a watch list, and right now, that's not the case."

"They might have been keeping their noses clean until now, but if they are dealing with Dante you know they will be into something illegal soon if they aren't already," Shelby said.

"Looking at the data I've gathered, that's possible. This trucking company has been growing by leaps and bounds. They started with twenty-five trucks, and as it stands today, they've grown enough to run over 10,000 trucks in all fifty states and even in some of the U.S.-owned territories. Not all the trucks are manned, but it's clear from their IRS filings that they are expanding quickly. I just can't seem to figure out where all their operating funds are coming from since the majority of their business affiliations isn't with the normal broker boards. The money appears to be from foreign-owned corporations that have nothing or very little to do with merchandise or the transportation of goods." Cody paused as he analyzed the data on his monitor. "Wow, I need to go Shelby. Good work, keep it up."

Before Shelby could respond, Cody hung up.

"Okay, that was a quick change of attitude."

Shelby hit the speed dial on her phone for Angelica. She knew her partner would want to know all the information she'd uncovered. Angelica's phone went to voicemail. "Huh, she must be talking with Cody." She disconnected and concentrated on following her two suspect trucks to Kansas City, Kansas.

◊◊◊

"Cody, run this Ohio plate for me right quick—MTB0005."

Cody entered the information into his computer. "It's a stolen plate, Angelica."

"I figured as much. Oh well, it doesn't matter right now. They took off right after they unloaded. Whatever they were carrying is on the trucks I'm following. I think they even transported some of the cargo from my two trucks to that Ohio plate truck. I can't be sure, though, because they made those transfers really fast. I don't even think I could have gotten a local unit there quick enough to interrupt the process. I'm headed north into Michigan on I-75; I don't have a clue where we are headed. Have you heard from Shelby?"

Cody finished entering the last of Angelica's verbal report into his computer. "Yeah, she gave me some really good information on that Shield Sheik outfit. In fact, while I was entering her report into the computer and checking out her information, something caught my attention. Shield Sheik does appear to be a legitimate company on the surface, and even when you dig a little deeper into their financials it's hard to notice. The only reason I noticed anything strange is because one of the companies doing business with Shield Sheik is in my own portfolio of investments."

"Oooh, Cody, our next up and coming business mogul with the fancy investment portfolio," Angelica chided.

"Never mind about my financial life. What I figured out is that the company is owned by a Saudi investment firm. They buy up failing companies, sell them to other investment companies, and invest money into new companies. In fact, a lot of the money that Shield Sheik is using to operate is coming from these companies and not from their transportation of goods. They are employing drivers and paying them to deliver loads, but the loads are not coming from legitimate trading outlets."

Angelica interrupted. "In other words, Shield Sheik is transporting God knows what, to God knows where, for God knows who, and getting paid and financed by a bunch Saudis with a shitload of money?"

"That about sums it up. Except it appears, on the surface anyway, that they are a legal investment company. The only way that could only be the case is if someone high up in our government has their fingers in the cookie jar."

"That's a scary scenario. Now, not only are we fighting against cartels poisoning our citizens with all these drugs, but now we have to find out what idiot in Washington is lining his pockets with foreign money so drugs can be transported around this country without being detected?"

"Oh, I think there is something more going on with Shield Sheik than just the distribution of drugs. You and Shelby are right to assume something funny is going on with that company," Cody conceded.

"Finally, a handler who agrees with my instincts." Angelica laughed.

"Yeah, putting Shelby on those trucks' tails was a smart move. I'm going to do more digging and watch their business growth platform online. Shelby also told me that she spent the night in a truck stop in St. Louis. I didn't want to alarm her at the time she was making her report, but a small gun store was blown up not too far from that truck stop last night."

"Do they have any idea who set off the bomb?"

"The feds are investigating it now, but nothing substantial has come over the wire yet. They think it could be a terror attack, but there is no proof yet."

"Did Shelby say something in her report that made you think about the incident? Or is it just because she was in the same area where it happened?"

Cody hesitated. "Well, both really, and also because she mentioned that she observed one of the drivers leave his truck at about two a.m. with a backpack."

"He could have been going to take a shower?"

"Yeah, that's what she suspected, but intelligence from the explosion scene said that the explosive device had been contained in a backpack. It was detonated remotely at around two forty-five a.m., about a mile and a half from that truck stop."

"I see. A lot of coincidences for sure."

"Too many."

"Let's keep this information under wraps until we have more evidence against Shield Sheik. Make sure Shelby tells you everything she observes. Even the smallest detail might be important. Don't let the brass know what she's doing either, just in case we have some sympathetic mole among us. I don't like what seems to be developing here, but maybe we can nip it in the bud before it gets any bigger. It's a shame Homeland Security hasn't done a better job on this."

"Well, their lives are overwhelmed with which ass to kiss in order to keep their jobs. It's an election year remember?" Cody said, irritated.

"Oh, I know. Politics and politicians are always the reason everything is in such a mess. We're just the pawns." Angelica let some of her impatience with the system show as well.

"I'll monitor her closely and keep things under wraps until we know more."

"Thanks, Cody. I'm not sure yet where we're headed in Michigan, but we are entering Detroit. I'll let you know where we stop."

"Gotcha! Be careful."

Angelica pushed Shelby's call button on her radio screen after disconnecting with Cody.

Shelby answered as if she was out of breath. "Hey, Angelica, what's up? I tried to call earlier, but I guess you were on the phone with Cody."

"Why are you breathing hard?"

"Well, we stopped in Kansas City, Kansas, and I just unloaded my bike from the back of the truck. It and the car should get me around."

"They may seem like inconspicuous vehicles, but both the car and the bike have been tricked out. They move fast and have state-of-the-art technology."

"You know I have a need for speed." Shelby became serious again. "The drivers and their wives are in the restaurant right now. I know they are planning to do something in this town. They made contact in the little store by the coffee machine with another man. I couldn't understand what they were saying. I'm pretty sure they were speaking Arabic, but their body language and behavior told me everything I needed to know."

"Are you sure they'll do something there? Maybe they just stopped for lunch?"

"No, they are planning to do more than eat lunch here; trust me."

"Please be careful, Shelby. I'm not sure what those people that you're following are up to. I wasn't going to tell you this, and Cody didn't tell you because he didn't want to spook you, but a gun store near where you parked last night was robbed and bombed last night. It happened around two forty-five a.m. this morning."

Shelby paused before speaking. "Holy crap, that was around the time I saw one of those men leave his truck last night. Do you think they are connected?"

"We have no idea. Cody is looking into it, but you'd better watch your back, and don't get too close to those idiots." Angelica warned. Then she heard Shelby start her motorcycle.

"They're moving, Angelica. I knew it. Talk soon." Shelby hung up.

"Shelby, be careful!" Angelica yelled, but then realized that they had been disconnected. *I should be watching out for her,* Angelica thought to herself. *But I have to keep track of these dimwits. I sure hope she uses the brain underneath those blonde curls.*

◊◊◊

The trucks drove for forty minutes into Leavenworth, Kansas. One of the trucks turned off and parked in a nearby truck stop, but Shelby followed the other truck to a military installation. What surprised her when they arrived was how easy it was for them to gain access. They showed some paperwork at the gate and were allowed to enter the base. Shelby knew that if she flashed her agent's badge at the posted guards, that she would also be permitted onto the base. But she also knew that it might raise suspicions with base security if they knew that she was following a truck they'd just let onto their post. She knew that she wasn't going to be able to follow the truck any further, so she decided to turn around and go back to her own truck in Kansas City.

She planned her next steps: *I'll load my bike and head back to where I left my truck. If their truck isn't there when I get back to the parking lot, then they're probably heading to York, Nebraska. I'll find them. I just wish I knew what the hell they're picking up at an American military post.*

◊◊◊

"Hi Angelica, this is Damian. Shades and Dante aren't moving at this point. I'm going to leave them for a few days. I need to get a few loads, and at least make enough money to pay my bills."

"Sure, Damian, do what ya gotta do. I'm keeping close tabs on these Glacier trucks over here in Dearborn. Looks to me like they've got a huge main terminal here for Shield Sheik. My boys here are delivering and picking up loads out of their warehouses."

"Yeah, I knew those Shield Sheik trucks had to have a main terminal somewhere. Do you have any idea what they are taking from Glacier Transport or what Glacier is getting from them?"

"Not a clue. I really want to get in there and have a look, but Shelby's following a couple of their trucks. She is uncovering some vital and frightening information. I don't want to blow the lid off this Sheik operation until I know more about what they are doing."

"I understand; you want to reel in the big fish."

"That's exactly right."

"Well, your two big fish here in Atlanta are staying pretty close to the bottom of the pond right now. I think they know the heat is on and they don't want to get fried. I'm going to take a few days and run some loads. I'll keep an eye on them, but I need to make some money right now."

"I understand, Damian. Just keep me posted if you happen to see them make any moves."

"I will, Angelica."

"We'll talk soon."

◊◊◊

"Hey, I know it's late, but when you get this message, please give me a call. It's important." Shelby hung up her phone and within seconds, Angelica called her back.

"Thank God you're okay. I've been on pins and needles wondering what you've been doing." Angelica said with relief in her voice.

"I'm fine, Angelica. Have a little faith in me. I just wanted to give you an update. I followed those trucks to Leavenworth, and one of them picked up something from the military post there. He had papers, which means if they are doing something illegal, someone up high knows about it. There is no way they are getting something on or off that base without permission, right?" Shelby asked.

"Depends on who signed the orders and what the orders are for, but it does seem strange that this new trucking company is hauling items for the military. It usually takes a lot of clout, plus a good reputation in the trucking industry to get military loads."

"I wanted to get onto the base and check things out, but I knew if I did, I might have blown my cover, especially if base security found out I was investigating a delivery truck. I think you need to get Cody to find out who authorized that truck onto that post. Something really underhanded is going on right under our noses. I can feel it."

"Yeah, you could be right." Angelica pondered for a moment. "By the way, where the hell are you?"

"Oh, I rode the bike back to where we were in Kansas City. I loaded it up, and now I'm rolling about a mile behind them on I-80 headed to York, Nebraska."

Angelica scolded. "Well, until we figure out what your subjects are up to, do not, I repeat, DO NOT make contact with them or put yourself in any predicament that will get you hurt."

"Don't worry, boss lady, I got this. I'm just keeping my eyes open and my mouth shut."

"The eyes open I can believe, the mouth shut, not so much." Angelica laughed.

Shelby huffed. "Fine, I see where your loyalties are. I guess I'll have to spoil Harley rotten just to get even."

Angelica laughed, but then got serious. "I want you around for a long time to spoil that kid of mine, so take care of yourself out there. Damian is taking a few days away from Dante's place to make some money, Shades and Dante aren't moving or receiving anything right now."

"That seems odd."

"Yeah, I think they know we're watching them."

"Could be, Shades needs to come out of his spider hole and face us."

"Fat chance of that happening, he's a coward. So, I'm stuck here in Dearborn until my trucks decide to move again. I did want you to know that Shield Sheik has a massive main terminal here in Dearborn."

"Really? Do they have a lot of trucks?"

"Yes, it looks to me like they have a few hundred in the terminal here right now. Those trucks aren't sitting still, either. I don't know where they are getting their loads or even what they are hauling yet, but they are moving something."

"Well, I gotta go right now, Angelica, we just pulled into the truck stop here in York. It looks like one of the trucks is parking and the other is taking on fuel. I need to go, call you soon."

Angelica didn't like the fact that Shelby hung up so quickly, but she knew she had to trust Shelby if her little blonde partner was going to make it as an agent.

◊◊◊

"What the hell is going on, Shades? Why am I staying in my own room now? Why can't I stay with you in our room?" Chrystal tugged at Shades' arm as he passed her in the hallway.

Shades stopped, hesitated, and then spoke to Chrystal. "Look, I have nothing to say about what happens to you right now. Dante wants you, and whatever Dante wants, he gets."

"I'm not just some piece of ass you can pass off to your boss anymore, Shades. I thought that I meant something more to you than that now. I thought I had earned the right to be your woman. I don't want to be with him, Shades; I want to be with you."

Shades pulled his arm away from Chrystal. "It's over, Chrystal. You belong to him now, and there is nothing you or I can do about it."

Tears welled up in Chrystal's eyes. "You bastard. You're no different than that creepy old snake of a man in there." She pointed toward Dante's office. "The only difference between the two of you is he has a fortress of slime protecting him from the cops, and you have to beg for a corner to hide in."

Shades slapped Chrystal so hard that she fell to the ground. "Shut up and just do what you're told. I have more important things to think about and deal with than you right now."

Chrystal put her hand to her red, swollen cheek and gritted her teeth. "You're not a man; you're a mouse that's going to be eaten alive by that snake."

Shades wanted to hit Chrystal again for her insolence but a twinge of his true feelings for Chrystal stopped him. He whispered. "Shut up, Chrystal, and just do whatever he says. I'm working on a few things. Just give me some space to deal with him. I can't take care of things if you're on my back, too."

With those final words, Chrystal fell to the floor and sobbed. Shades left to do Dante's bidding.

Through her sobs, Chrystal swore vengeance. "I hate you, Shades! I'll die before I give myself to that perverted old man. You've done your last deal over me."

Chrystal got up and went to her room. She grabbed a small bag of pills that she had in her purse. She went to the ice bucket where an uncorked bottle of expensive champagne had been left for her—it was a gift from her new admirer. She took the entire bag of pills and flushed them down her throat with several gulps from the bottle. In a few moments, her head began to spin and she dropped both the empty bag and the unfinished champagne. She felt numb; nothing mattered to her anymore. She opened her door and stumbled down the hall to the room she'd shared with Shades. She closed the door, walked over to the bedside table, turned on the lamp, and opened the door to the table in search of Shades' revolver.

It wasn't there. There was, however, a very sharp dagger neatly positioned along the inside of the drawer. "This will work," she said as she unsheathed the blade.

She walked methodically to the bathroom and removed her clothes, piece by piece. Once inside, she placed the dagger on the edge of the huge garden tub. She jammed the stopper into the drain and turned on the water. Steam rose from the near scalding bathwater. She lowered her naked body into the tub; the drugs and alcohol made her dismiss any discomfort from the water. She sighed with relief, knowing that soon her torturous life on earth would be over.

Chrystal picked up the knife and made elongated cuts deep into the radial artery of both arms. The dripping dagger fell from Chrystal's hand and landed flat on the mat next to the tub. She closed her eyes, let her cloudy mind drift, and her blood pressure plummeted. The water from the faucet mixed with the crimson blood and spilled over the side of the tub as her body submerged. Moments later, she was dead.

CHAPTER SIX

The chill in the air drove straight through Shelby's jacket and pants as she pushed to keep up with the truck that left the parking lot after fueling. She knew that it was going to be dark in a couple of hours, which meant that not only would it be colder, but she would be more visible because of the bike's headlight. The truck went south on Highway 81 for about two miles and then turned east on an old farm road. She wanted to follow them but knew she had to keep her distance or the trucker might become suspicious. Shelby held back, allowing only the flying dirt off the rear tandems to guide her to wherever the truck might be headed.

Shelby estimated they had gone about three or four miles down the rough and rocky road when the truck turned into a well-maintained farm yard. Not wanting to draw attention to herself, Shelby pulled her bike down into a road ditch to the north. Treading carefully in the ditch, she walked toward the farm until she could see through the barbed wire fencing. The eighteen-wheel truck was partially backed into an enormous white and blue building, which also housed lathes and drills. Several vehicles were parked near the house, with about half a dozen men gathered at the front of the truck.

Before long, the group of men disappeared into the machinery building. Shelby couldn't help herself; she gathered two of the lower fence lines together in one hand and two of the higher fence lines together in the other, which gave her enough room to slither through the small opening and into the yard. She moved quickly to the outside of the building. She peered through a crack in one of the seams closest to the corner and saw that the men were unloading what appeared to be a military hummer. Shelby wanted to get a better look at what else was in the building, but she knew that she would have to wait until it got dark unless she could find another way.

She continued to watch as much as she could through the small crack and noticed a small door near the front of the building that was open. The eighteen-wheel truck formed a barricade between the men and the door, blocking them from view. She leaned in for a closer look and saw a huge combine and corn wagon parked in front near the same door. Without thinking, Shelby moved toward the front of the building and through the open door, unnoticed. Once inside the building, she moved slowly behind the combine's gigantic wheels. Still uncertain she was completely camouflaged by the farm equipment or safe where she was, Shelby looked around and spotted some old dusty wooden stairs that appeared to lead up into a loft.

This is perfect, she thought.

She tiptoed up the rickety steps and into the loft. The men entered the building and became so occupied with checking out the hummer that they were unaware of being watched. Shelby pulled her cell phone from her pocket and tapped on the recording app. She moved across the loft, as quietly as a cat. She knew she couldn't shuffle, because the floor was made of old plywood and two-by-fours that were well weathered by the rain and snow. The gaps in the wood reminded her of the loft in the barn at her parents' place in South Texas. Shelby had learned from experience on that ranch that lofts were great hiding places from her brothers. She always had to remember not to shuffle her feet because the dirt from the top floor filtered through the cracks down to the bottom floor and would easily give her away.

She only had a few inches left to go in order to be directly overhead of the men when the voices stopped. Shelby froze. She hoped that she hadn't done anything to alert them to her position above them. With the cell phone still in her hand, she hit the pause feature and waited, hoping the talk would resume again soon.

I'm far enough, she thought, and lowered her body to the floor as gently as possible. Her nose was just atop a wide crack, which gave her an excellent view of what was below her. What she saw almost made her scream. There wasn't one Hummer in the building—there were four! Now she understood why there was so much sophisticated machine shop equipment in the building.

Three of the vehicles had certain sections of their bodies stripped down and parts were strewn around the building.

What in the world are these guys doing with these Hummers? she wondered. She knew she had to remain quiet and still until the men left the building—no matter how long that would take. Her attention was diverted when, to her surprise, a couple of women came in. Even if she'd been able to understand their language, she would have not been able to hear what they said. The deferential women spoke in whispers and only nodded when one of the men spoke to them. Then the women followed the men out of the building.

Shelby sat up. She was alone in the dimly lit structure.

◊◊◊

"You bastard! Because of you, Chrystal is dead!" Shades shouted at Dante.

Dante remained calm and leaned back in his leather chair. He was smoking an after-dinner cigar. He removed the Cohiba and blew smoke into the air. "Don't blame me for that whore's decision to end her life. I would have given her anything."

Shades pulled the gun from his waistband and pointed it at Dante. "You're going to pay for this. I should have taken you out a long time ago."

Dante didn't flinch. In a single move, he put his cigar on the edge of the crystal ashtray and pushed the alarm button under the front edge of his desk. Nothing happened. He pushed it again. Still, nothing happened.

"I disabled it before I came in here, you old fool. No one is coming to save your ass from me this time. Take a hard look around, Dante. This is the last time you're going to see it. It's all mine now."

Before Dante could utter another word or attempt to move, the hollow point bullet hit him right between the eyes—he slumped in his chair. Blood streamed down his cheek and pooled on the floor.

"There, you greedy, old bastard! The devil will meet you in hell."

◊◊◊

Shelby didn't move for a few moments until she was absolutely sure that everyone had left the building. Once she felt the coast was clear, she found her way down from the loft and over to the Hummers. She knew the men could return at any moment, so she pulled out her cell phone and began taking pictures of everything she saw around her. She eased over to the door so she could take pictures of the Hummer that was still in the truck. There was a desk in the corner, and she went over to it and saw several bills of lading and other paperwork piled on top. She was taking pictures of them when she heard voices outside the building.

Shelby made her way back into the shadows and hid behind the combine. She wanted to take more pictures and record more of the conversations she heard, but she also had to remain vigilant for the perfect time to sneak out into the now dark night. A roar gave her the opportunity she needed to escape. One man had climbed into the truck to drive the Hummer off the trailer. The other men stood around the truck, there to guide him out. The ample noise and the men's rapt attention on the Hummer was her cue to leave.

Shelby moved toward the open door she had entered through earlier and slipped out into the night. She was almost to the fence when she stumbled and her cell phone flew over the fence and into the ditch. "Shit." She scrambled to her feet and carelessly maneuvered her body through the barbed wire fence, catching a small portion of her coat sleeve on some of the prongs. "Damn it." She looked at the rip in her jacket. "I loved this jacket."

She knew she didn't have much time before the truck that had brought the Hummer to this farm would be returning to the truck stop. She began searching frantically in the tall grass and shrubs for her phone. Not only did the cell phone have the evidence she just collected, but it was her only source of communication back to Angelica and Jack.

Shelby had been searching for several minutes when she suddenly heard the eighteen-wheeler parked at building fire up. "Great the remote control. Maybe I can hide down here in the brush until they go by." Just then, Shelby's phone vibrated and she saw the light from it glowing less than a foot away. She reached down and picked it up. She quickly put it in her jacket pocket and zipped it shut. She had no intention of answering any calls right now.

She moved her motorcycle up the small incline of the ditch and put it up on the road. She could tell that the big rig was slowly moving away from the building and heading toward the road. Within a few seconds, she had mounted the bike, started it, and was well on her way down the dirt road before the big truck ever reached the end of the exit.

Shelby's heart pounded as she raced toward the main highway. She looked over her shoulder several times to make sure she was far enough ahead of the truck for the driver not to recognize her rear bike light. Shelby reached the stop sign at Highway 81, quickly turned her bike north, and sped to the truck stop. Once she knew she was far enough ahead of the truck, both her speed and her heart rate slowed. "Wow, that was a close one. I can't ever tell Angelica or Jack about that; they will skin me alive." Shelby laughed to herself.

When she finally pulled into the truck stop, the cold of the night air finally broke through her adrenaline rush. "Damn it, it's kind of cold out here tonight." Shelby moved her bike to the back of her trailer and opened the doors. She lowered the hydraulic lift and placed herself and the bike onto it. Then she pushed the remote control, and the lift took her and the bike up to the floor level of the trailer. She rolled the bike in past the car and into its own personal stand in the front portion of the trailer. She strapped the bike into place and then moved back to the rear of the trailer.

Shelby remembered when Betty had locked her in a reefer trailer where she could have died. Or when Betty again locked her and Jack in a trailer in Colorado. They *both* almost lost their lives that time. Those nightmares still haunted her whenever she walked the inside length of a box trailer. *I know I have to let those thoughts and fears go when I'm inside one of these babies, but it still creeps me out from time to time,* she thought, as she lowered herself to the ground on the lift.

After securing the lift back into place, and then closing and locking the doors, Shelby walked into the truck stop restaurant. *I'm hungry, and I know I must have a dozen phone calls to return.* She smiled to herself as she opened the door and went inside.

◊◊◊

"Angelica, this is Damian. When you get this message, please give me a call."

Angelica listened to her messages, hoping that one of them was from Shelby. She hadn't heard from her partner in several hours, and she was nervous with the way Shelby had abruptly ended their last phone conversation. She was also looking for the newest member of the DEA because her husband Jack had not been able to reach her, either.

Angelica decided she would try one more time before calling Cody. She did not want to call their handler; Cody would have to send out the calvary and both of their asses would be in slings. Thankfully, before she could reluctantly dial his number, her phone lit up with a call from Shelby.

"Where the hell have you been? I've been calling, Jack's been calling, and if you hadn't just called or answered one more time, I would have had to call the one person you don't want me to."

"Look, I'm sorry, but I was following one of the trucks on my bike. You will not believe it when I show you pictures of the cargo I got at the place where they unloaded that Hummer."

"Shelby, what did you do? You were told to follow them, but you did more than that, didn't you?"

"I was hiding in a ditch outside the barbed wire fence when I saw an opportunity to get inside this humongous machine shop. They never saw me. I had to hide out in the loft and behind some equipment, and it took me longer to get back to my bike than I expected, but I got great audio and photos. I had to hurry and get my bike out of the ditch; then I raced back to the truck stop before the truck driver saw me on that farm road."

"Shelby, if Cody gets wind of this...."

Shelby interrupted. "...but he won't. Not unless you tell him."

"Oh my God, Shelby Mathews, are you completely out of your mind? You are not supposed to be close enough to anyone or anything in order to take pictures. Have you completely lost all your senses?"

"Calm down, Angelica. Nothing happened to me except a small rip in one of my favorite jackets from that stupid barbed wire fence."

"You are going to be the death of me. I'm going to have a heart attack, and my sweet little Harley is going to be motherless."

"Oh stop, you know I'll be her momma if anything ever happens to you." Shelby laughed, but meant what she said.

"Shut the hell up, Shelby Mathews. It's time for you to rejoin my training classes. I can't have you out there pulling stunts like you just did."

"Why? I know what I'm doing, and I got some really great stuff. Angelica, seriously, I know I told you I wouldn't make contact with any of the suspects, and I haven't, except for those two women and their husbands in that truck stop laundry room. But I had to get those pictures and get as much information as I could about these people. These are some bad people, and they are planning some really terrible things. They've got six military Hummers in that building that they are taking apart. I'm pretty sure I saw explosives and detonating devices, among other things. The pictures should confirm what they have in mind. I took pictures of paperwork, including bills of lading, schematics, and even what looks like emails that were printed out. There were a couple of computers in there, too, but I didn't have time to get any information off of them. I recorded some of their conversations. I have no idea what they were saying. I think they were speaking in Arabic. This is a treasure trove of information, and if I hadn't gotten what I did tonight, it might have been gone by tomorrow, especially if they feel they have been compromised in some way. So stop being mad at me for not following orders, and be happy I got out clean. You would have done the same thing and you know it."

Angelica sighed. "You're right. You did the right thing. I'm proud of you, but it was still a dangerous thing to do without backup. How the hell am I going to turn that information over to Cody without explaining how you got it?"

"Just tell him I followed the truck, the truck unloaded, and left. After the truck left, I went into the building and checked it out. I got the pictures and left." Shelby explained.

"Yeah, but isn't that truck in some of those pictures?"

"Yeah, well just tell him it was another truck."

"I'll try, but Cody's not stupid. He knows bullshit when he hears it."

"He'll just make you keep me on for more intensive training. You will have to drop what you're doing and follow me around."

Angelica felt conflicted, and not just over how much to tell Cody. "You know, Shelby, we're on to something big. I'm afraid that they'll pull it away from us and insist that we continue with this drug investigation."

"No, Angelica, you can't let him do that. Isn't there some way that you can join me? Come so that we can follow these guys together instead of those drug dealers. This is really important, Angelica. I know these people are planning something really awful, and I want to stop them if we can."

"I hear ya. Let me talk to Rex and see what he suggests. We still have to keep an eye on these drug dealers because they are involved in some way with Shield Sheik, but maybe Rex can tell me how to handle Cody. You get some rest and keep an eye on those trucks. Don't tell Cody or anyone else about this stuff until I talk to you tomorrow. You email me everything you've got. Upload the recordings and send them to me too; use the app with the encryption that I showed you. We don't want anyone intercepting any of this information."

"Okay. I'll get everything to you as soon as I talk to Jack and calm him down. He's been blowing up my phone ever since we started talking."

"Sounds good, I'll talk to you tomorrow." Angelica hung up her cell phone. "How the hell am I going to get you out of this one, Shelby Mathews?"

◊◊◊

"Hi, Damian, this is Angelica. I've been busy talking on the phone with Shelby. What's up?"

"Well, I'm not really sure, Angelica. I did a couple of local loads today and then on my way home, then I stopped by Dante's place just to see if there was anything going on."

"Was he there?"

"I don't know, but there was some strange shit going on. At first, I thought I was hearing things when I heard the gunshots coming from Dante's mansion. But then I saw a big truck go in through the gate. It backed right up to the front of the mansion, and they loaded stuff out of the house into the truck. I could have sworn I saw it was Shades driving that big truck when it left. I followed it to a factory that Dante owns, but they closed the gates before I could get inside to see what they were up to. I know what they do in that factory—they have melting incinerators in there, like they have in steel plants. They use those hot furnaces to melt down plastics and cans for recycled materials. At least that's what they say they use them for. But I'm thinking tonight they are using them to get rid of a body, or maybe evidence of a murder."

"Thanks, Damian. I'll see what I can find out. That is quite a bit of suspicious activity. Keep an eye out when you can, and let me know if you hear or see anything else."

"I will, Angelica."

CHAPTER SEVEN

"**I** know you aren't supposed to get involved in my cases, Rex, but I really need some advice on how to get my and Shelby's butts out of this ringer she has gotten us into. Can you help me, babe, please?" She went on to tell him about her conversation with Shelby.

"Damn it, Angelica, you know better. The only advice I can suggest is to maybe put the pictures off on one of your CIs. That way, Cody won't be able to ask you who you got the pictures from because you can't and won't disclose your informant," Rex said in desperation.

Angelica was ecstatic. "Rex, you are a genius! I should have thought of that myself."

"Now, explaining to him how pictures from York, Nebraska ended up in one of your informant's hands, while you have a training agent in that same location might be a little harder to explain. But crazier things have happened in this business."

"Just coincidence. He can't prove otherwise."

"You'd better be careful, Angelica. Cody isn't me, and he won't hesitate to knock you down a notch or two if you get out of hand or if he catches you in a lie."

"I know, but the information and pictures that Shelby captured are so important. Baby, this isn't just about drug trafficking anymore. These drivers that she is following are some really bad guys—maybe even terrorists. You heard about that gun store bombing, right?"

"Yeah."

"We think it's the same guys that Shelby has been following."

"Oh, now that's even more damaging, Angelica. Why the hell aren't you turning this stuff over to Homeland Security instead of Cody? If you truly believe that those drivers are involved with some kind of terrorist plot, you need to contact Homeland now!" Rex demanded. "If you don't, I will. There is no telling what those people might do."

"I will, Rex, but you know how slow they are about checking out stuff we notify them about these days. Shelby and I are on to something really big with these two trucking companies we are following, and it's not just drug-related. We just want a couple of weeks to find out what they are doing."

"A couple of weeks, Angelica? A lot can happen in a couple weeks."

"I know."

"You'd better step lightly. If more things start happening, I think you'd better be prepared to expose what you know and fast," Rex warned.

"I think I'm just going to turn over everything to Cody in an email, but I'm not going to tell Cody to contact Homeland Security, or even that I think he needs to look over the information right now. I'm just going to send him the information and let him decide what to do," Angelica decided.

"That's not right, Angelica. You know how things get lost in the agency. What if he doesn't take the time to look over your surveillance photos and these idiots blow up half of L.A. or New Orleans this time? No, you can't do that. I won't let you do that. You tell Cody about the photos and information and tell him to send it on to Homeland. If they let it fall through the cracks, then it's on them and not us," Rex insisted.

Angelica hesitated. "Okay, Rex, I'll do it. Can I at least have a week to see what they are up to, first?"

"No. Pass that information along and do it today."

"Okay. But we are not giving up our tail of these guys until someone from Homeland Security takes it from us or Cody pulls us. This is Shelby's and my case."

"Fair enough. Now go do your job, and get off my phone so I can feed the baby. By the way, we both love and miss you very much. When you coming home?"

"I miss and love you guys, too. I can't say for sure when I'll be home, but it won't be too long. I'm sure Cody is going to give me a few days off for bad behavior after I turn this stuff in."

"It won't be all that bad, Angelica. Bye, babe."

Angelica looked at her cell phone. She ran through the list of phone calls she had made in the last couple of days. There was Cody's number. She hesitated for a few moments and then lit up his name with her finger. The phone immediately dialed Cody's phone. "Well, here goes nothing," Angelica said as she put the phone to her ear.

"You got Cody, what can I do for you today, Angelica?"

At least he sounds upbeat, she sighed "Glad you're in a good mood," she said.

"I am, unless you have something to tell me that will put me in a bad mood."

"An informant just sent me some interesting information. But before I give it to you, I want you to promise that Shelby and I will get to continue investigating these drug traffickers. Even if you have to contact another agency and they try to take over. Remember, my informant is the one who uncovered this information, and Shelby and I want to follow it through. We also want to continue investigating Shades because we think he's somehow mixed up in all of this." Angelica took a breath.

Cody waited for a moment for the information. "So, what is it?"

"First you give me your word that the case remains ours," Angelica insisted.

"Seriously, Angelica? You know I can't give you that kind of guarantee. I don't have that kind of power. Besides, if the information you are about to give me is that sensitive, the higher-ups will surely take control of it without your say so," Cody reminded her. "Just give me the encrypted information, and I'll let you know. I find it hard to believe that someone got you additional information about these drug yahoos that we probably don't already have."

"Come on, Cody, you can give me something. This *is* about the drug trade, but my informant has uncovered something more sinister going on, and it has to do with the military and foreign participants. I'm not talking about

Central America, the West Indies, or Mexico, either." Angelica tried to give him a taste of what she had in order to gain some leverage.

"What the hell, Angelica? Are you out of your mind? You know if you have vital information about some criminal activity going on, you are sworn to uphold the law. Now, tell me what you got and I will try and keep you on the case, but I can't promise anything."

"All right!" Angelica reluctantly told Cody everything that she knew, forwarded all the photos, and hoped that after he examined the information and turned it over to Homeland Security that she and Shelby would still have an investigation to run.

Cody called her back thirty minutes later. "So, what you're telling me, Angelica, is that an unnamed informant gave you this information and these photos. That this informant just happened to be in this, what looks like a machine shop, by him or herself, and took all these photos, recorded all of this conversation, and turned it into you just because it was the right thing to do?"

"Yes."

"I'm younger than you, Angelica, but I wasn't born yesterday. Did your informant happen to give a location of all this activity?"

Angelica hesitated. "Somewhere in Nebraska."

"Nebraska? Now isn't that a coincidence? Shelby just happens to be on a tail in Nebraska. Really, Angelica, you expect me to believe Shelby had nothing to do with this surveillance? I mean, how probable is it that some mentally-ill, tweaked, street worm trying to avoid a stay in a local lock-up might have compiled all of this professionally gathered intelligence? I don't buy it. I think you'd better come clean."

"Look, Cody, I gave you the info, and its serious stuff. Where it came from isn't important. It came from an informant. Now, when you hear from Homeland Security, I expect to know about it right away. Until then, Shelby and I will continue our surveillance." Angelica stood her ground.

"You'd better get that girl on a short leash, or both your jobs are going to be on the line." Cody hung up without saying another word.

Angelica called Shelby.

"Hey, Angelica, what's up?"

"What's up is that half my ass was handed to me by my husband this morning and the other half was just now handed to me by Cody. He's pissed."

"Oh. I'm so sorry, Angelica."

"Look, Shelby, I'm not angry. I totally get what you're doing and why, but you can't do this by yourself anymore. Please, until I can break away from my surveillance and join you, which I hope to do very soon, you need to stick to just tailing those trucks. Cody isn't stupid, and he knows that information came from you. If he wanted, he could have both of us yanked off these details right now and have both our butts sitting behind a desk. Don't do this to me, please."

"I won't do it again, Angelica. I will call you about anything that goes on. I promise."

"Good. Now, I'm in Ohio until these guys move. Once I get a chance, I'll break away from these trucks and hook up with you. Keep your eyes and ears open. NOTHING ELSE. Keep me informed as to where you are and wherever those trucks go."

"I will."

◊◊◊

"I don't care what you think, you pissant. Dante isn't here, and he left me in charge. If you have a problem with that…" Shades stood. He had been sitting behind Dante's desk in a new leather chair. The one he had shot Dante in a day earlier was so soaked in blood, so he incinerated it along with the old man's body. He pulled out the gun concealed in his lower back and pointed it at the man in front of his newly acquired desk. "I'll be happy to introduce you to my new enforcement team, Glock 43."

The man put up his hands and backed away toward the door along with two men who had been standing next to him, "Fine, Shades, but Dante never let me know he was leaving or where he was going. He won't answer his cell phone, and none of his security team is missing, so no one is with him. I'm his top security lieutenant. He never goes anywhere without security. Something isn't right here."

Shades put the gun down on the desk. "Don't worry about it. He told me he wanted a private getaway with his new girlfriend, Chrystal." Shades sat back down at the desk. "I think he went out on his yacht. He said he didn't want to be disturbed for a while." Shades moved a few papers that he had been looking through around on Dante's desk. "He has left everything to me, including his gorillas. So that means I'm in charge of you guys, unless you would rather I give you your final paycheck so you can hit the road. It's your choice. I do have other guys that I can bring in within the hour who can take over for you with no trouble."

"Why would I do that? I've been working for Dante for twenty years."

Shades stood up again and took aim at the men at the door. "Tucker, I don't really care how long you've worked for Dante. I'm in charge until he returns. Can I make that any clearer? We are doing things my way. If you don't like it, get the fuck out."

"Fine, but when's he coming back?" Tucker asked.

Shades waved the gun around at the men. "Don't know. I guess when he gets tired of banging his new fling. Which at his age, shouldn't take long," Shades scoffed. "Who gives a fuck when he comes back?" Shades sat back down. He pointed his gun at the men again. "Deal with it. In fact, you know what? I've decided to just get my own guards. You're fired. Get out of here! By the time my new guys get here, you and those goons had better be gone."

"Fine, Shades, we're going." The three men disappeared into the hall.

Tucker huffed in anger and talked as he walked out. "Something just isn't right here. Dante never would have left town or went on his yacht without security."

"When was the last time you saw him, boss?" one of the men asked.

"The day before yesterday, I was off yesterday."

"Who was in charge of Dante's detail yesterday?" the other guard asked.

With a knowing nod, he said, "Riggs. Stupid-ass Riggs. Let's find the son-of-a-bitch and find out what happened here yesterday." All three men moved through Dante's mansion until they came to a door that led to the back grounds area. There, positioned about two hundred yards north was another building where the security guards slept between rounds.

Tucker entered his security code on the keypad and the door opened. The men walked into the semi-dark hallway. To the right were several offices, to the left was a television lounge area. Tucker looked into the room and spotted the man he was looking for right away. "Riggs!" Tucker yelled. "Get your lazy ass up out of that seat and tell me what the hell went on around here yesterday."

Before Riggs could respond, Tucker grabbed him by the neck and threw him up against the wall. Several other security men in the room stood up and prepared to defend their partner. But after seeing who had Riggs by the neck, they quickly holstered their guns and backed away from the conflict.

"I asked you a question, Riggs, and I expect an answer," Tucker demanded.

Riggs choked and sputtered trying to breathe. Tucker loosened his hold on the man's neck, and Riggs gasped for air. After Riggs composed himself, he rubbed the area around his neck and spoke through several coughs. "What the fuck, Tucker? Why are you tryin' to kill me?"

"I want answers, and I want them now!" Tucker pushed Riggs up against the wall again, only this time, he had his gun out and pushed against Riggs' belly. "I want to know what the hell went on around this place yesterday. Where is Dante?"

"Nothing went on around here yesterday except that girl that Shades was banging killed herself in his bathtub. Dante didn't call for me all afternoon. I checked on him before I went off duty this morning, right before you got here, and Shades told me he was still asleep."

"So, you never physically saw Dante at all yesterday afternoon or evening?" Tucker put his gun away.

Riggs shook his head. "Nope, the only thing we dealt with was that girl's dead body. After the maid found her, Dante called me and told me to help Shades put the body in one of the trucks from the recycling plant."

"Dante told you to help Shades with the body? You talked directly to Dante?"

Still choking and coughing, Riggs answered, "Yes, Dante told me to get some of the guys together, wrap the body in sheets, and put it in the truck parked at the front entrance. He said that Shades would be hauling the body over to the recycling plant. So, that's what we did."

Tucker moved away from Riggs. "Did you talk with Dante after that?"

"Just once, when the job was done, and he said he was going to his bedroom."

"And you're sure it was Dante?" Tucker insisted.

"Yeah, man, it was Dante." Riggs rubbed at his neck. "What the fuck is this all about? Why did you almost kill me over that stupid little whore's body?"

"It's not about the body, you idiot. Dante is missing, and Shades claims that Dante went off with that girl—the dead girl you guys just told me was put in the back of that truck. I have a feeling that Dante did leave with Chrystal, but not on any yachting trip."

"So, do you think Shades killed Dante?" one of the other men in the room asked.

"Yes, I do." Tucker paced the floor.

"What you want us to do about it?" Riggs asked.

"I'm not sure we can do anything about it, at least not right now. Shades just fired me, and I'm sure he's coming for the rest of you. He's bringing in his own security team. I'm thinking our time here is over, but I have an idea. As much as I hate cops, I think maybe with their help we might be able to bring Shades down. Then we can come back in and take over Dante's operation once the feds have cleared things out."

Tucker looked at the seven men in the room. "I know where everything of any value is in this place. We have exactly forty-five minutes to get as much of it as we can before Shades' security team shows up. "Riggs, we can't get to Dante's computer in his office, but I know all the pass codes. Get your computer and bring it here."

Riggs left and went to his room.

"Harold, you and Jason figure out something to get back into that house quickly. There is a box in Dante's room that has keys and security lock codes for every building and vehicle here. The yacht codes and keys are there, too. Get that box and bring it to me."

The two men left.

"We could take Shades out, boss," Ram said.

"No, it's too late to try anything like that. Besides, he's holed up in Dante's office. That office is like a safe house. He won't leave there until his team arrives. By then we'd better be gone or we'll be in a gunfight for sure."

"What about the wall, gate, and grounds guards. Aren't they going to be a problem once we start hauling stuff out of here?"

Riggs came back into the room and opened his computer up on a table for Tucker. Tucker sat down in front of the computer and started punching keys. "Don't worry about them right now; we'll take them out one by one, should there be any resistance."

Soon, all of Dante's bank and other money accounts came up on the computer. Tucker punched in security codes and other vital information, which allowed him to transfer millions of dollars that had belonged to Dante over into other accounts that he could control. He changed passwords, he built files for important information that he thought he might need later, and then he deleted hundreds of files. Knowing that he didn't have time to completely wipe out everything and take all of the money that Dante had hidden, he closed the computer. "There, that will keep Shades busy for a while, trying to figure out where all of Dante's money went."

He got up from the table and looked through the window at the mansion. "Now, if those two guys will just get back here, we can gather a few loads of product, some stored artifacts, and unload a good portion of Dante's arsenal into the trucks we are going to confiscate." Tucker saw the two men racing out of the back door of the mansion. One was carrying a small, strong box in his arms.

"Good, they found it. Come on, men, we have twenty-five minutes to clean this place out."

CHAPTER EIGHT

"**O**h hell, what now?" Shelby reached for her phone above her head on a shelf in the sleeper. "Yeah, this is Shelby."

"Time to rise and shine, sleepyhead. You've got work to do," Jack said gently.

"Oh, hi, sweetheart. Yes, I know it's five a.m. and time to roll."

"You told me last night to call you when I got up this morning so that you could make sure you didn't miss tracking your trucks."

Shelby threw her covers back and bolted from her sleeper with her cell phone still at her ear. She peered through the closed curtains on her windshield. "Damn it! One of the trucks has already left and the other truck is leaving the parking lot now. I shouldn't have slept so long. Look, baby, I gotta go. I'll call you back in a little while. I have to catch my tail or I'm going to lose them. I love you."

Shelby felt bad about not waiting for Jack's reply as she pushed the end button on her phone and threw it on the unmade bed. She took off her shorts and tee-shirt and grabbed her jeans, a bra from the drawer, and fresh t-shirt from the closet. As quickly as she could possibly move, Shelby dressed, ran a brush through her hair, slid the curtains back from the windows in the front cab, jumped into the driver's seat, and pushed in on the air brake knobs. "No time for a pre-trip inspection right now, I gotta catch that truck."

Once again, Shelby's phone rang. She reached for her Bluetooth device and attached it to her ear. She moved her big truck out of the parking lot and then southbound on Highway 81. "Yeah!"

"You sound busy for so early in the morning. You aren't infiltrating another barn, are you?" Angelica teased.

"No, but I am in a hurry to catch up with one of my trucks. I thought getting up at five would be early enough, but I guess I was wrong about how early these jokers get going in the morning."

Shelby sped up. "I know where they are headed; the younger of the two women I talked to yesterday told me they would be heading home to Salina, Kansas, but I want to know where they go when they get to Salina. One of the trucks left already, but I still have a chance to catch up with the other one."

"Well, don't get yourself in a wreck trying to catch them. Once you get to Salina, you can track them down with your car. But remember…from a distance."

"I know, I know. Keep my distance. You're no fun anymore, so professional."

"Now come on. I'm fun; I just like to make the higher-ups *think* I'm doing things like they want them done. It makes them so happy," Angelica explained. "Look, enough chatting for now. I do have to get down to some serious stuff with you. I know that when you make your morning report with Cody that he will pass this information along, but I wanted to personally let you know that some really crazy shit is going down around the country. A community college parking lot in Kansas City, Kansas erupted in gunfire yesterday. It was one male gunman who opened fire on several students in the parking lot. Homeland Security is not disclosing specifics, but Cody says it was a foreign exchange student from Libya. She killed two and injured twelve before the explosive device she was wearing apparently went off accidentally because she was still shooting when the thing detonated. They say the explosion blew up some cars she was using as a shield, the two who lost their lives were hunkered down in one of those cars when the shooting started."

"She?" Shelby asked. "I was just in Kansas City yesterday, Angelica."

"Yes, I know that, and you were also in St. Louis when that gun store fire occurred. Just listen to everything before you get freaked out. Yes, it was a female. Cody said that Homeland Security is dragging their feet. They either don't know details or won't give any to him. Hell, he's come up with more information on his own by conducting computer searches for Shield Sheik. He'll fill you in on everything during your morning report call, but from the sounds of things, you've stumbled into a real hornet's nest. Cody wants me to continue following Glacier for a few more days since, from what he can tell, they are delivering several of their loads to Shield Sheik facilities. What I've come up with so far is that Shield Sheik's home terminal is in Dearborn, Michigan, but they might have other terminals around the country. That terminal in Dearborn is one big son-of-a-bitch, and from what I could tell while I was scoping it out, they've got hundreds, or maybe even closer to thousands of trucks coming from, going to, and parking in that yard."

"You told me it was large, but that is larger than some commercial lines. What are they doing?"

"That's what I'm trying to figure out."

"How is it possible for them to grow so fast? When I was running the roads, I never came across even one of these trucks. Now, you can't go into a truck stop or really anywhere without seeing at least one. The trucks aren't flashy, so you don't really notice them unless you're looking for them, but once you get to know what they look like, you realize that they are everywhere."

"That's what Cody is looking into. The problem is that the company not only isn't flashy, but Cody says they look 'too clean,' financially and business structure-wise. They are literally and figuratively off the charts."

"Damn it, that is really insane, and I'm out here chasing after them in my eighteen-wheel truck."

"You'd better watch your ass. We have no idea who these people are right now; nor do we know what they are up to. Keep your butt in the truck seat, and don't let them know you're watching them. We don't know what they will do, but we know what they are capable of."

"I got it, Cover Girl. Barbie will keep her ears and eyes open and her gun holstered to her hip. When do you think you'll be able to join me?" Shelby asked.

"Not sure just yet. A couple of days, I suspect. It really depends on where your trucks take you."

"Well, if that woman I was talking to was telling the truth, and they are headed home for a few days, it looks like I'm going to be on a thirty-six-hour layover. So, really, there is no need for you to hurry with what you're doing. I think all I'll have to do is simply find out where they live and watch their daily habits. I might even find a good restaurant for a nice meal."

"Sounds good. I really do need a little more time following Glacier. These idiots are driving me insane with all of their constant stops. I think they know I'm following them, and they want to piss me the hell off. Why can't they just rack up the miles and deliver their loads? I'm going to bust them eventually. May as well get it over with, right?" Angelica chuckled.

Shelby laughed. "Right." Suddenly, Shelby stopped laughing. "Hey, I gotta go. Call you back."

Angelica didn't like the sudden disconnection from her partner. "Shit, what the hell have you gotten yourself into now, Shelby Mathews?"

Angelica's cell phone rang. It was Damian.

◊◊◊

Shelby went past the two trucks that had pulled over into a small parking area just a few miles outside the Kansas state line. She backed her truck down and quickly pushed a few buttons as she spoke into her GPS. "Siri, where is the closest rest area or fuel station?"Siri responded, "Fuel stop, one point two miles away on the left."

"Thanks, Siri." Shelby absently replied to the woman's digital voice. "Good, I will only be about a mile ahead of them. Looks like my two tails caught up with each other. I just hope they don't change directions. I'll lose them altogether."

◊◊◊

"Hey, Damian. What's up?"

"Not much, but I did go by Dante's place last night and this morning before going to work. Did you ever find out whether there were any reports of gunshots or missing persons? There is some really strange stuff happening over there. I just saw a whole bunch of trucks leaving the mansion. Those trucks were being driven by some of Dante's upper-level bodyguards. It also looked like the guards at the gates were trying to stop them from leaving."

Angelica pondered the information. "To answer your first question, no, we haven't received any reports of gunshots in the area during the time you reported you heard them. Nor has anyone been reported missing, but I seriously doubt any of those criminals in Dante's organization would have any family that would care enough to report them missing."

"I know that," Damian replied.

"It does make me think that maybe something internal has gone haywire. If Shades took Dante out, or forced him to get rid of some of his henchmen in order to put himself further up on the food chain, that could be a problem." Angelica unintentionally voiced her inner thoughts, "I need to see if my handler will let me try and infiltrate Dante's mansion somehow. We need to find out if Dante is still around."

"I think I could get in there. Amber told me once that Shades had a girlfriend who was really nice to her. Her name was Chrystal. I might be able to act as a delivery person, delivering some flowers for Chrystal. I could see if I could get some information from her," Damian suggested.

Angelica thought about it. "One problem. How would you know that she's even there? Shades and Chrystal moved into the mansion because of the heat that is on Shades from the ATF, FBI, and the DEA, not to mention the local law. No, that would be dangerous. Besides, I'm sure she wouldn't answer the door. However, I might be able to get one of Shades' old girls that we busted and is still in lock up to try and contact Chrystal in exchange for time off of their sentence."

"Damn it, I wanted a reason to get close to that bastard."

"I know, but I don't want you to get hurt. His time is coming, Damian, and I promise I will get you in on the bust somehow. Right now, I want to know what is going on at that mansion."

"It's just…."

"Patience, Damian."

"Fine."

"What you're doing by keeping your eyes and ears open for me around there is awesome. I just can't stand the thought of that bastard hurting you, too. Just keep doing what you're doing and let me see if I can put pressure on one of his old girls."

"Okay. I'll see what else I can observe from out here."

"Thanks, Damian. I'll talk to you tomorrow."

◊◊◊

"That fucking bastard Tucker is a dead motherfucker." Shades looked over the ransacked arsenal warehouse. He took the lid to one of the empty wooden crates and threw it across the floor. "He's a dead man. I'm going to kill you, Tucker! There is no running from me." Shades threw several other items that were in his way. He turned to the new men he had now under his control. "You will help me find Tucker and the rest of those fuckers. They are all dead. Do you get me? Kill all of them."

"Yes, sir." The new men were too afraid of the maniacal man to refuse him.

"Check the other buildings and let me know if Tucker and his men got into them as well. The bastard took off in several of the company vehicles while we were talking in my office. I think he also took one of the company ten-wheel trucks. I saw that on the security monitor, but those bozos at the front gate just let him pass. Fucking idiots! I told them to not let him out of the gate with anything."

"We'll get them for ya', boss! Do you know where he lives?" one man asked.

"No, dumb ass, I don't know where he lives! I have to check the computer in my office to get all of that information. You think I have time to keep up with every security person I have on staff?" Shades grabbed the man by the nape of the neck and forced him to the ground. "Maybe I'll make you my computer wizard, bitch!"

"Yes, sir!"

Shades let go of the man after humiliating him. "Now, get the fuck up. I'll tell you what I want you to do and when I want you to do it. The rest of you assholes, check out the other buildings and bring me a report. Me and my new computer wizard bitch—we'll be in my office finding out if Tucker screwed with my money, too."

◊◊◊

Shelby hit the button on her headset. "Hey, Cody, how are you this bright and early morning?"

"Well, not as good as I would be if I were still in my bed sleeping. Seems I have to keep up with the two crazy women I've been assigned to keep in line."

Shelby couldn't tell if he was joking or not. "So, what have you got for me today?" she asked.

"I'm sure you already heard from Angelica about the trucks that I'm tracking and that we are headed to Kansas. Or at least until about fifteen minutes ago, I was following them to Salina. Right now, I'm stopped at a little truck stop just inside the Nebraska-Kansas line. My trucks are stopped a few miles back at a rest area; I didn't want to blow my cover, so I went on down the road a couple miles. I'm hoping they head this way soon."

"Yes, Angelica did let me know what you've been up to and some of it hasn't been good, Shelby. You are just a tail and nothing more, do you understand?" Cody insisted. "I also have you on my GPS tracking board, so I'm fully aware of where you are."

"Yes, sir," Shelby said.

"Please, don't call me sir—Cody is fine. I'm sure your trucks will be along soon. I'm also thinking that I may go against my better judgment and have you put some tracking devices on those two trucks when they shut down in Salina. I'm becoming quite concerned with the information that I'm gathering on my heightened searches pertaining to this massive, rogue trucking company. I think you stumbled onto something rather dangerous. Homeland Security dragging their departmental heels, but I should know sometime today or tomorrow if the company is legit. I should also know if any of that information Angelica gave me from you will be of any use."

"From me?"

"Never try to BS me, Shelby."

"Sorry about that, Cody, I just had to find out what they were doing," Shelby admitted.

"Look, I get that, but you're in training, and there are things you just don't understand about investigation and surveillance. We are investigators, not spies. We leave that spook stuff to the CIA. Sometimes we have to use more covert practices, but most of the time we just report what we see and hear. We may use informants for the rest of the dirty stuff. You are not trained to be undercover; I need you to remember that," Cody scolded. "It's not only about your safety. It's also about what will hold up in court."

"I understand, Cody. I'll play it cool."

"Good, now that I have you reined in, I have to say that I find what you have uncovered compelling. Why on earth would truckers have six military-issued Hummers on a farm in Nebraska? Something isn't right."

"That's what I think, too. Plus, these guys aren't delivering to normal delivery outlets, and their pick ups are off the beaten path; they're not using normal routes. I can't speak for the whole operation, but nothing about these two truckers seems normal. I'm hoping once they shut down in Salina that I'll be able to learn more about them."

"Shelby…"

"From a distance, I promise."

"That's more like it."

"Hey, Cody, I gotta go. My trucks just went by, and I need to catch up to them again."

"Drive safe," Cody replied.

"Got it." Shelby pushed in one her air brakes and put her truck into gear.

◊◊◊

"What do you think Rex? You think you can get one of your guys in Georgia to make a deal with one of Shades' girls in lockup?" Angelica asked.

"I don't know, Angelica. I have a few connections down there, but it's been a while since I've talked with any of them. I'll see what I can do."

"I just want one of them to call Dante's mansion and ask for Chrystal. Once she gets her on the phone, I just want them to have a normal conversation. I'm interested to see if Chrystal will give her any information about what's going on. Maybe the informant can ask if she can come to the mansion after her release or something."

"I'll see what I can do, baby." Rex agreed.

"How's my little pumpkin doing?"

"Harley is giving me a little attitude about taking her afternoon naps lately. She wants to sit in my lap all day. I can do most of my handler duties holding her, but not the computer work. She likes to play with the keys. I have to proofread everything. I sent a note to the director the other day and didn't notice Harley had added a few of her own keystrokes to the note. Director Allen was a little confused until I told him it was a secret encrypted message from Harley. Thankfully, he laughed."

Angelica laughed. "That's my girl, making points with the director for her parents."

"Yeah, right. Hey, speaking of Harley, she's whimpering. I'd better go see what's up. I love you, babe. I'll check with Georgia Corrections in a little while."

"Love you, too, sweetheart. Give Harley kisses and hugs from her mommy."

"You got it." Rex hung up.

Angelica looked at her phone. She loved her job, but she missed her baby and her husband.

Angelica watched as the Glacier trucks that she'd followed into a truck stop outside of Columbus, Ohio left the parking lot. She pushed in on her air knobs and put her truck in gear. "Now, where are you bastards headed?" she mumbled.

◊◊◊

Once she arrived in Salina, Shelby did her best to follow the two trucks to a Shield Sheik truck yard. The yard was located in what Shelby determined to be a normal industrial area of town. There was no attempt to hide the facility from public view, but she could tell that once a truck cleared the open outside gate, the driver would have to clear another gate with guards before entering. This wasn't uncommon, but with what she knew so far about Shield Sheik, there was nothing common about the company. She parked along the road a few blocks away from the entrance. She waited and hoped the two drivers and their wives would leave the facility in their personal vehicles soon. It didn't take long.

Shelby's phone rang. It was Angelica. "Hey, what's up, girl?"

"Shelby, Cody is on the line, too. We need to talk. Cody just got word that a car bomb went off in a Walmart parking lot in York this morning. No one was hurt, but we both agree that these might be some kind of test runs for something bigger," Angelica explained.

"Bigger? What the hell do you mean bigger?" Shelby sounded nervous.

Cody explained, "We are just speculating at this point. Of course, Homeland Security doesn't think it's anything beyond some lone wolf-types looking for attention, but with my cyber investigation of Shield Sheik, I believe there is a whole lot to be concerned about at this point. It's possible they are planning another big attack on America, like 9/11—maybe worse this time."

"Oh wow. This really is serious!"

Cody's voice remained calm and decisive. "We've got this, Shelby. Remember, we are professionals—there is no need to panic. Angelica is on her way to Pittsburgh from Ohio. I don't want to pull her off her detail just yet. Shield Sheik and Glacier are working together; we know that. I need you to keep your head down and eyes open for a few more days until we can get some further information on what exactly they are collaborating about. Can you do that?"

"Of course I can. I'm following my truckers and their wives. Right now they are in their personal vehicles. I know that I can't follow them all the way to their neighborhoods, but I can get a general location. Once I do, I'll get into my car and find out where they live. I'm not sure I'll be able to put those GPS trackers on their trucks right now. They turned their trucks in at a Shield Sheik yard in Salina. But I'll keep a close eye on these people and see what they might be planning," Shelby said.

"That's good, Shelby," Angelica said. "It shouldn't take more than a few more days to find out what these two groups are doing for each other. I know that Shield Sheik is delivering drugs and illegal goods for Dante and Shades in return for Glacier delivering loads for Shield Sheik, but we just don't know exactly what the loads are yet."

"Well, Hummers for one. If they have access to that type of equipment, they can certainly get drones, explosives, and chemicals. A foreign-owned trucking company with access to all of these illegal items—if you ask me, this whole thing stinks to high heaven," Shelby said.

"Yes, but it's up to us to diffuse this whole thing before anything really bad goes down," Cody insisted.

"How are we supposed to do that alone, Cody?" Shelby asked. "Where are the other 'alphabet agencies' in all this?"

"I'm working on that, I promise. You and Angelica just have to keep an eye on the targets for now," Cody said.

"I'm with Shelby on this one, Cody," Angelica sounded impatient with her handler. "You need to make it clear to Homeland Security that the information we are uncovering is crucial."

"I'm trying, Angelica; they're just not listening at the moment. Who knows why? Maybe they've got other situations on their radar."

"They'd better *start* listening, Cody—this could turn out to be a mess," Angelica replied. "Don't worry, Shelby and I will do our parts and keep watch. Remember however, if DHS doesn't come through, we have enough woman power to do things alone."

"I will, I promise. Don't remove the safety lock on those sidearms just yet," Cody tried to assure the women.

"I've got all my trust in you, Cody…Uh, oh, I gotta go." Angelica's tone sounded urgent. "I'll call y'all back later."

"She's turning into a Texan, Cody. Did you hear that 'y'all' come out of her mouth?" Shelby laughed, trying to make the moment lighter.

"Sure did, *y'all!*" Cody also laughed in an attempt to hide his concern for his agents. "I'll always look out for you and Angelica, Shelby, that's my job."

"I know."

CHAPTER NINE

"**L**ook, you son-of-a-bitch, I caught you red-handed exchanging money instead of a waybill for cargo. Now you can talk to me or you can talk to the feds, but I'm a whole lot nicer." Angelica stared in into the eyes of the man sitting across the table from her in handcuffs.

The man smirked. "I want a lawyer, *Angelica*," he spoke in a heavy Spanish accent.

Angelica stood and kicked her chair into the wall. "Fine, Señor Rodriguez, you can talk to the feds. I'll make my deal with your partner, Señor Sanchez. He seems a whole lot more cooperative."

"Don't bet on it, Angelica." Eduardo laughed.

Angelica slammed the door as she left the interrogation room.

One of the local detectives waiting for her in the hall asked, "Did you get anything?"

"No, he lawyered up. How about you?" Angelica was frustrated.

"Not much, but he did say that they were scheduled to meet up with some other trucks in Buffalo, New York. There's some kind of powwow there. He wouldn't say where exactly after he realized he'd just given up a piece of vital information. He's not very savvy. You want to give it a go?" The detective asked.

"No, I think I'll just let you and the feds handle these jokers. I'll hit the road and see if I can pick up their trail to Buffalo."

"Are you sure you don't want to try and get more out of these guys after all that hard work busting them?"

"No. What I should have done was bust these parasites in Birmingham when I first caught sight of them. I'll let you guys claim the bust and the paperwork. Send me an email with the report and I'll sign it." Angelica smiled. "I need to get going if I'm going to find those assholes."

"Good luck, Agent Brighten."

Angelica grabbed her coat and headed out the door. "Thanks, it's getting cold out. I just hope I don't get into any bad weather."

"Not supposed to snow until next week sometime."

"Good to know."

Angelica strode to the parking lot and got into her Charger. She started the engine and was about to leave when she decided to check in with Cody.

"Cody here."

"Hey, I know it's way early in the morning. I need to let you know we had a successful bust in Pittsburgh, but as we suspected, everyone lawyered up. Dante and Shades aren't going to be happy when they find out that several of their trucks have been impounded in the Keystone State. They're taking inventory on the trucks right now. They haven't found much in the way of drugs. What they *have* discovered are chemicals, which they are testing, and mechanical parts used to modify guns. They had a couple of containers of saltpeter, sulfur, and charcoal, which were not listed on any of the manifests."

"Gunpowder. So the locals have enough to hold them and confiscate their loads?"

"Oh yeah. Most of the waybills they were carrying are fabricated documents. What was listed on the manifests doesn't match the contents in their trailers. This is some scary shit, Cody. I'm used to dealing with drug traffickers and thieves, but this is different. Those Glacier and Dover trucks should have been loaded with drugs. Where are the drugs?"

"I'll bet Shelby's right; those drugs are probably on Shield Sheik trucks."

"Yeah, maybe. I'm going back to my truck for a few winks. Then I'm headed to Buffalo, New York in the morning. One of the perps let information slip about a group of their trucks meeting their somewhere."

"Do you know when?" Cody asked.

"No, and I don't know where in Buffalo. But I do know who; now I just have to get lucky and catch either a Glacier or Dover truck headed to Buffalo."

"Or a Shield Sheik truck," Cody noted.

"Yeah, I'll bet I can find one of those going there, too."

"Get some rest; call me tomorrow."

"Okay. Any word from Shelby?"

"No. She's been pretty quiet. Last time she checked in she told me she'd found the neighborhood. Apparently, most of the Shield Sheik drivers live in the same neighborhood. They live as typical Midwest family units—single-family dwellings, two kids, two cars, and a dog. I looked at tax and property records in Saline County. From what I could tell from the tax records, most of them are of Middle Eastern decent. Their homes are all within several blocks of each other. Shelby did some surveillance in the neighborhood. From what she observed, those associated with Shield Sheik didn't appear to associate much with the neighbors outside their inner circle. In fact, she was asked to leave the area by a couple of men when she was spotted parked on one of the public streets. She did as they asked, not wanting to cause problems or blow her cover. The closest mosque is in Lawrence, and they caravan there for prayer and services."

"That seems strange," Angelica said. "Living sequestered in a middle-class neighborhood."

"DHS calls these cells, 'no-go zones,' and they are popping up in neighborhoods all over this country," Cody said.

"What the hell is a 'no-go zone'?"

"Well, originally most sleeper cells were set up in apartments in big cities. Originally, in the late 1990s and early 2000s, radicalization targeted single young men who could live in the shadows of big cities with diverse populations. But with the proliferation of social media and the rise of rival groups, some factions started recruiting families to be placed in smaller cities and towns around softer targets. They start with a couple of families and get them settled in—some open small businesses like printing shops and some purchase convenience store franchises. Soon, other relatives join them and their community starts to grow. However, instead of assimilating, they start their own schools, civic centers, and in some cases build mosques."

"That doesn't sound so bad," Angelica noted.

"It's not, really. America is the land of opportunity. We've always welcomed refugees, and we should continue to do so. Like anything else, it's a few bad apples that ruin it for everyone else. It's not the fact that they are moving here or that they are practicing their faith. It's the factions that become radicalized that pose the greatest threat. When radicals insert themselves into an emerging Muslim community, they often try to persuade their new friends and neighbors to insulate themselves from Westerners. They form their own neighborhood watch groups in an attempt to keep law enforcement from patrolling their streets and set up jamming devices to keep law enforcement from monitoring their activities. In some cases, there have been reports of them handling their own legal matters, mostly misdemeanor stuff—as far as we know."

"Wow, create their own legal systems? Can they do that?" Angelica asked.

"No, not legally at this point, but they are pushing in that direction. Orthodox Jews and devout Catholics do have rules around culture and customs that are adjudicated in their own tribunals, but not when it comes to criminal matters."

"I can see how it can be a slippery slope. If we allow different groups to dictate their own laws in their own communities, then we could become a fractured country of different laws, not one nation under constitutional laws, right?"

"It's a possibility. But it's also complicated. Remember, different states have different laws and even individual counties and cities have different laws. State rights is our protection from an overreaching federal government. That may be why Washington has been allowing these communities to establish themselves. It's tricky for DHS and other agencies—respecting individual freedoms while keeping all U.S. citizens safe from terrorist threats."

"But at the end of the day, we are one nation following U.S. laws, which is why we have to insist that Homeland Security hold these communities accountable for any violations of our laws, even if conflicts with their religious laws. That's the whole point of the Supremacy Clause in the Constitution."

"Have you passed on the information Shelby gave you from Nebraska?"

"I've tried. They are not willing to concede that there is a problem."

"What the hell is going on? Do you think there is some sort of cover up?"

"I'm not sure. I'm doing everything I can to find out just what Shelby has uncovered, but I just keep hitting brick walls."

"Do you think it's a jurisdiction thing? We're beyond just hunting down drug dealers at this point. Maybe we stepped on the wrong toes."

"I haven't wanted to admit it, but I agree. Shelby has uncovered a hornet's nest."

"Are you going to pull Shelby and me?"

"No, not yet—for two reasons. First, Homeland Security and the other agencies I've contacted seem really tight-lipped when it comes to this stuff, which in itself pisses me off. After all, we're all supposed to be on the same side. They should be sharing everything they know with me instead of trying to divert our attention elsewhere. Second, I want to know who these people are and what they are doing here."

"I agree. Something smells to high heaven with all this."

"I'll keep you informed. If I hear anything from DHS, ATF, FBI, or the CIA I'll let you know," Cody said.

"Thanks. I'm going to my truck to sleep. I'm wiped. Talk to you soon."

Just as Cody hung up, information from DHS appeared on his screen.

◊◊◊

"What the hell do you mean you just lost two loads of Shield Sheik property?" Shades' voice over the cell phone blistered Rodriquez's ears. "I should have left you in that cell!"

"Look, boss, it was that DEA who busted us—Agent Angelica. She had the locals take us down before we were able to get our loads to the drop site. At least they didn't get the product, boss. It's still in the warehouse."

"Shut your trap!" They might not have gotten the product, but Shield Sheik sure isn't going to let us have that product without getting their loads in return."

"Brighten has the trucks and trailers secured in police impound. There's no way we can get at them."

"That bitch is dead. I've had all I can take when it comes to her. She keeps sticking her nose into my business," Shades yelled. "See what you can do about getting into that impound lot and getting those trucks out of there, or at least the loads. I don't want Shield Sheik pissed about this. Do you understand? I will take care of Brighten somehow."

"I got it, boss. I'll do what I can."

"Get it done!"

Shades ended the call and slammed the phone on the desk. "Something has got to be done about that bitch." Shades pointed to one of the men standing in his new office. "Get me all the information you can find on Angelica and Rex Brighten. I want to know where they live, if they got kids, everything!"

"Yes, boss." The man left the room.

Shades looked around the room. "I think it's time we make a little house call to Shield Sheik headquarters in New York. I want you to get Dante's, I mean *my* plane ready at the airport. We will make a trip to Buffalo tomorrow." Shades knew as long as the cops thought it was Dante on the plane, they would monitor his activity but not interfere without cause.

◊◊◊

"Morning, sunshine," Cody greeted a tired Shelby.

"Good morning, Cody, if you can call it that," a sleepy Shelby replied.

"What? You're not bouncing out of bed, ready to get that next bad guy around the corner?" Cody teased.

"Shut up, Cody. I'm not awake yet. I only had three hours of sleep. My gun is still in the holster in my sleeper, but I can promise you if you were here right now, it wouldn't be. Now, what the hell do you want?"

"Testy, testy! Do you always wake up like this? Poor Jack."

"Get on with it, Cody."

"Fine, I need your report. You should also know that Homeland Security is stonewalling us. Angelica and I agree it's probably time to pull you off this detail and put you back with her."

"No way, Cody! You can't pull me; this is too important. Something really bad is going on here. I don't care if Homeland Security is ignoring us. I have a really bad feeling about what is going on and so should you. Besides,

Angelica told me yesterday that she was going to try and wrap things up on the East Coast and join me in a few days."

"I know she told me last night, but plans have changed. Angelica made a big bust in Pittsburgh last night and looks like she's going to get into some hairy stuff in New York in the next few days. It all has to do with Shield Sheik, Glacier, and Dover—so you'll still be working on the case."

"Look, I know y'all think I'm just a rookie, and I may have been a little overzealous out of the gate, but Cody, don't make me drop this tail right now. I know I'm on to something here, and these people are leading me right into their plot."

"I know how you feel, Shelby, but I think you need to back Angelica up on her end."

"Please, Cody, give me one week. They come off of their thirty-six-hour break today. Let me follow them for a week and see where they go and what they do. If I can't find anything else out about them, then I'll back off, I promise," Shelby pleaded.

"I don't know, Shelby."

"One week, Cody, please. I promise."

"Fine, but just one week. Regardless of what you find, I'm pulling you."

"Thanks, Cody. I just have to find out what these guys are doing."

"Remember, you're restricted to tailing—that's all!"

"I understand."

"I'll let Angelica know. I sure hope she doesn't get shot or something while her backup is off chasing tail somewhere."

"That is a terrible thing to say. I'm trying to do what is right, so don't try and lay a guilt trip on me."

"Now, how about your report?"

"There isn't much more to report from last night. I staked out their neighborhood from a distance. I'm being careful since they caught me on their street. Lucky for me it wasn't the two men I met at the truck stop in St. Louis. They are really protective of their neighborhood—they call it a neighborhood watch, but it's more than that, Cody. They are policing their own streets, and many of them are armed. I stayed out about five blocks but never saw another local."

"No locals at all?"

"None."

"I better check with the PD there and see what's up. Were you in the county or city limits?"

"Both, actually. Some of the property is in the city limits and some of it is in the county. But I didn't see the locals or the county patrol around any of that area."

"Okay, I'll check on that. What's the plan for today?"

"They finish out their down time today. I'm fixin' to shower, dress, eat, and head toward their yard. I think I can use a parking lot a few blocks away from their truck yard. I'll wait for them there."

"Okay, stay safe and let me know what's up."

"I will. Thanks, Cody."

◊◊◊

"Angelica, it's Damian. Give me a call when you can. I've got some information for you." Angelica listened to Damian's message on her cell phone and then called him.

"Hey, kiddo, what's up?" Angelica said when Damian answered.

"Hey, Angelica." Damian sounded half asleep.

"I'm sorry, Damian, I didn't mean to wake you up."

"No problem. Hey, I have some really important information for you. I saw a couple of SUVs leave Dante's place last night. They went to the airport. It was not Dante on that plane, Angelica. I haven't seen Dante in a while now. Shades got on that plane with some new security guys. I'm just speculating here, but I think Shades took Dante out and now he's running the show."

"No shit? That is news. I think I can get Cody to find out their flight plan."

"No need, I went into the office at the airport. I have a buddy who works there. He makes sure the planes get out of the hangars, and he usually knows what flight plans have been filed. He told me everything. That plane is headed for Buffalo, New York, but no return flight filed yet. That's all I know."

"That's great intel. I'm headed to Buffalo right now. I'm going to have the locals see if they can find out where the occupants of that plane spent the night."

"I've got an idea. I'm going to pretend to be a repairman and see if I can get into that estate."

"No way, Damian! You can't do that—it's too dangerous."

"I'm not even sure I can get in, Angelica; I'm just going to try. The only people in that place right now are a few security guards. If I'm right about Dante, then we can get the locals involved and bust Shades," Damian reasoned.

"I understand what you're trying to do, but you can't, Damian; you could be discovered. I can't protect you if you trespass. Dante was bad enough, but if Shades is in charge and you get caught up in there, he will torture you. He's evil."

"Fine, I'll wait 'til you get back down here," Damian lied. "But we might not get another chance."

Angelica didn't like how easily Damian gave into her. "Swear to me you'll wait."

"I'll wait," Damian lied again.

Angelica still didn't know if she believed him, but she let it go. "Just keep watching the place when you can, and let me know what's happening. Swear you won't go in there."

"I swear." Damian's fingers were crossed. "I gotta go get a load, but I'll check in soon. You be careful up there in New York."

"I will. Call me soon."

"I will."

CHAPTER TEN

Shelby knew after her earlier conversation with Cody that she couldn't tell him she had done a little more than surveillance the previous night. She couldn't tell anyone what she had discovered or how she had discovered it, especially if she still wanted to stay on Shield Sheik's tail.

As she waited in the parking lot only five blocks from the Shield Sheik truck yard, Shelby went over her journal entry from the previous night. She'd decided that since she couldn't literally make a full report on her activities to Cody without getting fired, that she would simply write them in a journal:

I entered through a small opening in the fencing around the truck yard. The facility had apparently been abandoned for the night. No other trucks seemed to be coming in, at least for the moment. I had already checked the place out before my entrance, taking note of the guard at the gate, the guard near the main entrance to a warehouse on the grounds, and the guard rolling around the property on a four-wheel golf cart-type vehicle. No other guards appeared to be present from the outside, but I wasn't sure of others until I entered the warehouse. I had to find out what was being held in that warehouse. Quietly, I searched around the building for an entrance into the warehouse, but there was nothing I could have used to enter without making my presence known. I almost gave up hope of getting access to the building and was preparing to exit the property when a Shield Sheik truck appeared at the entrance gate. The guard quickly cleared the driver for entrance and he pointed out the warehouse, apparently for either loading or unloading. The driver maneuvered his truck over and backed it into position at the dock with the help of the guard from the warehouse entrance. The guard on the roving four-wheeler pulled up next to the dock and then got onto a forklift, while the guard who had spotted the truck into position opened the dock overhead doors. I'd found a small hiding space near the side of the warehouse where I watched as the team of only three men, driver included, unloaded pallet after pallet of wooden crates of all sizes. Several of the pallets had barrels on them, but from my vantage point, I couldn't tell what was in the crates or barrels. One crate did come off one of the pallets. Its contents spilled out onto the dock, and the guards and driver quickly gathered a bunch of small arms. I continued to watch as they emptied the almost completely filled trailer into the warehouse before deciding that I needed to leave the property. This is very disturbing to me, especially the secrecy of this operation and the now two locations that I have uncovered and the dangerous contents that these facilities hold. I want to tell my superiors what I have uncovered, but for whatever reason, they are more concerned with my safety and their jobs than they are concerned with the safety of our nation. I don't understand why Homeland Security hasn't uncovered this, and even when they've been given ample information, they refuse to look into these places. I will continue to track and expose as much of this as I can until I am pulled from this case. Hopefully before that time, I will be able to get someone to listen to me.

Before Shelby could make another entry into the journal for the day, she looked up and noticed that the two trucks she had been following a few days before were now on the road again. Shelby threw her journal into her passenger seat, put on her seatbelt, pushed in on her air breaks, and proceeded out to the street. "Wait for me, boys."

◊◊◊

"Hey, Cody, can you find out from someone at the airport in Buffalo where Dante's private jet pilot and passengers might be staying?" Angelica requested before Cody could even say hello.

"Sure, is Dante going to be in Buffalo, too?" Cody asked.

"Yeah, one of my informants told me that Dante's plane left Georgia last night and heard a flight plan was filed for Buffalo. I figured it was kind of a coincidence, but if they are there to meet with their drivers, maybe even with Shield Sheik, I could just follow them instead of trying to guess where the meet-up is going to take place," Angelica explained.

"Excellent idea. I'll get back to you in a minute."

"Great. Oh, and also see if a passenger manifest was filed?"

"What are your suspicions?"

"Nothing really, I'm just curious. Use your pull with the FAA if you have to."

"This sounds like more than mere curiosity."

"I have a suspicion that one of those passengers is Shades, and he's impersonating Dante to stay under the wire."

"Okay, that's going to take me a little longer, but I'll get you the hotel information first."

"Thanks."

"How did you figure out Shades might be on that flight and not Dante?"

"Something the informant said. In fact, is there any way we can find out if Dante is still alive or not? Do we have anyone on the inside anymore?"

"I haven't gotten anything over the wire about Dante lately. Our insider was outed some months back. We haven't been able to get anyone back in there yet. What makes you think Dante is dead?"

"I have an informant who is keeping tabs on Dante's estate; he mentioned that he hadn't seen Dante in a while. He's also that same guy who let me know about Dante's plane going to Buffalo. He got a glimpse of the passengers as they loaded, Dante was not on the plane, but Shades was."

"So, you think Shades took out Dante? Maybe he was just going in his place?"

"I don't know, maybe. There's just a lot of weird shit going on at that place according to my informant."

"Well, I'll see what I can find out. Keep me apprised of what you discover. This could be a major break for us in the Shades' case. If he's exposing himself by pretending to be Dante, it will be easy to bust him outside that estate," Cody remarked.

"Yes, it will." Angelica looked forward to the day she would finally be able to put cuffs on Shades for Amber's murder. "I'll keep you informed. Hurry up with that hotel information. I've already got my charger unloaded; I'm ready to roll."

"Just a few more minutes. What? No crotch rocket?" Cody joked as he worked his computer for the information Angelica had requested.

"Too damn cold for a bike up here. I need to go back down south."

Cody interrupted. "Call ya back."

"Great, I'll wait," Angelica said, frustrated.

◊◊◊

Shades' guard came into his hotel suite with a laptop computer and a tablet of paper. "I've got everything you want on Agent Brighten, Shades. She's living in Dallas, Texas with her husband, Rex, and a baby girl named Harley. She's been an agent with the DEA for 10 years. Her parents live in Temple, Georgia." The young man powered up the laptop and typed in the Dallas address of the house that Angelica and Rex had just bought a few months earlier.

"This is what I'm talking about. Finally, someone who can actually get me the information that I want. How did you do this?"

Puffed up with pride that he had just scored some points with his new boss, the young guard boasted, "I was a government hacker until I went rogue on them a few months back. I got tired of the shitty hours, the shitty pay, and all those suits taking credit for my work. Most of them couldn't find their way around Google without help, let alone hack into private information on a DEA agent."

"Well done, credit is given where credit is due here." Shades handed the laptop back to the young man. "See what you can find out about what she's working on, where she might be, who her handler is, and if she's got a partner."

"It might take some time. I'll need to hack directly into the DEA's database. They have some pretty tough firewalls, but I've done it before—most recently for my previous employer. They needed me to access the Department of Defense and get them a manifest so they could get accesses to equipment to military bases."

"Very impressive."

"Well, in fact, it was my previous employer, Shield Sheik, where I learned about you, sir. I figured you could use someone with my expertise. Well, I'd better get started trying to get what you need from the DEA."

"I see you're someone who does his homework. I expect you to do more than try, son. Get it done. I want that information." Shades went to the balcony window and pulled back the curtain. "I want to know if that little bitch knows where I am today." Shades suddenly let go of the curtain. "What time is it? When is the meeting with Martinez and those Arabs?"

"It's twelve-thirty, sir. The meeting is set for two." The young man left the hotel room.

Just then, Shades' cell phone rang.

◊◊◊

Damian approached the guard shack of Dante's estate in the white plumber's van he had borrowed from a friend. Several other times, he'd wanted to do what he was doing right now; he was tired of watching for months from outside the wrought iron gates. His heart raced as he spoke to the guard. "I'm here to fix the bathroom on the second floor for Dante Holt."

The guard looked at his sheet. "I don't have an order from Mr. Holt for a repair today."

"Well, Mr. Holt's house manager contacted our office about two weeks ago, but you know we've been really busy. I told him we wouldn't be able to get to him for a couple weeks, but I would get to him as soon as possible." Damian held his breath.

"I'll need to check on this." The guard called up to the main house. Because of all the new people Shades had put into place, the guard wasn't sure exactly who was in charge of the house itself. He also thought perhaps the work order had been misplaced, he hadn't gotten his copy, and he sure didn't want Shades pissed off. "Are you sure?" the guard said into the phone. "I don't want Shades pissed off at me if there is something that needs to be fixed…"

"Look, if there is a work order problem on this, I can come back in a couple weeks. I got other jobs I need to get to, I don't really have time for all this security crap just to fix a leaky tub." Damian started to put the van in reverse.

"No, no wait." The guard waved his hand while still talking on the phone. "I'm sending him up. All he's here to do is fix a leaky tub; you guys can keep an eye on him. I'm sure the paperwork just got misplaced." The guard hung up the phone, opened the gate, and pointed to toward the house. "Go straight to the back entrance of the main house. The butler will meet you there."

Damian nodded to the guard and drove the van forward. He looked around as he drove. Dante's estate was beautiful, but Damian knew if he had as much illegal profit as Dante had, he'd be living the high life, too. Damian's heart was still pumping hard when the back of Dante's mansion came into view and a well-dressed older man guided him to a parking space. Damian parked the van.

This is it; I'm in. Now all I need is to find some evidence that will put Shades and Dante away for good.

"Right this way, sir. I can't seem to find the work order requesting this service, but since Master Dante left a couple weeks ago, nothing has been in order. Master Shades has been changing everything as of late; nothing is as it should be. I'm sure Master Dante will put things right when he returns."

"So, Mr. Holt isn't here?" Damian asked.

The man walked Damian into the rear kitchen entrance of the mansion. Damian was awed at the size of the place. "No, sir. And, there hasn't been any word from him since his sudden departure with that Chrystal woman. Some are saying they eloped; others think something else has happened to them. But it's not my job to gossip, just to run this place. Now, which bathroom was it you were hired to fix?"

Damian looked at a piece of paper he had written on for a prop. "I'm not exactly sure, the ladies in my office just said a second-floor bathroom."

"Oh dear, that does present a problem since there are eight on that floor in the west wing, and seven on the east wing. I'm sure it must be one on the west wing since those are used primarily for guests. Master Shades and his friend Chrystal had been using that wing for some time, until Master Dante left with the Chrystal woman. Master Shades has since taken up residence in Master Dante's east wing, but I haven't noticed any leaking tub in that wing." The butler walked Damian to an elevator. "I'll take you to the west wing. You'll have to check out all the restrooms."

Damian entered the elevator after the butler. "Okay. I can do that."

The man appeared rather irritated with the situation as he pushed the second-floor button and then stood back for the doors to close. "Master Dante is not going to like any of the changes Master Shades has made when he returns. Things have just been a complete disaster and so unorganized with Master Dante absent."

"I'm sorry to hear that." The door opened to the second floor, and Damian walked out into the hall. The butler stayed on the elevator, holding the door ajar. "I've several things to attend to. I'm sure you can find your way to each bathroom. If you can't locate the problem tub, or you need anything, just pick up one of the intercom phones in any of the rooms or hallways. They are connected to the security office; they will notify me and I'll be available to assist you."

"Thank you. Do you want me to go to the east wing if I can't find the leak here?" Damian asked.

"Yes, I suppose that would be okay." The butler, still holding the door, pointed to a long hallway that led to a pair of wooden double doors. "Straight down that hallway, through those double doors, that's the way to the east wing. Be sure and let security know you're going into that wing before you head that way. A security alarm will go off if those doors are opened without notification."

"Okay, I think I can manage things from here." Damian walked to the first door on his right and tried to open it. It was locked.

"That's a supply closet." The butler said as he let the door start to close. "The next one, please, sir."

Damian let go of the doorknob, smiled, gave a slight salute to the butler, and walked to the next door. Before opening the door, Damian looked up and down the hallway and took a mental note of all of the security cameras present in the hallway. He spotted several cameras. *This isn't going to be easy,* he thought as he opened the door to the first room.

Damian looked around the room as he entered it for security cameras. There didn't appear to be any, but he couldn't be sure. *I'll just have to risk it,* he thought as he went through the drawers and closets in each room.

Damian's search of the place had netted him nothing until he came to the bathroom that Chrystal had once occupied. Trying to appear as if he was actually looking for a plumbing leak, just in case he was being monitored, Damian looked at the pipes behind the toilet. He was not surprised when he located several spots of what appeared to be blood behind a toilet next to the tub in that bathroom. "Well, what do we have here?"

Damian searched the medicine cabinet behind the mirror over the sink, trying to find something he could use to get a sample. He located a cotton swab and an empty toothbrush holder. He opened the cabinet below the sink. He saw lotions, bath salts, and other items a woman might use in the bath. Damian rubbed the swab into the dark stain to get a sample. He then went through every drawer in the entire bedroom, bathroom, and closet shelves. He took photos of everything he thought was noteworthy. He saw a strap hanging from the top of a dresser. He reached up and brought down Chrystal's abandoned purse. Her wallet was in it, and he pulled out her driver's license. *Now, why would a woman leave her driver's license behind if she was off getting married?* Damian thought. *Maybe she isn't off getting married to Dante at all. Maybe they are united in death somewhere at the hands of Shades.*

When Damian found nothing else to search in the rooms he'd been given access to, he picked up the intercom phone and called the security desk. "Yeah, this is Frank Baldwin. I've checked all the restrooms on the west wing, and there doesn't seem to be a leak here; your butler told me to notify you when I needed to enter the east wing."

"Hold on a minute," the security guard on duty said. "You're to wait until I can clear it with the head of security. I need to call him."

Damian didn't like the sound of that response. "I can't hear you very well; there seems to be something wrong with this connection. Did you say go ahead?" Damian was determined to get into that east wing with or without permission. He headed toward the double doors and pushed on them.

"No, wait!" The guard yelled just as Damian opened the double doors. Damian could hear a loud alarm going off in the security room.

"Thank you," Damian said as he dropped the phone and went through the doors. He quickly took out a can of black paint from his tool bag and began coating the lens of each camera he located in the hallways. He figured the security guards hadn't turned the monitors on in the east wing yet, since they first had to turn off the alarm he just set off. He knew he wouldn't have much time to search, especially once they realized their cameras weren't working. He set out to find Dante and Shades' sleeping quarters.

◊◊◊

"Yes, Cody. I found the hotel, and I'm watching the building right now." Angelica stopped talking. "Hold on, Cody, I think they are coming out of the building now."

"Fine, let me know when you want me to call back…"

"Wait! Well, look at what we have here. I do believe it's Shades himself coming out of that hotel. I'm going to move in a little closer to make sure," Angelica said as she put her Charger in gear.

"No, Angelica. Hold back and wait for backup. You don't want to spook them. You know they must have lookouts," Cody insisted.

Angelica knew Cody was right. "Fine, I'll let you know where this tail leads me. You'd better have plenty of locals ready to back me up when I get ready to make this bust. Shades is going down today."

"I'm on the horn now with Buffalo PD; they have several units standing by. Take it easy, Angelica. We need a nice clean bust." Cody did his best to calm Angelica down.

Angelica pulled out just as Shades' small caravan of vehicles passed her car. "We are heading south on Delaware Avenue, Cody."

"Just stay with them, but don't get too close," Cody advised.

"I was tailing vehicles while you were still letting your mommy wipe your nose," Angelica chided him.

"Very funny. Look, I've got Shelby calling on the other line. I have you on the tracker. Don't hang up. Stay with them and I'll put Shelby on hold and transfer your tracker over to the PD tracker for the dispatchers so they can get the locals out there with you."

Cody left the line open and Angelica could hear him talking with Shelby. "Is this an emergency? I'll call you back in five minutes." Then she heard Cody again, this time speaking to Buffalo PD. "I just transferred her tracker to your monitor. Do you have her spotted? Hold on, I'll ask her." Cody picked up the open line to Angelica. "Are you heading right on Church Street?"

"Yes, but now we just turned left onto Lower Terrace," Angelica responded. "I think we are heading toward the harbor area."

Cody didn't respond right away; Angelica could hear him talking to the police dispatcher again. "Okay, yeah, good. You got her? No, I'm going to keep you on the line for a little while, just in case something happens. Yeah, thanks."

"Okay, Angelica," Cody said to her, "they are tracking your vehicle and several units are headed your way."

"Make sure they ARE NOT coming in with lights and sirens." Angelica paused and then shouted, "Oh shit, Cody, they just spotted me. I have to give chase. Tell PD to keep tracking me. Damn it, one of the vehicles just broke away. I'm going to stay with the two in front of me. Oh damn, another one just broke away. I knew I should have gotten a closer look at that bastard Shades; I don't know which vehicle he's in. Cody, I'm going to stay with this vehicle. See if you can get Buffalo PD to locate a silver four-door; it looks like a newer model Chevy heading onto the I-5. The other vehicle was also a four-door, but it's a dark blue Dodge Caravan. It made a U-turn and is now headed north on Lower Terrace. If Shades is in one of those vehicles, they will probably head straight to the airport. I'm hoping he's still in this brown SUV I'm following. We are still traveling. "

Cody was doing his best to communicate everything that Angelica was saying to the PD. "Yeah, on the I-5, not sure which direction on the I-5. She went under the five and is still in pursuit of the brown SUV. Vehicle is not stopping, but it's doesn't appear to be breaking traffic laws, either. She's doing her best to keep the vehicle in her sights. Yes, thank you." Cody came back to Angelica on the phone. "How are you doing, little lady?"

"I'm doing just fine, Cody. Looks like my pursuit is about to end. They just pulled up into valet parking at the Marriott Convention Center. Everyone is getting out of the vehicle. Some are even staring at me; they know I was following them. Shit, Shades didn't get out of this vehicle, any word from the PD if they located any of the other vehicles?" Angelica was furious that Shades had slipped through her hands again.

"Nothing yet, Angelica. They have airport security watching Dante's plane, but no sign of either vehicle yet." Cody tried to comfort Angelica. "We'll get him, hang in there. Are you going to question the men in that brown SUV?"

"No, that would be a total waste of time; they aren't going to say anything. He knew I was in Buffalo, Cody. How did he know that? Everything they did today was planned. He's probably meeting with his *compadres* right now, and they are laughing their asses off at me. That's okay. I'm going to nail that son-of-a-bitch pretty soon—you can bet on that, Cody my man."

"So, you still want the PD to keep an eye on the airport?" Cody asked.

"Yeah, and have them photograph every passenger that boards that plane. I want a flight manifest of passengers and the return flight plan. I suspect that Shades will drive part of the way back to Georgia and then catch his plane back to Atlanta from another airport. Or, he might get a ride from one of his drug smuggling buddies. Bastard. I should have known he wasn't going to go down easy."

"Don't be too hard on yourself, Angelica. I do have some good news. I had the airport authorities give me a list of all the private planes flying into Buffalo in the last couple days. They did mention that there were a higher number of private arrivals than normal. Two were from Saudi Arabia, three were from Mexico, one was from South Africa, and five others were from different states in the United States. Dante's was included in the five from the U.S."

Angelica sat in her car outside the Marriott. She wanted to go inside so badly and bust those bastards, but she knew it would be useless. "I wonder how many of those planes flew into Buffalo for that meeting Rodriguez was bragging about?"

"Don't worry about that, Angelica. You need drop this for now—head back to the truck stop and load up your car. I just got word Dover, Glacier, and Shield Sheik are heading to Virginia Beach to make an exchange, and you need to be there. I'm pretty sure this whole thing in Buffalo was a decoy to get you off their tail."

"Me, too. Okay, I'm heading to the truck stop. Did you ever call Shelby back?"

"Oh, damn. I forgot. Gotta go. Call you back."

◊◊◊

"Look, I don't want to keep hitting you, but Shades wants to know who you are and what you're doing here." The man said as he put his fist into Damian's gut again. Damian was bruised and bloody over most of his body. He was hanging by a thick rope attached to a cross beam in the ceiling of a poorly lit, cold, concrete-walled room with a steel door.

Damian coughed up more blood that eventually dribbled from his mouth and onto his bare chest after the blow. "Fuck you. Tell Shades to come ask me himself if he wants to know so bad. He's nothing but a drug dealing murderer."

The man hit Damian again—this time in the kidneys. Damian groaned in pain before passing out. Realizing that he wasn't going to get anything else out of his prisoner, the man and his partner left the unconscious and bleeding Damian hanging. "We'll be back in later to finish this conversation, or to finish you."

"Did you lock that door?" The man pointed down the hall to the room where Damian was being held.

"Of course, but that guy ain't going nowhere." The man shrugged his shoulders. "He can't even hardly breath, let alone walk." The men laughed.

"I need to call Shades and let him know this guy ain't talking to us." He pulled out his cell phone. "Yeah, tell Shades this guy ain't talking." He paused to listen. "I don't know, he just ain't." He paused again. "He just says he's not talking to anyone but Shades." Another pause. "The guy is almost dead; we beat him really badly." Another pause. "Yeah, he's secure in the basement. He might last another two or three days, but I can't promise he'll last more than that." He paused. "Okay, we'll leave him until Shades gets back. Does he want me to try and keep him alive?" He listened. "Okay, we'll give him some food and water 'til y'all get back here."

CHAPTER ELEVEN

Angelica sipped her coffee and listened to the news on the television inside the Virginia Beach truck stop café. She wasn't in any hurry since the drug deal that she was going to try and bust wasn't supposed to go down for several hours. She bolted upright in her booth when she heard that another terrorist attack had occurred—this time in Pittsburgh. "Damn it." Angelica quickly called Cody.

"Why didn't you call and tell me about the explosion at the impoundment lot in Pittsburgh?" Angelica demanded.

"I just got the information myself. I was just about to call you. It turns out that Shades had some of his lackeys try and get the trailers and trucks out of the impoundment lot yesterday. They failed miserably, all of them were arrested, but then this morning, someone broke into the place again and blew it to pieces. It looks like whoever that stuff belonged to in those trailers decided if they couldn't have it, no one could. They also blew up the warehouse where we suspect Shades' drugs were being stored."

"Looks like Shades pissed off one of his customers. Do you think that stuff belonged to Shield Sheik like Shelby is saying?" Angelica asked.

"I don't know, but Shelby is one smart cookie. She's still tracking those two drivers. So far they've dropped off some of what they were carrying in Clinton, Oklahoma; Lubbock, Texas; and Hobbs, New Mexico. They picked up some stuff outside of Hobbs at the chemical deposit plant. She is currently following them into Arizona. It's very possible that she is on to something, Angelica. I need you two to get teamed up again ASAP. This thing that she is on to is pretty big, and Homeland Security is still turning a blind eye to it. They don't think there is anything to what she's uncovering."

"She's smart, all right, and if DHS isn't paying attention, it's political. I think she's got something, too, but I can't break away from what I'm doing on this end right now. I'm also a little concerned about my informant from Georgia. I haven't been able to get a hold of him and that really bothers me. I may have to head down that way after I finish with this bust here in Virginia Beach. I have not seen one Glacier, Dover, or Shield Sheik truck in this truck stop all morning. Are you sure that they are supposed to be meeting here for an exchange?"

"Yes, from all the intel that I've been getting, there is a big deal going down at four this afternoon right there in Virginia Beach near the harbor." Cody suddenly broke away. "Something is wrong here—I just pulled that information up again on my computer; there is something really strange about the wording in this memo." Cody punched at a few keys on his computer keyboard. "Damn it, Angelica. You hang tight there for a little while—don't go to that harbor site just yet. I think I got a hacking piggybacker. In fact, are you packing?"

"Yes, I have my service revolver strapped to my side, under my jacket." Angelica felt for her weapon.

"Good, you need to be very vigilant, I think someone is tracking you through my computer. I'll get back to you in a few minutes."

Angelica was nervous. *How is it even possible that someone could be tracking my every movement through my own employer?* she wondered. *Aren't there firewalls and stuff like that to prevent such things from happening?* Angelica needed to talk to her husband. She punched up his name on her cell phone.

"Hi, baby, just needed to hear your voice," Angelica said when Rex answered the phone.

"What's going on, Angelica? We just talked this morning." Rex was suspicious.

"Oh, nothing really. Cody just informed me that not only did some terrorists blow up the trucks and trailers I had impounded in Pennsylvania, they then blew up a warehouse full of drugs. And now—he seems to think someone is tracking my every move through his computer. He said it's some kind of hacking piggybacker, or something like that. Do you know what he's talking about?"

"Well yeah, but it's pretty difficult to piggyback through government firewalls, unless you have actually worked on or been into those systems. Sometimes it can be accomplished by obtaining identifications and pass codes, but that's still pretty hard to do. If it has happened, the person who is doing it is connected to the government in some way, or else is one hell of a hacker. Does Cody think you're in danger?"

"He didn't really say; he just told me to stay strapped and vigilant. He seems to think this bust I'm on is a set up job. I'm beginning to believe him since I haven't seen hide nor hair of any Glacier, Dover, or Shield Sheik trucks. Plus, although Cody doesn't think so, I could just tell from the looks on those guys' faces in Buffalo that they knew all along I was there."

"You'd better be careful, Angelica Brighten, you mean the world to me and our little girl. I don't care what Cody says; you always trust your instincts over what your handler says. He's not there; he doesn't see what you see, or feel what you feel. You trust your own instincts always, you understand me?" Rex demanded.

"I am, baby, I promise." She sighed. "I wish I could come home right now."

"Then come home."

"Oh, you know I can't right now. Drugs are flowing into this country like water over a waterfall. Shelby is tracking some suspected terrorists who may very well be involved with Shades and his drug deals. To top it off, I haven't heard from Damian in a couple of days and I'm worried about him. See? If I come home now, the whole United States might get blown up. I really miss you and Harley, but I have another two or three weeks out here before I can come in for a break. I think once we get a handle on what Shades and Dante are up to, and find out what those yahoos Shelby is chasing are up to, both Shelby and I will be able to take a break and come home for a while."

"Don't stay out there too long, Angelica. I know you like being back on the job, but don't burn yourself out so fast. You can't save the world all by yourself."

"I know that Rex; that's why I got Shelby out here with me."

"Funny, you just be careful and take care of yourself. I mean it," Rex scolded.

"I will." Angelica looked at her phone. "Hey, babe, I gotta go. Cody is calling me. I love you. Give Harley hugs and kisses for me."

"Always do. Love you, too."

Angelica punched in the call from Cody. "What's up, Cody?"

"This is serious, Angelica. I just sent two armed patrol units to your location. Someone did hack into my computer and they are tracking you. The police are going to escort you to your truck, inspect it for explosives, and escort you out of Virginia Beach. I want you to come to our office here in Springfield, Virginia so that I can reprogram all of your electronic components and your truck. It's only about three hours from where you are right now."

"Fine, I've lost my tail anyway. If I'm not going to make any more busts on this case for a while, I'm heading to Georgia to find my informant. After I find my informant, I'm heading west to run with Shelby," Angelica insisted.

"I was going to suggest the very same thing," Cody said. "See you in a few hours."

"Right." *I can't believe my entire case blew up and that I'm back to square one.*

◊◊◊

"Boss, I'm telling you, we have been waiting for two hours now, and Agent Brighten hasn't shown up."

Shades was fuming. "Where's that computer guy? Send him to my hotel room now!"

Within a few minutes, the young man who had been hacking for Shades entered the hotel room with a laptop computer. "I'm sorry, Mr. Shades, some-how they found out that I got into their system." The young man put the computer on the table in front of Shades. "They have completely shut me out. They have even disconnected the tracking system on Agent Brighten's truck. I don't know how they found out; I was very careful not to cross through any firewall alerts."

Shades looked at the scene on the laptop. He sat back in his chair and puffed on a slim cigar. "Well, looks like we'll just have to wait until they reconfigure their entire computer system and try again, won't we? How long do you think it will take for them to reprogram everything?"

The visibly frightened young man responded as honestly as he could, "It's really hard to say, Mr. Shades. They'll have to reprogram the computers, phones, and GPS tracking systems, which means that they'll require Agent Brighten to bring her truck and electronics to the agency for downloads and reprogramming. It could possibly take a few days, unless they try and Band-Aid the system with just a reboot and reprogram from the main frame. I doubt they will do that since it's a government agency."

"So where is the agency located where Agent Brighten might be headed to for reprogramming?"

"Springfield, Virginia, sir."

Shades looked at the two men who had entered his room with the bad news about the botched ambush. "Do you think it would be possible for you two fuckheads to find out if Brighten is headed to Springfield without screwing it up?"

"Yes, sir, we can do that, sir."

"Good, when and if you locate her and her truck, I want you to follow her. I want to know where she goes and what she's doing. I have to fly to California and take care of some business there with Shield Sheik at the border. We have a new shipment coming in from Baja, and I want to personally make sure that the men Shield Sheik asked our Mexican friends to smuggle into the country with our product made it safe and sound. Shield Sheik is turning out to be a great ally, but they are asking for a lot of favors lately.

"We'll take care of it, boss. What about the prisoner at the estate? You want one of us to go back and deal with him?"

"I want you, and the men I have assigned to you, to do what I just told you to do. I will take care of things at the estate. Unless there is some reason you want to get back to Georgia?"

"No, sir." The men left Shades hotel room. "We are on Brighten right now, sir."

◊◊◊

Angelica entered the DEA office. "I'm here, Cody, let's get this mess straightened out. I need to get to Georgia. It's been too long since I've heard from my informant." Angelica threw her phone and placed her laptop on Cody's paper-covered desk.

Cody offered Angelica a chair. "Why so concerned with this particular informant? Most of the time informants don't want to be located."

"He's a special case; he's helped me out a lot. He's kind of a friend, too."

"You know that's not allowed when it comes to informants, Angelica. You have to remain objective in case that 'friend' gets his ass in a ringer," Cody scolded.

"Forget I said 'friend.' I'm legitimately concerned. He's given me a lot of information on Shades. By the way, did you happen to find out anything about Dante? In one of my last reports, my informant told me about some really suspicious activity going on at Dante's mansion. Was Dante on that plane that landed in Buffalo? My informant seems to think something has happened to him. It was all in my report."

Cody tapped the keys on his computer. "I don't have any reports of anyone around the Georgia area who's familiar with this case making any mention of spotting Dante. Not at his mansion, not at the airport, and not at any of his usual hangouts."

"Interesting. Did you send anyone to check out that warehouse that my informant told me about? Or that ten-wheel truck that he suggested Shades was driving? He did say he saw them load a couple of elongated plastic wrapped items into that truck before making a delivery to that warehouse."

Cody stopped talking and leaned back in his chair. "Now, how do you suppose that I accomplish that kind of investigation, Angelica? That takes search warrants, warrants take a judge, and a judge wants probable cause, none of which you have. The only thing you *do* have is the suspicious word of an unnamed informant."

"Yeah, I know. Guess while I'm in Georgia finding my informant, I'll check out that warehouse for myself."

"Don't go getting yourself in a jam, Angelica."

"I won't." Angelica thought for a moment before continuing. "You don't think Shades has a hit out on my life, do you? I mean with this hacking thing, tracking me to Buffalo, and then to Virginia Beach?"

"It has crossed my mind. I think you need to sidestep that trip to Georgia and go on out to California. Shelby is going to need your expert help out there, I can feel it."

"No way. I have to find Damian." Angelica covered her mouth, knowing she had just divulged her informant's name.

"So, his name is Damian?" Cody said with raised eyebrows.

Cody and Rex were the only ones besides Shelby who knew that name. Although Cody had been helping her track Shades down, it was obvious he didn't know, or at least hadn't yet connected the name Damian, the husband of Amber Nichols, and Amber's murder at the hands of Shades. "Yeah, didn't mean to give that one away."

"Be more careful. I might be a double operative." Cody broke the tension with a laugh.

Angelica rolled her eyes and tried to smile at Cody's attempt at humor. Angelica stood up and stretched. "How long is it going to take to get all this electronic shit and my truck reprogrammed? I need to get on the road."

"Not long, maybe a couple of days." Cody sat up when his phone rang.

Angelica sat back down in her chair. "A couple of days? You've got to be kidding me."

Cody pointed to his phone and put his finger to his lips, as a sign that Angelica needed to be quiet. "It's Cody, what's happening, Shelby girl?"

Angelica perked up, she whispered at Cody. "When you finish talking to her, I want to talk to her, since you have my phone."

Cody transferred his conversation with Shelby to his computer speaker so Angelica could hear. "Angelica is here; I just put you on speaker."

"Hi, Angelica. I was going to call you later."

"Hi, Shelby, Cody saved you a phone call. Had to come in and get my computer worked on at the office. So, what's up?"

"Well, things are going pretty well. I told you about all the places we stopped for deliveries and pick-ups after we left Kansas. We also made another drop in a little town outside of Tucson called Benson. I saw several Dover trucks there. It was late when I finally followed them across the California state line. Then they picked up some stuff from some Glacier trucks at a truck stop here in Blythe. I'm so glad we finally stopped, I'm ready for a nap."

"Did you happen to observe anything they were unloading or loading, Shelby?" Cody asked.

Shelby had seen a lot of what they were loading and unloading, but she couldn't tell Cody. Instead, she logged it all in her journal. "Not too much, lots of boxes, several really large ones, pallets wrapped in heavy plastic. Unfortunately, I wasn't close enough to make any kind of identification of the cargo. The plastic-wrapped pallets were transferred into the Dover and Glacier trucks. The other items were transferred from Dover and Glacier trucks into the Shield Sheik trucks."

What Shelby could not divulge to Cody is that she knew exactly what they were loading and unloading because she had gotten up close enough to see. The plastic wrapped items on the pallets were boxed flat screen televisions. But, one of the drivers from Dover used a knife to cut into the plastic, ripped back one of the flaps on the box, dug into the box with his hands, and pulled out several large plastic bags of white pills, some contained white powder, and one bag that contained cash: American currency. After checking out his product, he put it back in the television box, taped it up, and put the plastic wrap back into place. The men then went to the items that had been exchanged with Shield Sheik. The Shield Sheik driver inspected his items, which included ammo, guns, and drones. Shelby spotted the chemical barrels sitting at the back of the trailer. She figured those were the containers Shield Sheik had picked up in Andrews County, Texas.

"Do you have any idea where they are headed?" Cody inquired.

"No, but if I understood Arabic or Spanish better, I think they might have been discussing it in the truck stop café earlier when I went in to get some dinner. The only thing I really understood from the conversation was the number seventy-eight. I don't know what that means, though."

"Hold on," Cody said. He brought up a road atlas on his computer. "Shelby, it's possible that they are going to cut back down on Highway 78 to

Interstate 8. Highway 78 connects with Highway 86 and leads into El Centro. I really doubt they will continue on 78 into San Marcos, that is a scenic route, not a really good road for big trucks to be hauling."

"That is if they continue into California," Angelica added.

"Yeah, if they do continue into Cali, I see here on my map what you're talking about, Cody. I have no idea what they plan on doing. Waking up every hour on the hour to make sure they haven't left the truck stop is tough. I sure could use some help out here, Agent Brighten," Shelby teased.

"I'll be out there soon. I have to go to Georgia first. I have an informant I need to make contact with over there."

"Well, hurry up. I want you to get out here so I can do more than just watch these trucks."

"Hold on, cowgirl, I'll be there soon," Angelica joked.

"By the way, Cody, I heard on the news something about an incident at a Lubbock bookstore. Something about a firebomb because the store refused to sell books written in Arabic."

"Here's what I know," Cody said. "A man went into a small independent bookstore with a box of books. The owner said the man had a very thick accent. He guessed the guy was from the Middle East because the books he had in the box were in Arabic. The man wanted the bookstore owner to carry the books in his store. The owner looked at one of the books, but said 'no' because he did not know what the books said or what they were about. He offered to keep one to see if he could find someone to translate it. The man snatched the book away from the owner and left the store; he was obviously quite upset about the owner's response. The owner thought nothing of it, until the bomb went off later that night when the store was closed. The back door was jimmied with a crowbar. The bomb was placed inside and detonated."

"Well, at least there weren't any casualties," Shelby said.

"There was one," Cody said. "This information was not released to the media. The man who wanted his books in the store had the bomb strapped to his body. He blew up himself and half of the back of the store."

"So, instead of one big attack, we're seeing a series of smaller ones," Angelica observed.

"That does seem to be what's happening," said Cody. "In Buffalo, New York, a shooting was averted at the airport when a gunman tried to take a gun out of his checked bag at the baggage claimed area. Someone saw what was happening and alerted a security guard who was nearby. In Clinton, Oklahoma, a young mother of two children was confronted by her ex-husband. The Iranian national wanted the children and their passports. He wanted to take them with him back to Iran. She refused, locked him out of her parents' house, and called the police. He broke into the home, held everyone hostage for several hours, and then shot her. A police sniper took him out."

"I guess the grandparents will be raising the children," Angelica said.

"It reminds me of that movie, *Not Without My Daughter*. That was based on a true story," Shelby said.

"There was another incident," Cody said. "Outside of Hobbs on the New Mexico-Texas border. At first, the locals thought it was just an electrical fire in a records room of a chemical plant. Upon further investigation, it was deemed as arson. The fire was started soon after a records clerk questioned a trucker who had driven in to pick up some potentially radioactive material from the plant. She suspected that the bill of lading that the driver presented her was forged. He came out of his truck and when she tried to call for security, put his arm around her throat and snapped her neck. Before anyone knew what was happening, he took his order to the loading dock and got his load and left. No one suspected anything until they spotted the smoke coming from the records office. A small cigarette lighter was found at the bottom of the record clerk's wastebasket. It had been triggered remotely to ignite. The fire wasn't big enough to do much damage to the property, but the people in the area are nervous. The picture of the tags taken by the security cameras were also bogus."

"Hold on, let's think about this for a minute. "St. Louis, York, Buffalo, Lubbock, Clinton, and Hobbs. Anyone see a pattern forming here?" Angelica suggested.

"I've been thinking the same thing, partner. Think about it—every place Shield Sheik goes…," Shelby began.

"…destruction follows," Angelica finished her partner's sentence. "But why, Cody? Is Shield Sheik trying to prove something, or are all of these incidents just coincidences?"

"No, not all of them. There's been a string of crimes all over the country that on the surface seem to be unrelated—bar shootings, mall shootings, car and building bombings, shootings at parties or art shows—some have been averted through the help of the public and diligence on the part of local law enforcement, many have not. I'm not really sure what their end game is with all of this, but I want both of you to be very careful. Whatever these people are up to is dangerous. DHS isn't going to be any help; they don't think it's a national problem. They see these events as local crimes, but there is a thread— and that thread is Shield Sheik and their associates," Cody explained.

"So, I've been right all along. These guys that I'm following are terrorists? I feel really uncomfortable right now," Shelby said.

"Don't freak out on us now, Shelby. We still need you to continue following them. Angelica will quickly finish here on the East Coast. She'll be joining you out west in about a week. Can you handle things until then?" Cody asked.

"Yes, I've got this. It just makes me nervous knowing that I'm dealing with terrorists who are so determined that they will sacrifice their own lives."

Angelica tried to comfort her partner. "Just follow, Shelby. Don't try to be brave. I'll join you soon. We will nail these bastards together, even if Homeland Security wants to sit on their hands."

"I will," Shelby said. "Listen, y'all, I gotta get some sleep. I'll check in tomorrow and let you know which direction we're headed."

Angelica could tell by Shelby's tone that she was hiding something, but she didn't want to confront her with that knowledge in front of Cody. "I'll call you tomorrow."

"Get to bed," Cody interjected before hanging up.

After Cody disconnected from Shelby, he sat back in his chair and clasped his hands at the top of his head. "So, what are you thinking?"

Angelica got up from her chair and moved to the door. "I think I need you to call me a taxi, since I can't use my truck, my car, or my motorcycle right now. I need to get to a hotel for the night. You have twenty-four hours to fix my stuff, because this thing is bigger than that little girl can handle without some backup. I just hope she doesn't do something stupid like she did in Nebraska."

Cody picked up his keys off the desk and threw them at Angelica. "Take my car. I'll take your Charger home tonight. I'll call in a few techs to work on this stuff tonight. I'll have you out of here tomorrow night. Do you really have to go to Georgia?"

Angelica caught the keys with her free hand. "Yes, I do. I don't have a choice there, unless he calls sometime tonight and lets me know he's okay. I'm going to do my best to get my business in Atlanta done quickly, and then head out west with Shelby. I know she needs me."

"I'll get the computer stuff finished quickly, you have my word."

"Thanks, Cody. She's a smart woman, a little wet behind the ears, but too smart to do anything stupid," Angelica said in an effort to convince herself as well as Cody. She left his office.

Cody turned back to his computer and reached for his cell phone. "I hope you're right, Angelica."

◊◊◊

"Hey, boss, we found Agent Brighten. She is in Springfield, Virginia, at the DEA's main office. She's in the DEA building, and someone moved her big truck and trailer into a huge garage area."

"Fine, keep an eye on her. I am headed to California. You keep me informed of her movements. I'm sure she's going to be in Springfield for a few days."

"Got it, boss."

Shades hung up his cell phone and boarded his newly acquired plane. Dante's private pilot spoke respectfully to Shades, "We are fueled and ready for what looks like a smooth flight to San Diego, sir."

Shades took his seat in one of the luxurious reclining seats at the front of the plane. The private stewardess placed a half-filled glass of Jack Daniels with two cubes of ice in front of Shades. "Your drink, sir."

Shades took a sip of the cold liquid. "Thank you."

CHAPTER TWELVE

"Look, boss, we lost her for a little when she left Springfield, but we caught up with her, and she's heading into Atlanta as we speak," Shades' man reported.

"Fine, you stay with that bitch, and don't you dare let her out of your sight. I want to know everything that she does, every place she goes. I want to know it all, do you understand me?" Shades ordered as he entered the vehicle that would take him to meet his new partners.

"We've got it. We won't lose her again." The guard attempted to cover his conversation with the driver. "No, stupid, she went left. THERE, over there!" The guard returned to his conversation with Shades. "We got this, boss."

Shades hung up his phone in disgust. "Idiots! I'm not sure any of them have half a brain." Shades yelled at the driver, "Take me to the warehouse outside of Tijuana on the U.S. side of the border. Do you know where it is?"

"Yes, sir. I've been there many times. Tito is my boss," the Mexican national replied.

"Good, maybe someone can get something right today," Shades mocked. "Don't make me late."

"Sí," the driver replied. "No problem."

◊◊◊

"No, not again." Shelby reached for her cell phone and turned off the alarm. That alarm had awakened her every hour on the hour for the last thirty-five hours. For whatever reason, Shelby's tails had not left the truck stop with their trucks. She saw them make their initial exchange when they first got to the truck stop, but nothing else had occurred since then. They were just hanging out at the stop.

Exhausted, Shelby glanced at the time. "Five freaking o'clock in the morning. Ugh!" As had become her hourly routine, Shelby got up out of her sleeper, pulled back her curtain, and checked to see if her tails were still parked. "Good, they're in the same place, maybe I can get a little more rest." Just as she let go of the curtain, she caught a glance of a man climbing out of the cab of one of the trucks. She quickly pulled the curtain back again away from the window. "Damn it! Couldn't they give me just one more hour of sleep?" Shelby replaced the curtain, removed her sleeping clothes, brushed her hair, rubbed toothpaste over her teeth, rinsed with mouthwash, and spit into an empty drink cup next to the microwave.

She grabbed a clean pair of jeans, a bra, socks, and a t-shirt from the closet. After getting dressed, Shelby grabbed her make-up bag, threw on just enough to appear presentable to the public, pulled her sleep curtain back away from the windows, and secured them with the snap ties. She turned off her generator, started her truck, aired up the brakes, and moved her truck to the fuel island. "I'm not leaving this damn truck stop without some coffee."

◊◊◊

"Here, I brought you more food and water—boss's orders. If it were me, I'd let you starve to death." Shades' guard put the food on the floor in front of Damian who was still hanging from the ceiling rafter. The guard disconnected the restraining device that had kept his arms above his head for hours. Damian fell to the concrete like jelly. His legs and arms were still numb from the lack of circulation. With a few swipes of his wrists against his body, Damian freed the rope around his wrists and then reached for the water. He was so thirsty, but when he reached for the bottle, he couldn't hold it.

"Don't get too comfortable. Shades wants you alive until he gets back, but I'll be back in a little while to hang you back up." The guard laughed. "I'm sure when he does get back, food and water will be your last concern."

The guard left the room and secured the steel door behind him. While Damian waited for the feeling to return to his extremities, he looked around the room again, hoping for an escape. All he saw was the door; there was no other way in or out. A five-gallon bucket sat in the corner of the room, with a folding metal chair right next to it, nothing else.

When he could finally feel the pain of the blood flowing back into his fingers, he fumbled with the water bottle lid until it came open. He turned the bottle upside down into his mouth, guzzling the liter of water down as quickly as it would come from the plastic container. "Ahh, water!" Nothing had ever tasted so good to Damian.

Next, he reached for half of the sandwich the guard had left. He ate the whole thing in two bites. He reached for the other half. He threw the empty bottle to the ground and used his now only half numb hand to shuffle his way across the floor to the metal chair. He took the last bite of the dried-out sandwich and placed both hands on the chair for stability as he turned his body over, forcing himself into a kneeling position in front of the chair.

Tears came to his eyes as he felt the pain running through his legs. He forced himself up onto one foot from the kneeling position and pushed himself to stand. "OH! DAMN IT! This hurts so freaking much." Damian managed to stand up on both feet, but his legs still felt like Jell-O. He put his hands on the metal chair and slowly lowered himself into a sitting position.

Damian finally broke down and cried. He had cried many times since Amber had been killed, but this time was different, this time he let everything go and prayed. "God, if you're there, I hurt so bad. God, if Amber is with you, and if I can't find a way out of this hellhole, let her know I'll be there soon. Tell her I've missed her, tell her I tried to take out the SOB who took her from me, but I think I'm in quite a mess right now. I know we haven't really talked much since I was a kid, God, but I sure could use a little help getting out of this situation."

◊◊◊

Angelica knew when she walked out of the broker's office that something was terribly wrong. "Where the hell are you, Damian?" she said out loud as she put on her sunglasses and mounted her motorcycle. The weather between New York and Georgia had changed drastically over the trip. It was somewhat chilly in Atlanta, but it was snowing in New York. Angelica hit the start button on her Kawasaki 1000, backed it out of the its parking space, and drove out of the parking lot to the main street. She decided she'd go to Damian's house first to see if he was there. If not, she'd check out Dante's estate. Since he was not at work, she figured those were the only two places he could be.

◊◊◊

"Cody, you were right. We are headed south on Highway 78. From the road signs, it looks like we are headed to El Centro. The last sign I saw was about ten miles back; we are seventeen miles out," Shelby said over her Bluetooth headset.

"They are probably heading south of San Diego, but be sure and call me right away if you don't go west on Highway 8," Cody instructed.

"I'll let you know. Have you heard anything from Angelica?"

"No, not since she checked in when she got to Georgia this morning. I have no idea when that woman sleeps."

"She doesn't," Shelby responded. "I gotta go. Call ya back."

Shelby turned into the parking lot of a hotel across from the truck stop where her tails were parked in El Centro. She watched as the trucks pulled in behind the stop, but they didn't park. She couldn't see too much after they went behind the building, so she got out of her truck, walked across the street to the truck stop, walked behind the building, and hid by the trash receptacles.

While she stood there, the two drivers of the trucks that she had been following got out of their trucks. They shook hands with some other Shield Sheik drivers who were waiting by their parked trucks. Shelby wasn't close enough to record or even hear what they were talking about, but several pieces of paper were exchanged between the drivers. To Shelby, they appeared to be invoices or bill of lading forms. The men spoke for a few more moments, hugged each other, and then returned to their respective trucks. Shelby quickly left her hiding spot and ran back to her truck.

Just as Shelby opened her door, mounted her truck, and slid into her driver's seat, she locked eyes with the young Arab woman she had met in St. Louis. "Shit." Shelby tried to look away before the woman realized who she was, but it was too late. Shelby could tell from her eyes that she had recognized her. She hoped the woman wouldn't say anything to her husband about seeing her again.

Shelby reached for the button on her dashboard touchscreen and called Cody.

"What's up, Shelby?" Cody asked

"We are headed westbound. Oh, and the woman who I met in St. Louis? The nice, young one? She kind of got a glimpse of me when I got back into my truck here at the truck stop."

"Why did you get out of your truck?" Cody asked, sternly.

"I had to pee, Cody," Shelby lied.

Cody adjusted his tone. "Oh, well do you think she recognized you?"

"I don't know, but we locked eyes. I know she saw me. I just don't know if she remembered me, or if she will tell her husband."

Cody heard the worry in her voice. "I wouldn't worry about it. Just make sure you stay well enough behind them so they don't see you following them," he advised.

Shelby wanted to tell Cody about the paper transfer, but she knew that would have to be saved for her journal. She would share everything with Angelica when she got out west to meet up with her. "I won't. Look, I gotta go, traffic is pretty congested. I'll call back when we land somewhere."

"All right, stay safe."

◊◊◊

Angelica spotted Damian's truck parked along the street in front of the house he was renting. She pulled her motorcycle into the driveway and parked under his carport next to an F-150 Ford pickup. Angelica felt the hood of the pickup with her hand; it was cold. She went to the side door of the little bungalow and knocked. "Come on, Damian. Answer the door." Angelica knocked several more times before trying the doorknob—it was locked. "Where are you, Damian?" Angelica checked every window in the place. Most had closed shades; the others yielded no evidence that Damian was here or that anything sinister had happened to him at his home.

Angelica went back to her motorcycle. Discouraged, she placed her sunglasses over her eyes.

"Hey, are you looking for Damian?" A voice came from behind her as she was throwing her leg over the seat.

Startled, Angelica quickly dismounted her bike and felt for her service weapon attached to her hip. "Yes, who's asking?"

The white-bearded man with scruffy hair beneath a well-worn ball cap with a Marine insignia stepped back in a hurry when he noticed Angelica placing her hand on her sidearm. "Whoa! No call for all that. I'm looking for Damian as well. Are you a cop? Is he in trouble or hurt or something?"

Angelica quickly scanned the man, along with a side-to-side glance of the perimeter. She let her hand relax off of her gun. "Can't be too careful these days, Marine. Semper Fi. Before I answer any of your questions, who are you?"

The scraggly dressed older man offered his hand to Angelica. "Semper Fi! I'm Rascal Newman, United States Marine, First Sergeant, retired. I live just across the street there." Rascal pointed to his brown and tan wood-framed house. "Damian borrowed my van a few days ago; I haven't seen hide nor hair of him since."

Angelica shook the old man's hand. "Glad to meet you, First Sergeant Newman. I am, or was, Staff Sergeant Angelica Brighten. I gave eight years of my life to our blessed Corp," Angelica said with pride. "To answer your questions, yes; I'm looking for Damian. He's my friend. I'm not a beat cop, but I am an agent with the DEA. Damian isn't in any trouble that I know of, and I'm trying to find him to make sure he's not hurt. When did he borrow your van?"

"Oh, it was about three or four days ago. I can't remember exactly. But he told me he just needed it for the afternoon. I trust Damian; he's always brought back what he's borrowed from me in the past. This time, I'm worried something has happened to him."

Angelica looked around the neighborhood. "Me too, Rascal. I'm going to find him, though. He didn't mention where he might be taking the van, did he? Or, what he might be using it for?"

"No, he didn't really say what he needed the van for. He did put a duffle bag of tools in the front seat of that old plumber's van when he took it. I told him he could use whatever tools or plumbing supplies I had in the back of the van, but he said he had what he needed in his bag. I don't know; maybe he was going to fix someone's plumbing or something. Maybe it turned out to be a bigger job than he thought," the man offered.

Angelica thought over the information from the man. "What color is your van?"

"Oh, that old thing used to be white, but now it's more rust than anything else." Rascal laughed through a smoker's cough.

Angelica nodded her head. "I think I know where he might be. I hope I'm wrong, but I think I know." Angelica got back on the motorcycle.

"You'll be sure and let me know about Damian, won't you? I've been awful concerned about him," the old man pleaded.

"Yes, I'll let you know first thing when I find him, and your van." Angelica maneuvered the two-wheeler around until she faced the street; then she broke the machine's loud muffler motor off with the starter switch. She unzipped the side pocket of her black leather jacket and pulled out a business card. "Call headquarters if Damian shows up here."

"I will. Honestly, I'm not concerned with that old rusty contraption of a van, just Damian. He's such a nice, helpful young man," the Marine yelled over the motorcycle engine.

Angelica adjusted her glasses again, gave the old man an affirmative nod, and a military salute. "You have my word, First Sergeant Newman. When I find him, I will let you know."

Angelica made a beeline for Damian's stake-out point near Dante's estate.

◊◊◊

"Boss, we just followed Brighten to a blue house in south Atlanta. I'm not sure why she went from a trucker's broker's office to this little house. She also talked with some old dude, a neighbor who came from the other side of the street while she was there. Whoever she was looking for never came to the door, either. She's on the move now. It's crazy; she carries that little motorcycle she's riding in the back of that eighteen-wheel truck she's been driving. Is that what they do with all the money the government gets from us when they make a bust?"

"Oh, shut up, you idiot. Just keep her under surveillance. I'm almost to my meeting with Shield Sheik and Glacier. Let me know if anything really important happens. Otherwise, I'm going to be really busy for the next few hours."

◊◊◊

It took the trucks Shelby was following about three hours to reach their southern turn onto Highway 125. Shelby hadn't been this close to Mexico since her nightmare escape some years earlier. She knew that if the trucks she was following crossed the border she would not be permitted to cross with them. A sense of relief flooded her body with that knowledge, along with a small twinge of disappointment that she might lose her tail.

Shelby snapped to attention when the two trucks she'd been following in heavy traffic suddenly exited. As she inched her way to the exit that the two trucks had taken, she could see the tops of their trailers making a right-hand turn onto the main street. She looked at the crowded thoroughfare of the exit that they had taken and Shelby knew that if she went down the same exit ramp that she would blow her cover. As she continued on past the exit, she noticed from the overpass that the two trucks had turned left into a gated warehouse area.

She called Cody on her Bluetooth. "Cody, no time to chat. Can you Google the closest truck stop to Highway 125 and San Miguel Road? Hurry please, I'm almost to the border."

Cody heard the nervousness in her voice. "Okay, from your location, there is a truck stop at Otay Mesa Road and Piper Ranch Road. It's not far from you. I'm punching it into your GPS. Your navigation should be set right now." As soon as Cody said this, Shelby's navigator voice spoke out. "Make a right turn in…"

"Thanks, Cody, my tails just turned off on that road. I have to get to the truck stop. I have to use my car for a little while and track them down," Shelby rushed. "I don't want to lose them."

"That's fine, Shelby, but don't break procedure. No foot surveillance, no recordings, and definitely no crossing the border with the agency's property—that includes you!"

"No problem there, Cody. I've had enough of Mexico for this lifetime. Look, I need to go. I have to get my bike out at the truck stop. I have to track those trucks down again before I lose sight of them."

"Be careful out there. I have a few agents in the area for backup if you get into any trouble. But you're not, right? Just be careful."

Shelby disconnected from Cody without confirming his instructions.

◊◊◊

Angelica looked over the area around Dante's estate. "I just don't see a white van anywhere, Cody. I need you to call the local PD to see if you can get me some day aerial reconnaissance from the last couple of days. If not, see if they can get a chopper in the air over Dante's estate. I need to know if there is an old rusty white plumber's van parked there."

"I'll check, Angelica, but what the hell is going on?"

"Just do it, Cody, get back to me as soon as possible," Angelica demanded.

Angelica took her bike on a slow ride around as much of Dante's estate as was possible to view from the street. The estate reminded her of Pig's compound in Louisiana, but this estate was smaller because it was located closer to Atlanta proper. Angelica checked out every possible gap in the fortified fencing. She spotted a couple of places she thought she might be able to squeeze through but knew that the place was most likely under heavy surveillance.

"Damian, if you've been taken prisoner in that place, I'm going to beat your ass."

◊◊◊

Damian had all the feeling back in his arms and legs when Shades' man came through the steel door, this time leaving it somewhat ajar. Sarcastically, the guard complained, "I guess I'll need to take that chair with me when I go. We don't like making our unwanted guests comfortable." The guard went to the center of the room and pulled down the rope that had kept Damian standing upright over the last few days. The guard pointed his gun at Damian with his free hand. "Get over here."

Damian slowly got up from the chair and shuffled slowly to the armed man. Without warning, Damian charged the guard; he knocked the man to the ground, and the gun flew out of his hand. Damian put all his pressure on top of the guard. "Like hell I will." Adrenaline coursed through Damian's body and he used his fists to beat the man in the face.

The man fought as best he could from underneath Damian's body. He even grabbed for the gun which was only a few inches away, but to no avail. Anger, fear, and determination caused Damian beat on the man until he went limp.

Damian got to his feet. He was panting from the struggle. He wiped the blood and sweat from his face and picked the man up off the floor. Damian took the handcuffs from the guard's back pocket and put them on him. Then, he dragged him to the hoisted rope, pulled down on the rope, connected the cuffs to the rope, and hoisted the guard up into the air until he could just barely touch the floor. "There you go, you bastard. See how you like that for a while."

The guard had no comprehension of what Damian had just said or done. He simply hung in the dark concrete room with his bloody face beaten beyond recognition.

Damian grabbed the guard's handgun off the floor. He slowly opened the door and peeked out to make sure that no one was waiting outside in the hallway. He quickly located the first of many security cameras and knocked it to pieces with the butt of the gun. He walked through the maze of halls and rooms, opening as many of the doors as he dared along the way. He knew that he would eventually locate a stairwell or an elevator. His persistence soon paid off. He found a door with an exit sign and a push latch. He cautiously pushed on the door, which led into a dusty, dirt-covered underground parking garage.

It looked as if it hadn't been seen or used by anyone in months, possibly years. The place was nearly pitch dark with only a small amount of light from under the metal overhead garage doors, which probably came from the security yard lights. If he did not exit quickly, the guards would find out where he was. He let go of the door and ran into the darkness toward the light from the overhead doors. To his disappointment, they were all secured, most likely automatically controlled from the guard shack. But Damian knew that all garage doors had manual opening capabilities in case of emergencies. The darkness indicated that it was probably night time on the other side of the doors, so he knew he would have to feel along the walls to find a manual lever to open them. Unfortunately, his adrenaline boost was wearing off, and he was exhausted.

He leaned against an old relic of a truck and patted his way along the top of the bed. It felt to him like an older model pickup. He climbed into the bed of the vehicle, lied on his back, and closed his eyes. He still had to wait for Shades. The guard said that Shades would be back in five days. He knew he'd been in that hellhole of a room for at least three of those days. He would hide out in this abandoned parking lot and hope that the guards didn't know that this garage even existed.

◊◊◊

"I can't do anything about it, Angelica, the only aerial reconnaissance they have over that particular property is from a week ago. They said you're welcome to come look at it, but they won't be able to put a chopper in the air until the morning."

"Shit, Cody, that might be too late. Hell, it might be too late already," Angelica's voice was becoming frantic.

"You need to come clean with me, Angelica."

"I think my informant is in Dante's estate. I've combed this city looking for him. I even went by his house today and a neighbor told me that Damian borrowed his old white van. Cody, don't get upset, please, but my informant is Amber Nichols' husband. You know, the girl Shades killed? She's the reason I'm so interested in personally busting the son-of-a-bitch."

Cody couldn't believe what he was hearing. "You employed a member of the family as your CI on this case? That's not only wrong, Angelica, that's really bad for your career. How could you do such a thing?"

"I didn't employ him as a CI, Cody. He was already down here staking out the place, when Shelby and I arrived. I told him not to do anything stupid, but I did tell him to let me know if he saw anything suspicious." A tear fell from Angelica's eye onto her cheek. She wiped it away quickly, *Marines don't cry.* "I never asked him to go onto the estate. In fact, I explicitly told him *not* to. I don't even know that he's in there, but I do know that he wants Shades in a bad way, and that he might do anything to get at him."

"I get it, Angelica, but you knew his mindset, and you did ask him to give you information. You didn't tell him he couldn't get involved; you let him go ahead and do what he was doing, which might just get the man killed. This is serious."

Angelica remained silent. She hated to admit that Cody could be right.

"Look, from the last known aircraft flight log we have on Dante's plane, it landed at San Diego International last night," Cody said. "So, if Shades somehow got to an airport outside of the surveillance we had on him in Buffalo, chances are that he's in San Diego, not Atlanta."

"San Diego?" Angelica repeated. "Shelby's…"

Cody realized at that moment what Angelica was getting at. "Damn it, I thought I was on top of this! Shelby's in San Diego and so is Shades." Cody broke away for second. "Shit, I know you're concerned with Damian, but you need to get your ass to California, like yesterday. I don't want to lose an agent, and it's all our asses if you're not out there with Shelby. Something big is going down. Shield Sheik, Shades, Glacier, Dover, and even the cartels are most likely involved."

"I know, I'm going back to my truck now. What about Damian?" Angelica said with some reluctance.

"I'll get some of the local agents working on this within the hour. He might not even be in there. We'll run an aerial shot of the place tomorrow and see if we can find that white van. If there is an old rusty plumber's van parked somewhere on that estate, I will have local agents prepare a search warrant, and try to go in and get him out. Now go to California. I'm pretty sure Shelby needs you."

CHAPTER THIRTEEN

"Check every fucking room and every crack in this place. I want that fuckhead found. Shades is going to blow his top when he finds out that we let this asshole get loose." Carlos, the head security guard, barked out orders to the twenty men who canvassed the estate.

The two guards who discovered the body of the man that Damian had beaten to the ground carried him out of the holding cell and threw him onto the ground. "What about Ralph?" one of the men asked.

"Let him drown in his own blood. He shouldn't have let the son-of-a-bitch overpower him," Carlos ordered.

Every guard searched the estate from top to bottom, but just as Damian had predicted, no one checked the hidden underground parking garage. The door was hidden from most of the commonly used halls, and the old parking garage had never been placed on any of the estate's maps. It was only common knowledge among Dante's older security staff members. Shades had gotten rid of all of them days prior.

"We've looked everywhere, Carlos. He probably got out somehow, maybe through one of those holes back in the trees."

"You'd better hope to hell not. Shades is due back here in two days. Find him! I'm going back to the main gate. Call me if you locate him."

As Damian slept, the search continued.

◊◊◊

"This is really important, boss. That agent has been circling the estate now for hours on her motorcycle. She's looking for a way in, I think. She's been on the phone, probably to her superiors. Do you think they are going to try and make a bust on this place? Why do you think she's checking out the place so hard?"

"I don't know…" Shades paused for a moment. "…wait, let me check on something with Carlos and call you back."

Shades hung up with the man tailing Angelica and called the guard shack on the estate. Carlos saw the caller ID. He really didn't want to tell Shades that the prisoner had escaped, but he answered the phone anyway, "Carlos here."

"Carlos, did you guys ever check out the stuff in the duffle bag that the prisoner had on him? Or his wallet? Did you get his name?" Shades seethed.

Carlos quickly picked Damian's wallet up off the counter. "Yeah sure, boss, his name is Damian Adams according to his driver's license. He has a class A CDL driver's license, too. Why?"

"Just keep that bastard under lock and key until I get there tomorrow," Shades demanded.

Carlos didn't have the courage to tell Shades that the man had escaped.

"I know exactly why she's hanging out at the estate. I'm going to kill me two birds with one stone. Damian Adams is the asshole who took off with one of my girls, Amber Nichols. The Feds are trying to hang me out to dry because I killed that little piece of trailer trash. This is a good thing. I'll just give Angelica a call tomorrow and let her know that she has to come to the estate personally if she wants to get her friend. This couldn't have played out better if I had planned it myself." He hung up the phone before Carlos said anything else.

A few minutes later, Shades received a call from the men he'd sent to tail Angelica.

"Hey, boss, we just passed the Georgia state line. We are following Brighten westbound on I-20."

"What the hell? Why didn't anyone tell me that she's taken off?" Shades screamed.

"I thought Carlos would tell you…"

"You worthless piece of shit! Stay with her, don't you let her out of your sight. I'll deal with Carlos." Shades hung up the phone.

I have to think... I can't call her right now; she'll turn around and go straight back to the estate, bringing her agent buddies with her. No, I need to keep her away from the estate until I can get back there tomorrow. He called his men back, "You, idiots stay with her. Let her go as far as she plans to go; it's getting late there, so I suspect she will be taking a nap somewhere. Keep an eye on her; don't let her see you. I'll call you tomorrow with further instructions."

"Yes, sir."

◊◊◊

Breathing hard, Shelby slid through a broken section of the cinder block wall that surrounded what appeared to be a Shield Sheik or Glacier trucking yard. She picked up her backpack from the ground, where it landed before she made her entrance. She couldn't tell who owned the yard since there were an equal number of both types of trucks in the lot. There were even a few Dover trucks. Metal cargo shipping containers littered not only the entire concrete dock that surrounded the entire building on all four sides but the fence line as well. The place was packed with shipping containers. Shelby wondered how they managed to get anything done in a place where things were so unorganized.

Shelby found it very easy to maneuver her way through the yard under the cover of dusk. The sun hadn't completely left the sky and the moon hadn't quite made its appearance on the West Coast. Like a prowling cat, she made her way to an area where she'd observed a group of people gathered during the drive-by on her motorcycle.

She stopped when she heard voices. She checked to make sure her cell phone was in her front pocket and found a secure spot close enough to the conversation.

Shelby hit the recording app on her phone and inched as close as possible to the crowd of people. Her two drivers were among the crowd. Since the men gathered spoke different languages, they attempted to speak to each other in English. Still, it was difficult for Shelby to understand much of what they were saying. An analyst at DEA would make a transcript from the recording.

"We have to stay here until the bosses finish with their meeting," one of the drivers said.

"I think we will be headed to Tijuana to unload this cargo. Then we will gather our brothers together and bring them to America!" another driver stated.

Many of the other drivers cheered at the statement. "Yes, Allah is good. We shall take America for our prize."

Some of the other drivers in the crowd didn't cheer; Shelby assumed they were Mexican nationals. They appeared to ignore or not understand what was being said.

Suddenly, several of the men's phones rang at the same time. Shelby tried to listen to some of the conversations, but most of them were in languages that she didn't understand.

"We go now," one of the drivers said as he motioned for the other drivers to mount their trucks and follow him.

Shelby shoved her cell phone into her pocket and ran as quickly as she could to the wall opening where she'd entered. She took off her backpack and threw it through the opening, and then slid through the slim space after it. She grabbed her backpack off of the ground as she ran to her bike, which she had parked beside a tree. After shoving her helmet down onto her head, Shelby started the bike and rode out toward the street that she knew the trucks would be filing onto shortly. From the little bit of information she had gathered from the conversation, she knew they were probably headed to Tijuana, Mexico. She decided she'd follow them as far as the border.

Since the trucks were going to the border entrance, Shelby decided that she would get ahead of them. She could park in one of the lots near the border as they filed into Mexico. *I'll just take pictures of the trucks, watch them go into Mexico, and wait for them to return.* She desperately wanted to stay with the trucks to find out what they were doing, what they were hauling, and possibly discover some of the big players who might be involved in the operation. However, Shelby would never go into Mexico again, and not just because of Cody's warning. *I almost died in Mexico. Besides, I'm not allowed to cross the border as a DEA Agent without my government's permission.* She hashed out her plan as she continued to travel south. When she arrived, Shelby parked the bike in a pay-by-the-hour lot near the border.

She'd made it in time to watch as the trucks pulled up to the border patrol gates. Because many of the trucks were registered to Mexico and driven by Mexican nationals, the guards at the border simply let them pass without inspection or concern of any cartel affiliation.

When Shelby saw the last of the trucks pulling toward the border, something in her snapped. Without a second thought, she ran toward the last truck in the line. When the truck stopped momentarily, Shelby jumped onto the deck behind the cab. There wasn't much space between the box trailer and the cab of the truck, but she managed to hide herself in the space. She prayed no one was paying attention.

Her mind was racing as she thought about what she had just done. *Shelby, what the hell are you thinking? You are on your way into a country that you swore you would never return to, ever! Jump off, as soon as the truck slows down. You're not that far from the border. You can sneak back across and everything will be fine.*

But she had come this far and she knew that she couldn't stop now. She was determined to find out what was going on with these trucks. She was going to find out who was involved. She took a few deep breaths as she waited for the truck to travel the distance it needed to go to get to its intended destination.

Within a few minutes, the truck that Shelby had been riding on slowed down. Shelby didn't know if it was because of traffic or if the truck was approaching its destination. She wanted to make sure that she got off the truck before it possibly went through any kind of checkpoint. The truck was lining up with other trucks in a parking lot near a huge well-lit building. Shelby waited until the driver parked before exiting her hiding space. She knew that the driver would use his mirrors to back into place. She prayed that no one in the other truck beside them would notice her.

When Shelby heard the air brake release, she jumped from the space behind the cab and slid under the truck to hide between the rear wheels of the tractor, keeping as close to the wheels as possible. Luckily, no one saw her, but she was back in Mexico. She knew from her surveillance that a group of drivers were headed to a restaurant where they were supposed to meet with several high-ranking members of this unnamed drug and terrorist organization. The restaurant was at the other end of the parking lot.

Once all the drivers had cleared out and she felt that it was safe, Shelby climbed out from under the truck and went to the back of the semi to survey her surroundings. She turned her head with her back against the trailer of the truck as she gasped for air. She felt as if she'd been holding her breath for the last thirty minutes.

Shelby, what have you done? How in the name of God are you going to get out of here without getting spotted, or worse yet, killed? Jack's going to be so mad at you; Angelica is going to kill you, if you're not dead already; and Cody, well Cody will just make sure that your career as a DEA Agent is over for good. Oh, Lord, you are such an idiot. Why couldn't you have just stayed in the truck like you were told?"

Shelby finally calmed down and took another look at the restaurant from behind the truck. *Well, since it's a restaurant in a public place in Mexico, I should be all right,* Shelby tried to convince herself. *I'll just mix and mingle with the other patrons in the place.* When she entered the crowded, loud cantina, mariachi music was playing, smoke filled the air, and there was a heavy aroma of frying meat and stale beer. But everyone there was dancing and happy.

Shelby tried hard to blend in, but she caught the eye of a couple of locals as they stood by their treasured spots by the bar. "Hey, señorita, come over here, I will buy you a drink," one man said.

The other one said, "No, over here. I will buy mamacita all the drinks she wants."

Shelby smiled, waved, and quickly moved on through the crowd away from the bar area.

She scanned the large place until she finally spotted the group she was looking for. They were off in another part of the room all by themselves. Shelby saw a half-filled mug abandoned on a table and grabbed it as a prop— she didn't want to appear out of place. She was thirsty, but she would wait for the bottle of water that she was carrying in her backpack to quench her thirst.

Slowly, she maneuvered through the place. She was only a few feet away when she got a break. A booth of four people cleared out, and she quickly sat down in the side that faced the crowd of men she was trying to identify.

A waitress came by, cleared away the dishes, and wiped the table. In broken English, the young woman asked, "What you want?"

Shelby was surprised, but then thought, *eating dinner in this place could really be a great cover.* "Do you take American money?"

The waitress laughed. "Yes, we take American dollar. What you want? Fajitas good, you want beer?"

"Yes, fajitas and a cold beer, that would be great," Shelby said, nervously. She pulled the two twenties from her pocket. "Will this be enough to pay for the food and beer?"

Again, the woman laughed. "Oh, yes. You get very drunk with that much. Be right back with your food and beer."

While Shelby waited for the woman to bring her food, she looked over at her subjects gathered in the isolated corner. To her surprise, a nice-looking slender black man turned around for a moment to shake hands with some-one behind his chair. It was Shades! Sitting next to Shades was a man Shelby would never forget: Tito. He was the man Pig had hired to kidnap her into Mexico. She and Tito never spoke to each other because she'd escaped before getting the chance to make his acquaintance, but the mug shots she saw of him when she joined the DEA were burned into her brain. She still became anxious whenever she thought about the destruction the cartel leader caused while her trucker friends and family fought to get her out of Mexico. There were several other cartel leaders seated at the table. Shelby recognized them from photos she had been required to memorize during her early days of agent training. Other men at the table were not so recognizable. One particular man, of Middle Eastern descent, sat separately from the Americans and Mexicans. Several men wearing scarves stood around him. They were different from the men Shelby had been following who wore nothing on their heads. Shelby could tell that the standoffish man was important by the way the others de-ferred to him. She overheard one of the men call him Omar. She wanted to take her cell phone out and take a picture of him but concluded that would be too dangerous. She also needed to stay out of the eyesight of the two drivers she had been following.

"Thank you," Shelby said to the waitress as she placed the hot plate of sizzling beef, beans, and rice down in front of her.

She then placed a very beautifully painted covered ceramic dish next to the cold mug of beer. "You need more, you tell me."

Shelby handed the woman one of the twenties. "I think this will be plenty of food, thank you."

The woman took the twenty. "I bring you more beer. You want change?"

Shelby shook her head. "No, it's yours." The woman smiled and left the table.

The large plate of food sizzled and crackled, sending a savory aroma to Shelby's nose. *Oh, how I love fresh beef fajitas.* She took a sip of her beer. Then she opened the covered dish and found homemade tortillas. She'd always wished she could make light and fluffy tortillas like the ones that she now pulled from the dish.

◊◊◊

Angelica couldn't believe that she might possibly be the cause of her friend Damian's death. *Why did I encourage him to continue to do surveillance for me? I was just being selfish. I'm an agent for the federal government, for heaven's sake.* Angelica berated herself all the way to California. She was equally worried about Shelby. She pushed a button on her Bluetooth and the call went straight to Shelby's voicemail on the first try. She hoped her partner was talking to Jack or Cody. *I'll try again in a few minutes.*

Angelica was cold and tired. She was depressed and disappointed in her performance on her first assignment back on the job. The case was falling apart; Shades was on the run; Shelby, the trainee who she was supposed to be training, was off on her own; people wanted to kill her; and now one of the nicest guys she had ever met might be hurt or dead because of her. *What else could go wrong?* She turned into a rest area. Angelica knew that she had to get to Shelby before something happened to her, but she wasn't going to get there running on very little sleep. Angelica locked her doors, crawled back into her sleeper, removed her shoes, and then got between the sheets and the blankets fully clothed. Before her head hit the pillow, Angelica was fast asleep.

◊◊◊

Sipping at the last of her second mug of beer, Shelby watched as the men talked and exchanged money and handshakes. Several of the Middle Eastern men began to file out of the restaurant. Shelby realized that was her cue. She got up and started toward the door. Her waitress spoke to her. "You have good night, nice lady."

Shelby waved goodbye. "Gracias."

Outside, Shelby could see that many of the drivers were simply standing around by their trucks. She knew she would have to get around the new gathering without being seen. They were her ride back into the U.S. She saw an alley that went to the side of the parking area and into the street. She hoped that she would be able to go around the back of the trucks and then come in from behind them. To her relief, it was just as she had hoped, but she didn't want to get in behind the truck cab too soon. It was quite possible that a big exchange of drugs and merchandise might take place right there in the parking lot.

Shelby found a newspaper stand at the corner of the street with a bench right next to it. It was directly in front of a store that was dark and apparently closed for the night. Shelby sat on the bench and scanned the Spanish newspaper. She couldn't understand most of it, but she didn't care. She looked at the pictures of car accidents, politicians, and items for sale.

She jumped when she heard a loud pop. *A gunshot? What the hell?* Shelby took cover behind the little store. She was shocked to see two vans full of men pull up to the restaurant. All of the men exited the vans. The men from the earlier gathering were now hugging the men who were pouring out of the vans. Several more gunshots went off in the air, but Shelby realized it was from the men firing into the air. They seemed to be celebrating their friends' arrival. *So, these are the brothers they were coming to get.* Shelby thought.

It wasn't long after the gunshots that the rest of the gathered men exited the restaurant. Just as Shelby suspected, the large group of men walked back to the trucks. Several forklifts emerged from a building to the right of all the trucks in the parking lot and the workers set about emptying the Shield Sheik trucks into the warehouse. As she'd observed in the U.S., the pallets appeared to contain televisions and appliances. Shelby knew that the boxes were just for show. She was certain they contained more money and drugs.

Eventually, the Glacier and Dover trucks were unloaded. The plain, brown cardboard boxes concealed the contents, but the labels and warning stickers indicated they contained explosives. Once the items were all distributed, the men who had come in the vans climbed into the cabs of the Shield Sheik trucks. Because there were so many, several climbed into the cabs of some of the Glacier and Dover trucks. Shelby was in shock as she witnessed guns, explosives, and possible future dangerous criminals being loaded into trucks headed for the United States.

It feels like my country is in danger, but no one seems to care, she lamented. *Does anyone even know this is happening?*

Shelby waited for all those who had gathered at the rear of the trucks to finish closing and securing their doors. When the last man moved to the front of his truck, she jogged across the rear of the parking lot. She had only a few moments to get onto the deck. First, she made her way to the rear end of the tractor and hid in the wheel area again. Then, just as she was about to make her move to her hiding place on the deck, the passenger door opened. A man jumped out of the truck and stopped right in front of the passenger tires directly across from where Shelby was sitting in the dirt underneath the truck. She heard laughing coming from the truck cab. Shelby wondered if she'd been discovered and prepared to run, but she soon heard a zipper and the sound of drops hitting the dirt. The man was peeing next to the tire! *Thank God I can't see all that,* Shelby thought.

When the man finished and returned to the cab, Shelby took her chance and mounted the deck. The driver of the truck was still talking with other drivers at the front of the truck, so she figured she was safe. Since this was the last truck in line, chances were that no one would notice her slumped down behind the air-brake cables between the cab and the front of the trailer—at least she hoped not.

The air was becoming chilly as the truck hit the road back to the States. Shelby was glad that she was going back home, but she was extremely troubled by the cargo the trucks contained. She was going to have to fess up and tell Angelica what she had discovered and how she was able to see it all go down in the first place. She might get fired, but she didn't care. *These men and the items they are carrying are a danger to the American people. Each place they've stopped, this group has used these weapons to wreak havoc on American soil.*

Getting across the border wasn't going to be all that difficult because Shelby knew that the border patrol officers were stretched to the max and probably wouldn't care even if they did notice her on the deck this time. The hard part was going to come when she had to get off the truck.

It wasn't long before Shelby realized she'd have to jump off a slowly rolling truck. She had to plan it just right. When the truck stopped at the border patrol station, as predicted, the border patrol officer simply let the truck go right on by. Once the deck passed the gate line, Shelby jumped from the driver's side of the truck. She didn't look back; she just kept running until she was safe in the parking lot where she'd left her motorcycle. She paid the parking attendant, who evidently had noticed her daring feat. "You know you can just drive over the border. You don't have to try and kill yourself by jumping on and off of trucks."

"Oh, you saw that, huh?"

"Yeah, and I saw you get on that truck earlier. What's up with the Evel Knievel stunts? You're a beautiful woman, why would you want to take a chance of getting yourself hurt like that?"

Shelby took her change from the man. "Thanks for the compliment, but life just wouldn't be worth living without a little danger."

The man shook his head in disbelief. "Some people."

It hadn't taken Shelby long to get back to the truck stop on her motorcycle. She lost her trucks while retrieving her bike, but quickly located them as she raced down the freeway. Thankfully, several of the trucks pulled into the very truck stop where she was parked.

She opened the doors of her trailer and rode the bike onto the hydraulic lift, but before she could push the button to lift the motorcycle and her up into the trailer, an arm locked around her neck and a hand covered her mouth. Shelby struggled to free herself, but it was useless.

A deep voice with an unmistakable Middle-Eastern accent spoke into Shelby's ear, "I don't know who you are, who you work for, or what you think you were doing taking unauthorized rides on one of my trucks, but next time you should be aware of the vehicles *following* those trucks. I will not warn you again, stay away from my trucks. Next time I will kill you. Do you understand me?"

Shelby nodded her head as much as she could to confirm that she understood. "I'm going to leave now, do not turn around for two minutes." The man let go of Shelby and was gone as quickly as he had come.

Being a woman, Shelby couldn't help but be scared, but being a trained agent she knew that she couldn't allow her natural female instincts get the better of her. She did obey the perpetrator's command not to look around for a few seconds, but when she felt the man had gone, she quickly pushed the button to lift herself and the bike into the truck.

Still shaking, Shelby finished locking up her trailer. She scanned the area to make sure she was indeed alone. The man was long gone, but he'd left something behind. A wool, tan and blue colored scarf was on the ground near the truck. Omar, if that was his name, was wearing a similar scarf at the leaders' table in the restaurant. She walked calmly, but cautiously to the front of her truck. She got in, started the engine, and locked every door. She was suddenly very tired. She grabbed her gun and crawled into her sleeper. Sleep didn't come easily as she lay there obsessing. *Was my cover blown? Omar obviously knows what truck I'm driving. The name of the fictitious company that I worked for is plastered on the doors. Did he think I was a cop, or just some crazy lady trucker hitching a ride into Mexico?*

Shelby was concerned and frightened, as she logged everything she could remember from the night into her journal. *Should I give up the chase?* she wondered. *Will he be watching me?* She needed to talk to Angelica and tell her everything, but that conversation would have to wait until the morning. She now understood why having a seasoned partner was so critical. *These criminals use more than trucks to get around.*

CHAPTER FOURTEEN

"**H**ello?" Angelica said into her cell phone. Not wanting to remove her warm body from her sleeper bed, Angelica pulled at the covers until they were around her neck, covering every part of her body, but her head.

"Good morning, Agent Brighten. Well, it's eleven o'clock on the East Coast, so it's still morning."

The sound of Shades' voice over her personal phone caused Angelica to throw the covers from her body and bolt straight up in bed. "What the hell do you want, Shades? How did you get my phone number?"

"Now, is that really any way to talk to someone first thing in the morning? I mean really, I know you've had a rough couple of days and all, checking out my estate and trying to find your friend Damian. That sleeper of yours can't be that comfortable, and there really aren't too many accommodations for truckers at a rest area. Perhaps you should be at a truck stop; there are several really nice ones in Mobile, from what I understand." Shades knew exactly where she was and what she had been doing.

Angelica looked out her window—there were no vehicles or trucks in the rest area where she was parked. "How do you know what I've been doing? Are a carload of those creeps of yours following me?"

"Well, yes, Angelica, I did have some of my associates following you for a while, but I have since requested that they return to my estate. There was no further need to follow you, since I am en route back to my home as we speak. I have great plans to unite Damian Adams and his little wife Amber very soon. Perhaps, if you can make it in time, you would like to join us for the happy reunion?"

"You bastard! I knew you were holding Damian prisoner at Dante's estate. If you hurt him in any way, I will see to it that you hang."

"Oh now, now, Angelica, such big threats from a DEA agent who doesn't even know that she's being tracked. Hell, I even know where Rex and little Harley are right now."

"You keep my family out of this, Shades." Angelica tried to control the fear in her voice.

"So, I can expect you for dinner tonight then? I will be sure and save the entertainment for you. Just so you understand, the estate is now mine. Dante is no longer with us. Oh, and if you have any ideas about calling the local cops, that would be a really bad idea for not only Damian, but your family, and your new little partner Shelby's family as well. You see, dear Agent Brighten, I have been doing my homework. You are way out of your league dealing with me."

"I'll see you tonight, you bastard." Angelica hung up her phone. She brushed back her hair with her hands, pulled on her jacket, and put on her shoes. She didn't have to remove the sleep curtain from the front windshield, because she hadn't taken the time the night before to put it up. She unzipped the sleeper curtain, sat in her driver's seat, put on her Bluetooth earpiece, punched in Cody's number, pushed in on her air brakes, and made her way back to I-65 eastbound to Atlanta.

"I was just about to call you, Angelica. I saw where you shut down in Mobile early this morning, so I decided to wait to call." Cody continued without letting Angelica speak, "My local agents and the local police in Atlanta have been hard at work since last night, looking for that van. This morning, around ten o'clock, they spotted the van on Dante's estate. The local police are getting a warrant right now. They have plans to storm the place in a few hours."

"That's all fine and dandy, Cody, but I already know Damian is being held on the estate. I got a call from Shades about five minutes ago, and he's headed to *his* estate now. He's not in California anymore. He killed Dante, and he plans to kill Damian. I'm on my way back to the estate now. He said that if I don't come alone to dinner tonight, he will not only kill Damian, but he will kill my family and Shelby's family. He claims he knows where they live.

He told me exactly where I was this morning and exactly what I was doing in Atlanta. He's had some of his goons following me since you fixed the tracking system. You have to call off the raid, at least until I get there," Angelica explained.

"Wow, this changes everything. He's one mean son-of-a-bitch. I'll contact the locals and have them hold off until you can get there and in position. I'll also call Rex and Jack to let them know that we're sending security details for your families. I'll let Shelby know what's going on and to just stay on task."

"Yes, Shades is very dangerous, and now he has our personal information. Tell Shelby that Rex will call Jack and explain everything—that she doesn't need to worry. Tell her I'll be out there in California with her just as soon as I put Shades either on death row or six feet under."

"I will pass along the messages," Cody promised. "How long until you get back to Atlanta?"

"It's four and a half hours from Mobile to Atlanta. I left the rest area thirty minutes ago, running as fast as I can without attracting the attention of any state police. I guess I can be outside Dante's estate in four hours."

"Okay, I'll make sure that the local agents and cops wait for you."

"Good, make sure they stay clear of the estate, too. Shades warned me not to call the police in on this, so I don't want him to get jumpy. If he sees any units around, he might kill Damian before I can stop him."

"I got you on that; making those calls now." Cody hung up.

◊◊◊

The last truck pulled out of the parking lot at the truck stop. Shelby had been watching them as they filed out of the stop. She looked to see if any vehicles were following them before she pulled out and began her tail. So far, everything looked fine. She couldn't decide if she should follow them or not. She was completely confused as she pulled onto the highway and saw the trucks about half a mile in front of her. She wanted to talk to Angelica about her situation, but when she called in her morning reports, Cody told her that Angelica was sleeping and to give her a few hours. Shelby figured Angelica would be in California within a couple of days so she could talk to her then.

But what about right now? Am I doing the right thing by continuing to follow these trucks?

The ring of her cell phone startled her out of her thoughts. It was Cody. She pushed his name on the touch screen.

"How are you doing, Shelby?"

"Okay, Cody. What's up?"

"I've got some good news and some bad news. Which do you want first?"

"I don't know, Cody, just tell me what is going on." Shelby was in no mood for games.

"Well, okay then. Is something wrong, Shelby? You don't sound like yourself today; you seem a little stressed."

I think I just need a break. I know that following these guys is import-ant, but I'm tired. I kind of want to go home for a little while. Shelby kept her thoughts to herself and instead said to Cody, "I guess I'm just a little tired."

"This probably isn't going to make things any easier for you either, but Angelica is on her way back to Georgia. I don't know if she told you or not, but Damian, you know the man who was married to Amber?"

"Yeah, I know Damian. Is something wrong, did he get hurt or something?"

"We're not sure. Apparently, he's been keeping an eye on Dante's estate, looking for Shades. Somehow, he got himself inside the estate, and now we think he is being held prisoner. In fact, according to Shades, he is being held prisoner. Shades called Angelica this morning. He threatened to kill him, her family, you, and your family if she didn't come back to the estate tonight."

"Damian is being held captive at Dante's estate? Shades has threatened to kill her, me, and our families if she doesn't go back to Georgia? That doesn't make any sense. I just saw Shades last night!" Shelby immediately panicked and began firing off questions. "Do Jack and my boys know that they could be in danger? How does he know where we all live? How did he get Angelica's phone number? Does Rex know? Do you have plans to keep all of us from being killed or hurt by that monster? I need to get off the phone and call Jack. I need to drop this tail and head home. My family may need me."

"WHOA! Shelby, girl, take a breath. Be calm. Everyone is being notified. You can call Jack as soon as we get off the phone. We don't think there is any need for alarm right now. We have locals that are going to go into the estate with Angelica when she gets there. We hope that we will be able to capture Shades and his men *and* keep Damian alive at the same time. We do have plans in place to protect you, Angelica, and your families if it comes to that. Right now, I want you to calm down. I want you to first of all tell me why you didn't mention in your report this morning that you saw Shades? Where did you see him, Shelby?"

"I saw him in a restaurant I was eating in last night. I simply forgot to mention it this morning, that's all." Shelby told a half-truth.

"Did he see you?" Cody inquired.

"I don't think so, but…" Shelby stopped herself from telling Cody everything.

"But what?"

"Oh, I'm not sure. But…I think maybe one of the guys he was sitting with saw me," Shelby confessed.

"Why do you think he saw you? Did you recognize him? How would he have any idea who you are, unless Shades saw you and told him?"

"No, I didn't recognize him; he isn't in any of the pics we have. I'm not even sure he knows I'm a DEA agent, but when I got back to the truck stop after dinner, this man grabbed me. He threatened me, saying that I need to stop messing around with his trucks."

"Messing around with his trucks? What the hell were you doing near the trucks, Shelby? You know you're just supposed to be tailing them. We are talking about Shield Sheik trucks, right?"

"Yes, Shield Sheik trucks. I wasn't really messing around with the trucks. I just walked around them going into the truck stop. I was hoping to hear something; there were a whole bunch of them in San Diego last night."

"What did the guy look like and how did he threaten you? Was he driving a truck? This isn't good, Shelby, you should have told me earlier," Cody lectured.

"I know, I know. I should have told you, but I thought I could talk to Angelica and she would tell me what to do. I don't think my cover is blown.

I've been really careful to watch out for him. I think he might be a high up—an owner or some kind of "wise guy" from Shield Sheik. He's definitely Middle Eastern; he speaks English very well, and I don't think he drives a truck. I overheard someone call him Omar. He told me that he didn't know who I was, or who I was working for, but if I messed around with his trucks again he would kill me," Shelby hoped it wasn't obvious she was omitting details.

"That's just great, Agent Mathews. I am here for a reason. You are supposed to tell me everything. I'm going to have to find a seasoned agent in L.A. who can ride with you, or maybe I should just bring you in and send you home. You're going to end up getting yourself killed," Cody fumed.

"This is the very reason that I didn't want to tell you everything, Cody. I make one little mistake, walk by some trucks, and you're ready to pull me off this case. Fine, I'm tired of being threatened. Get yourself another agent to follow me around in a truck or send me home. I don't care anymore, my family and friends are being threatened. Maybe it's time you did pull me off this case and send me packing." Shelby was so frantic and worried about her loved ones that she'd lost all semblance of patience and professionalism.

"The trucks are on their way through L.A. right now; it looks like they are planning to make a stop somewhere in the Long Beach shipping cargo warehouse district. Do you want me to keep following them until you can get a replacement here, or just stop pursuing this case altogether? I realize that I'm a rookie, and being a rookie means I'm still learning. I'm going to make mistakes, Cody. These people that I'm tracking are dangerous, and there is something going on here way beyond my pay grade. So far, though, I think I've done a pretty good job figuring out what these crazy assholes are planning. I'm not a child, and I won't be treated like one anymore. You are the man in charge, so do what ya gotta do."

Cody was silent for a few moments. "I'm sorry, Shelby; you're right. You're a really great agent, and you're doing more than any rookie agent I have ever worked with my whole career. I should remember that you are learning, and that you will make mistakes. Just understand, I'm only trying to keep you alive; that's *my* job. I'm not a rookie anymore, but I did make a rookie mistake in letting you continue out there by yourself without Angelica. That is why I've been so paranoid about everything you do. If something happens to you, I have to not only answer for it but live with the fact that I could have prevented it."

"That's great, Cody, you've got my back; I get that. But if we're going to continue working together, no more threats. Either pull me off this case or let me try and do this job the best way I know how, mistakes and all."

"I don't want to pull you. Look, I know you're right about Shield Sheik. Keep following them. I don't think your cover has been blown. We'll deal with that if they start to show signs that they're aware of your presence. You'll know when that happens because they will start evading your tail. I will look into what information I can find about Omar and what his affiliation is with Shield Sheik," Cody said with confidence in his new agent.

"What about Angelica, Damian, and our families? Will you keep me posted on what's happening?" Shelby pleaded.

"Of course, I'll let you know the minute I hear anything. Your family is safe. We will keep you and them informed about everything. Angelica and the locals will be pulling off an all-out assault on the estate tonight. I'll let you know how that goes. You keep yourself safe."

"Thank you, Cody. I'm sorry that I got upset with you. I know you're only trying to do your job."

"Thanks, Shelby, for doing a great job for all of us."

◊◊◊

Carlos cringed when he heard Shades' SUV pulling up to the estate gate. "Damn it, has anyone located that bastard yet?" Carlos yelled over the walkie-talkie.

None of his men responded in the affirmative. They'd all been looking for Damian for at least twenty-four hours and still, no one had a clue as to his whereabouts. "Shit, Shades is here. Every one of you jackasses who doesn't have a perimeter protection post, get your asses to the guard shack. I'll be damned if I take this hit on my own. Especially since I didn't lose the son-of-a-bitch."

Shades was already in his office unloading paperwork from his briefcase into a security safe. He turned to his personal bodyguard. "Get Carlos on the horn, tell him to come see me now."

"Yes, sir." The bodyguard placed the call to the guard shack, "Boss says he wants you in his office now."

"On our way," Carlos replied.

Within a few minutes, Carlos and several other security guards entered Shades' office.

Shades sat in the chair behind his desk.

"You wanted to see us, boss?"

"Well, I wanted to see you, Carlos, since you are the head of security here. But I guess it doesn't hurt that you brought a few of the other guys with you." Shades looked at the other men. "Why did you bring the others with you, Carlos?" Shades sat up in his chair and folded his hands on his desk. "What's going on around here?"

Carlos wasn't sure how to tell his boss the unfortunate news. "Not exactly good news, sir. You see, the prisoner..."

Shades stood, leaned over his desk, and interrupted Carlos, "The prisoner what, Carlos?"

"He's missing, sir. One of the men went down to the cell to feed him like you ordered, and the next thing we know, the guard is half-dead and the prisoner is nowhere to be found. We've looked everywhere." Carlos nervously tried to explain the situation to his irate boss.

Shades grabbed a glass vase off the desk. He tossed it as hard as he could in the direction of the men who had come into his office. Most of the men were able to avoid a direct hit, but the glass hit a wall and shattered on impact, sending flying shards into the group. "You fucking idiots! You lost my prisoner? How does that happen?" Shades ranted.

"We are sure that he hasn't left the property, boss, but so far we have been unable to locate him." Carlos tried to explain, "He's still here; I'd bet my life on it."

Moving swiftly, Shades grabbed Carlos around the throat. "You and these fucking morons had better get the hell out of this office and find that motherfucker or it will be your life."

Carlos responded with a cough, "Yes, sir."

"Get out of here. Find him, or I will shoot all of you."

Carlos and his men left.

Shades looked at the Rolex watch he had stolen from Dante. "Approximately two hours before Agent Brighten arrives. I wonder where that bastard is hiding?" Shades sat back down in his chair. He started to play with a sterling silver pendulum that adorned the desk while he pondered his predicament. "Come out, come out, where ever you are, Damian Adams."

◊◊◊

Angelica backed her truck into a parking spot at the truck stop. She quickly removed her motorcycle from the back of the trailer. She'd made good time rolling back to Atlanta, but she needed to make contact with the local authorities, and then the officers who would be going in with her to get Damian away from Shades. She rode her bike to a prearranged location to meet with the heads of the Atlanta SWAT team, police, and the local DEA.

Angelica rolled up on the police units and SWAT van. When she took off her helmet, her long dark brown hair billowed in the air, and then came to rest alongside her.

The agents were taken aback by this beautiful woman blazing in to lead the charge on such a sweet bike.

A man in a three-piece suit put his hand out for Angelica to shake. He reminded her a little of Denzel Washington. "Welcome, Agent Brighten. I'm Agent Baldwin. We talked on the phone earlier today."

Angelica shook the man's hand as she tried to place him. "Nice to meet you, Agent Baldwin. I think we met once before. Maybe a training class in Springfield?"

"Perhaps, I've been to a great many of those during my time with the agency." The man pointed to a beautiful middle-aged woman in uniform. "This is Commander Grands; she's in charge of the SWAT Unit. She will be in charge of front assault and entry. Just to let you know, the warrant has been obtained, and everyone is aware that it may potentially take gunfire to enforce the judge's signed order on Shades."

"If I know Shades, he probably wouldn't even show his face while the search is being conducted," Angelica said. "I don't know if you know this, but he's wanted in connection with the death of a woman named Amber Nichols Adams. The man we are rescuing today is her husband. I suspect he was trying to take justice into his own hands and got caught. He may well die for his attempt."

"Yes, we are aware of Shades' background. We've wanted to make a bust on this place for years." He went to his car and pulled out a roll of blueprints. He spread them on the hood of his car. "Dante has been on our radar for a long time, but we just couldn't get enough evidence for a warrant. Maybe, now we can take him down as well," Agent Baldwin elaborated.

"I doubt that you'll be able to arrest Dante today. Shades informed me that he killed him," Angelica said. "My informant suspected as much earlier this week. All that may remain of Dante is some charred remains in that recycling plant down the road from his estate."

"I'll have some of the agents check that out," Agent Baldwin replied. "So, how would you like to proceed with this search warrant?"

Angelica held her motorcycle helmet in one gloved hand. She used her free hand to illustrate her plan. "I'll go to the gate first; he's expecting me. In fact, he demanded that I come to dinner. I want you and the teams to hold back for just a little bit. Maybe ten minutes, give me enough time to get him to let his guard down a bit. Then you and your teams come full force into the compound."

"How many men do you think he has?" Commander Grands asked.

"The most we have ever been able to calculate from aerial surveillance has been twenty, but there have been personnel changes. I would figure on around thirty men. Now, most of these guards are new hires. When Shades took out Dante, he fired or got rid of most of Dante's men. It's really hard to tell if all of them will even put up resistance," Angelica pointed out.

"Yes, Agent Brighten is correct; we've had several of Dante's ex-employees in our office, giving us information on Shades," Agent Baldwin agreed. "It is very possible that most of the ex-cons will not put up a fight. They are new, and Shades hasn't had time to build much of a loyal employee base."

"Don't let your guard down, though; these men may surprise you. After all, some have nothing to lose but their new job," Angelica added as she walked back toward her motorcycle.

"What about you, Agent Brighten? You will be in there all by yourself for at least ten minutes without backup. A lot can happen in ten minutes," Agent Baldwin said.

Angelica mounted her bike, pulled her hair into a bun, put her helmet over the bun, and secured the strap beneath her chin. She started the motorcycle. "No worries, Baldwin, Shades is a man. I'll deal with him like any woman deals with a man when she wants something." With those final words, Angelica smiled, put down the bug shield on her helmet, and rode off toward Dante's estate.

Commander Grands was smiling when Agent Baldwin looked back at her. "What did she mean by that, Commander?"

"It's a woman thing, agent." She put on her helmet and began barking orders at her two teams of police officers.

Agent Baldwin stood stunned for a couple seconds before getting into his vehicle. "I'll never understand women."

CHAPTER FIFTEEN

"**D**amn it!" Shelby said as she slowly moved through thorn bushes growing along the fence of an overseas shipping cargo container facility. Shelby was familiar with these types of buildings from when she drove her own truck. She picked up and delivered merchandise from similar places throughout the U.S. Much of the merchandise stored in these facilities was brought there after clearing a custom search at the ports.

Shelby's cell phone rang; she forgot she had it in her back pocket.

She whispered, "What's up, Cody? I'm a little busy right now."

"I just noticed that your truck isn't moving on the GPS tracker, and you're parked in a lot near the coast in Long Beach. Everything okay?"

"Yes, Cody, everything is fine. I'm in a bunch of thorny bushes outside of a holding facility. I told you the trucks were headed here earlier."

"Yeah, I remember, but come on, Shelby, you know you're not supposed to be doing surveillance outside your truck."

"Just trust me, Cody, I'm not in any danger. I can't even get into the place without the proper paperwork. I'm sure not going to climb this fence, but I can see the trucks and what they are doing from this vantage point. Don't be paranoid. In fact, just wait by the phone for a few minutes. I'll take pics of the stuff that they are loading and unloading and text them to you."

"Okay, as long as you're not in any danger."

"I'm not. In fact, I look like an idiot to most of the cars driving past. There isn't much cover out here, but it's too public for anyone to make much of a stink about me being here," Shelby assured her handler.

"I get it," Cody yielded. "Text me those pictures."

After disconnecting, Shelby continued to watch the loading process. She was very surprised to see cargo boxes that she knew from her training with the DEA contained military weapons.

"What the hell? I thought those kinds of things had to be held and picked up at customs." She took several pictures with her phone and then sent them to Cody along with a text message.

> Get on the horn with the ATF for a surprise inspection of this place. They are loading 100s of wooden military boxes into these Shield Sheik trucks. They don't say made in the U.S.A. on them.

Shelby was taking additional pictures when she got a text from Cody.
> The writing on the boxes is Chinese, Russian, and Arabic.

Shelby quickly texted back.
> Looks like a treasure trove of foreign guns & explosives headed to the American streets. Is the ATF even doing their jobs?

After a minute, she received Cody's response.
> It appears as if several agencies aren't doing their jobs.

Shelby texted the last of the photos and called Cody back. "I guess this is what you get when you mix politics with law enforcement," Shelby said when he answered. She continued to watch the activities of the Shield Sheik trucks.

"You've got that right. I'll pass these along to the ATF. I haven't been getting much inter-agency cooperation. Like you said, politics."

"I know we're supposed to look for the good in people, but there is a lot of evil in this world. Greed, money, and power struggles will never allow us to live in a world without borders. Our cultural differences can get in the way. We can be tolerant, but we can't afford to be naïve," Shelby said.

"I hear what you're saying, but I think a lot of people just want peace. Unfortunately, it's hard to work toward that when so many countries resent America and our way of life." Cody replied.

"Yeah, not everyone shares our view that we are the greatest country in the world. That's too bad because historically, America has been called upon when the world is in crisis. We've fought in wars trying to settle conflict in other countries throughout history. Would it have been better to stay neutral?"

"Well, that's an interesting question, but I doubt we'd be in a better place if we'd just allowed atrocities to take place in other countries without offering assistance," Cody replied.

"I majored in American History in college, and my dad and I talk politics all the time. After years of conversations, we still haven't gotten it all figured out." Shelby laughed.

Before Cody could respond Shelby noticed a man walking in her direction. "Crap, Cody, I guess it's time to go. I just got spotted by a rent-a-cop."

Cody heard a man's voice in the background, "Hey you! What are you doing there? This is private property!" The security cop yelled toward Shelby.

As Shelby ran to her truck, she said to Cody, "I'll call ya back in just a sec. Thankfully, the cop didn't notice me until after they finished loading the last of the trucks. I got more pics. Gotta go!"

◊◊◊

"I'm here to see Shades." Angelica removed her helmet and flashed a sly smile. "I have an appointment with him."

"You're Agent Brighten?" the front gate attendant asked. "He's been waiting for you. Sorry, I have to search you before I let you in—safety reasons you know." He pointed to Angelica's motorcycle. "That bike will have to stay out here. LeRoy will give you a ride up to the main house in the golf cart."

"Okay," Angelica said and moved her bike off to the side. She parked it next to the gate in the grassy area. She turned the motor off, placed the magnetic key under the fuel tank near the seat, dismounted, and put her helmet on the bike's seat.

Angelica turned to walk back to the guard booth, and the guard leered at her. She backed away slightly, but the man grabbed her. He forcibly made her turn, and she found herself facing one of the two rock pillars that framed the driveway. He placed her in an arrest position and frisked her. He rubbed his hands all over her body, including areas that Angelica would have stabbed him in the face for if she'd had a knife on her person. Luckily, he did not feel the cell phone that Angelica had hidden in the lining of her leather jacket.

"Well, pretty lady, looks like you're all clean." He leaned in and whispered in her ear, "Perhaps after Shades finishes with you, you and I can have some fun." She felt his breath in her ear.

In one move, Angelica stomped one of her steel-toed biker boots onto the guard's sneaker-covered foot and raised her other knee into his groin. While he was doubled over in pain, she stepped behind him and kicked him just hard enough in the ass to make him fall forward into the pillar. "I doubt it," Angelica said with confidence. She strode to the guard who was waiting to take her to the main building.

The driver of the cart gave Angelica a scared look. "So, I see the DEA trains their women really well in self-defense."

"Some—it's mostly a Marine thing," Angelica boasted.

"Remind me not to mess with you," the driver stated. When they reached the main entrance to the mansion, he told her, "Go through those two doors there into the foyer." The guard pointed as Angelica got off the golf cart. "There is an elevator to your left with a guard. He'll take you to Shades."

"Thanks," Angelica said. She watched as the guard left and headed back down the driveway to the guard booth at the front entrance.

Once the guard was out of sight, Angelica pulled the cell phone out of her pocket and typed in the words: "I'm in." She sent the text to Baldwin and slipped the phone into her boot. She knew she wouldn't have more than ten minutes before all hell broke loose, so she ran through the doors and turned left—almost running straight into Shades.

"Surprised to see me, Angelica?" Shades said with a smirk on his face.

"Well the guard *did* say there would be a staff member here to escort me in," Angelica quipped.

Shades didn't appreciate her humor. "Well, I would have met you at the door, like a gentleman, but you ran in here so fast. You must be in a hurry to join me for dinner."

Angelica followed Shades toward a dining room that had been lavishly prepared with a dinner for two. Shades put his hand out for Angelica, offering her the opportunity to enter the room first. Angelica really didn't have time for all the games, but she wanted to know where Damian was being held so she played along.

"Shall we?" Shades said.

Angelica walked to one of the seats and waited as Shades pulled the chair out for her. She sat down. Shades moved to the chair directly opposite her. He swirled, sniffed, and tasted the wine the waiter had poured in his goblet. Shades nodded and the waiter poured wine into the two wine glasses. He put the wine in a bucket and then removed the silver lids from the serving platters.

"Look, Shades, this is all fine and dandy, but I'm not here to wine and dine with you. I want Damian back. What do you want in exchange for him?"

Shades sipped at his wine. "But, Angelica, you said you would come and have dinner with me. Look at this fine meal I've had prepared for us. We can talk about Damian after we eat."

Angelica had no appetite. She took a sip of her wine. "Just tell me where he is, Shades. Is he all right?"

Shades laughed. He gave the waiter a nod and the servant put veal, risotto, and steamed asparagus on Shades' plate. Then he stepped back. Shades took a bite of the meat. "This really is quite good, Angelica, you should try some of it. The veal is cooked to perfection; I must give my cook a bonus for this one."

Angelica put down her wine glass and stared at Shades from across the table. "Is Damian okay? I want to see him."

Shades slammed his fork on the table and sat back in his chair. "You are in no position to make demands, Angelica." He sat up straight and picked up his wine glass. "He's here, Angelica, you will be with him soon enough. For now, relax and enjoy the meal."

"What do you want for him, Shades?" Angelica persisted.

"What I want is for you to stop talking about him. Tell me something I don't know about your family." Shades baited Angelica.

"You leave my family out of this." Angelica stood up and put her fists on the table. "You may think you have me over a barrel here, Shades, but think again. I will blow your fucking brains out if you even go near my family."

Shades laughed; he knew he had pushed an emotional button. "Sit down, Agent Brighten of Dallas, Texas. Rex and little Harley have nothing to fear, unless you try and take me down," Shades promised.

"So, that's it, Shades, you want me to just let you get away with killing millions of people with your drugs, including girls like Amber. So in exchange for Damian, you want me to just leave you be?"

"Well, yes, that would be great, but I don't think you're in a position at this moment to call the shots. It really wasn't smart of you to come here alone. I might not let you leave." Shades laughed.

"Oh, I'm leaving here with Damian today. Whether I let *you* leave is the real question." Angelica glanced at her watch.

Shades realized that Angelica had double-crossed him. He jumped up and moved swiftly to the windows in the dining room that overlooked the front gate. "Grab her." Shades ordered his bodyguard.

"Let me go!" Angelica fought against the strength of the huge bodyguard.

The guard finally contained Angelica and held her from behind. Shades walked to where they were standing, raised his hand, and slapped Angelica across the face hard. Angelica's head swung to the side. He'd split her lip open and her hair matted itself in the blood that now flowed from her mouth.

"You didn't follow the rules, Angelica. You weren't supposed to bring others to this little dinner of ours. It was supposed to be a private dinner."

Angelica continued to fight the bodyguard. "Fuck you, Shades. Where is Damian? They are going to storm this place any minute now."

Shades ignored Angelica. "Take her upstairs to the panic room. Don't leave that room for any reason. I'm going to escape through the basement. I'll be back for both of you once the cops have cleared out."

The bodyguard wrestled Angelica to the staircase that led to the second floor. Angelica fought with every step made. "Let me go, you fat bastard."

Carlos busted into the dining room. "SWAT is here, sir!" After seeing that Shades already knew what going on, he ran from the room, barking orders.

Shades ran to the elevator. He pushed the button for the basement.

◊◊◊

Damian had slept for what seemed like days. When he finally woke up in the back of the pickup, his mouth was dry from thirst. He had no idea what day or time it was, or exactly how long he'd slept. It didn't matter at this point; he was extremely thirsty, so he decided to take a chance and venture out of his hiding spot to find something to drink.

Once inside the hall, he knew that he could easily be spotted by any one of the security cameras that were still functioning. He moved cautiously toward a bathroom he'd spotted when he first entered the underground garage. Once inside, he drank as much water as possible from the sink.

"Look, Max, we have been down this blasted hall a million times; there isn't anyone down here. I don't even think anyone remembers these old security officer rooms."

"This used to be where the security officers lived?"

"Yeah, one of the older guards was down here with me yesterday. He told me that when Dante, the guy that used to own this place, built the new guard house, the guards slept out there instead of here. The only thing usable down here in this musty old basement is that holding cell, or torture chamber, whatever you want to call it." The men were talking just outside the bathroom door.

Damian held his ear to the bathroom door, being careful not to draw attention to his presence.

"Shades will kill us, and I do mean kill us, if we don't find this guy."

The other man spoke out. "I'm about ready to find another job; I don't like working for that psychopath. I don't know what the rich son-of-a-bitch is into, or how he makes his money, but you can be sure it ain't legal."

"I'm with you on that. Shades doesn't pay enough for this shit. We've been looking for this Damian guy for the last two days. He's nowhere to be found. I think he got out of the compound somehow."

Suddenly, the men's walkie-talkie went crazy with chatter. "SWAT and the cops are here! Every man for himself!"

The two men looked at each other. They dropped their conversation and ran for the door that led to the stairwell. "We'd better get out of here. I can't afford to get busted again," one said as they rounded the corner.

Damian heard the men leave the hallway in front of the bathroom. He decided to slip back into the underground garage. He knew that Shades was slippery and that he and Dante would have had some kind of a backup plan for getting away from the cops in case they ever did make a bust on the estate. Damian had a feeling that the underground garage was part of that plan. He was determined not to leave the mansion without taking Shades down.

◊◊◊

Angelica fought, scratched, and eventually bit the guard hard enough that he let one of his hands go from her arms. "Ouch, you bitch." The man checked out the teeth marks that Angelica had left on his wrist, while still maintaining a hard grip on one of her arms.

Angelica lifted her steel-toed, black leather riding boot and kicked backwards as hard as she could into the man's knee. "Let me go, you fucking gorilla!"

The man yelled out in pain. He let Angelica's arm go, as he tried to balance himself on the steps. Angelica took the opportunity to run down the stairs as fast as she could to the elevator. The bodyguard nursed his leg for only a second before pulling his gun from its holster. He fired at Angelica. "Stop!"

Angelica kept running. The elevator opened and closed just in time for one of the bullets from the bodyguard's gun to miss her. Having some idea of the place from the blueprints that she had looked over while talking with Agent Baldwin and Commander Grands, Angelica pushed the button to the basement. The place was huge, with all kinds of hidden spots, thanks to Dante. She had no idea where Shades would go once he reached the basement, but she knew that it would have to contain some kind of an escape. She wanted to catch Shades, but she also needed to find Damian.

Angelica reached into her pocket and grabbed her cell phone. She typed in a text message to Agent Baldwin:

Headed to the basement, tracking Shades, armed bodyguard in the dining room, no sign of Damian yet.

CHAPTER SIXTEEN

"Shelby, I don't want to alarm you, but there was a massive explosion near a Blythe, California shopping mall last night. Several people were killed and hundreds were injured," Cody said.

"Are you serious?"

"Yes, and this one *has* been confirmed as a terrorist attack. There are also unconfirmed rumors that small EMP drones were used inside the mall prior to the attack, taking out most of the electrical grid and electrical devices, which prevented the people in the mall from contacting the police about the attack. It was complete chaos."

"That's awful, did the EMT's get there in time to help?" Shelby asked.

"Yes, they did finally get there, but that wasn't the only thing that prevented the first responders from being prompt to the scene. It was later discovered that some sort of jamming device had been placed on the police department building. It jammed the radio communications between the police and the dispatchers inside police headquarters."

"How is that possible?"

"Remember those Hummers that you spotted in that barn in Nebraska? They are investigating it, but it looks like they used one of those jammers we use on our own military Humvees out in the field. I guess they were going for the maximum number of casualties."

"The more I think about this, Cody, I think these terrorists are performing these sporadic attacks, like some sort of practice run. Maybe they're planning something much bigger? Maybe, Shield Sheik is part of that plan?" Shelby added.

"I've been thinking the same thing."

"Why do these people hate us so much that they want to kill us?" Shelby wondered aloud.

"It's impossible to know. Most people don't aspire to that level of hate. Look, I have to go now, but I just wanted you to be aware of what's happening. Watch your back and stay vigilant."

"You got it, boss man."

◊◊◊

Damian leaned against the truck that he had used for a bed. He heard the chaos erupting above him and wanted to get out of the underground garage. However, he just couldn't shake the feeling that he should just stay put.

Damian heard the doorknob click, and then the door from the hallway opened. He squatted down, moved quietly behind the truck cab, and hid behind the driver's side door. Footsteps strode confidently through the darkness then stopped. After a momentary silence was the sound of a small metal panel door swinging open. The sound reverberated as the door hit the wall. Next, Damian heard the clicking of a breaker switch being engaged. The florescent shop lights in the ceiling came on. Damian hunkered down further; he was not going to make himself known until he saw who had joined him in the garage.

The figure moved to the garage doors and pulled at the metal handles that kept the doors from rolling up. Damian took the opportunity to see if he could identify who was there. He did his best not to make any noise, but the garage was too quiet. Even his breathing and heartbeat seemed to break the silence.

Sensing that he wasn't alone in the room, Shades turned from what he was doing. "Who's in here?"

Damian recognized the voice. The voice that had left numerous threatening messages on Amber's voicemail. It was the bastard who killed his beloved Amber!

"Yeah, someone's in here." Damian came out from his hiding place with the gun he had taken from the guard pointed at Shades. "Finally, after all this time, I have the chance to give you what you've got coming, Shades."

Seemingly unaffected, Shades turned back to the garage doors and commenced pulling on the handles. "So this is where you've been hiding, Damian. You know, my men have been looking for you for a long time. I never thought about sending them to look in here. This place was supposed to be a secret..."

Then Shades turned swiftly from the garage doors, pulled his gun from his side holster, and shot Damian before the young man knew what happened. Damian fell back as blood spurted from his stomach. Before he hit the ground, he fired at Shades and the bullet grazed the man's shoulder. The errant shot was enough to distract Shades, and Damian slid across the floor to take cover behind the wheel of the pickup truck. He tried to press on the wound with his free hand.

Shades jumped behind another vehicle that was parked close by.

"Wow, Damian, you're still really salty about Amber! She really wasn't worth it, buddy. She was just a little whore; you could have done much better."

Damian took a deep breath in an attempt to still his anger, "Shut up, Shades, don't talk about Amber that way. I loved her; she was my wife." Damian punctuated his sentence by taking another shot at Shades.

Shades ducked out from behind the car just long enough to press the knob on the wall to engage the automatic garage door opener. The doors to the underground garage squeaked and grated in protest. After years of neglect, they moved slowly. "Damian, I really don't have time for small talk so why don't you just crawl over there and die? I'm out of here."

Before Damian could get another word out of his mouth, Angelica came through the hall door into the underground garage. She'd heard the gunfire from the other side of the basement. Shades quickly took a shot at Angelica.

Angelica dove for cover on the other side of the pickup from Damian. "Shades, it's all over, there is nowhere to go. Give it up," she announced.

Damian heard Angelica's voice. "Angelica, I'm over here."

"Oh, looky here, a family reunion," Shades said as he slithered his way toward the driver's side door of the vehicle that he was planning to use for his escape.

"Shades, you're a dead man!" Damian yelled. "Angelica, he's over there in that left back corner behind that old Jeep."

Angelica looked under the pickup and saw Damian's bloody body near the truck wheel. She climbed under the truck to where he was. "I'm here, Damian."

Damian was growing weaker, and his feeble attempt at pressure could not stave off the flow of blood. His hand shook clumsily as he handed Angelica the guard's pistol. "Get that bastard, Angelica—get him for Amber."

Angelica placed the gun within reach. She opened her leather jacket as she cautiously watched the corner where Shades was apparently hiding. She tore at the button up white cotton shirt she was wearing. The material ripped, exposing the bottom portion of her bra. She took the cloth and placed it under Damian's bloody hand—the one that had been covering his wound. "Push on that as hard as you can, Damian. We have to stop the bleeding. Don't give up on me."

"Don't worry about me—get that asshole before he escapes, please. For Amber," Damian said as his breathing began to slow.

"You stay with me, Damian. I'm going to get us out of here. I will get Shades; you have my word on that." Angelica scanned the garage for evidence of what Shades might be planning or where he might be hiding. "Come out, Shades; it's only a matter of time before we take you down and you know it."

She grabbed the gun that Damian had given her and made a dash for the other side of the garage, dodging Shades' bullets as she ran.

"You're pretty fast, Angelica, but not fast enough. It would probably be better for you and your family if you just let me go."

"I warned you before, Shades, you leave my family out of this, or I will kill you."

"Dallas is so beautiful this time of year."

Shades opened the driver's side door of the old Jeep; he smiled with satisfaction when he saw the steering wheel. Without getting all the way into the vehicle, he reached in and pressed on the Jeep's gas pedal and pumped it a few times. Then he reached up and turned the key in the ignition. At first, the vehicle didn't want to turn over, but all of a sudden, it roared. Shades put the old dusty vehicle into drive. He hunkered down in the seat and used the butt of the gun to smash out the driver's side window. He fired several shots at Angelica.

Angelica saw that Shades was planning to leave the garage, she quickly came out of hiding and took aim at the Jeep's side and rear windows as it pulled out of the garage. She sprinted after the Jeep as it sped down the driveway toward a hidden rear entrance, which was partially concealed by bushes and brush. Angelica kept shooting at the Jeep, but Shades kept driving.

Realizing that it was no use, she stopped firing and let Shades go. She hoped the SWAT team would get him when he arrived at the gate. Angelica put the gun in her back waistband and rushed into the garage. She breathed a sigh of relief. The local police on the detail heard the gunfire and rushed in, following the sound of the shots to the secret garage. "We have ambulances on the way. The whole place is under control by the SWAT team. No casualties on our part, but lots of hurt or dead ones on the other side," Sergeant Nichols told Angelica.

Angelica knelt down next to Damian; she took his head and put it in her lap.

Damian spoke softly. "Did you get him, Angelica? Did you get him for Amber?"

Angelica didn't want to lie to Damian, but she couldn't bear to tell him that Shades had escaped again. "We got him, Damian. You just stay with us; don't waste your strength, the ambulance will be here in just a minute. Do you hear the sirens? They're almost here, Damian, now stay with me."

Damian spoke softly again, "Amber, Amber, I've missed you." Damian pushed one last breath from his lungs and then went limp in Angelica's lap.

"No, no, Damian. Come back!" A stream of tears fell from Angelica's eyes. Memories of her first love dying in her arms in Iraq came flooding back.

An EMT helped Angelica to her feet as the others in the garage took over Damian's care. Angelica walked to the open doors. She wiped the tears from her eyes and grabbed her cell phone to call Agent Baldwin. "Did you get that fucker at the gate, Baldwin?"

Baldwin was confused. "Which one?"

"Shades! He was driving an old hunting Jeep. He should have come straight at you if he was going to get out of this place."

"He never came through here, Angelica; maybe he's still on the compound."

"Shit!" Angelica shouted. "Well, I need some of your men to come to the north side of the mansion; there is a garage down here. If this garage can be hidden, then it's possible that there is a hidden exit as well. I want the whole perimeter of this fucking placed searched, and I want it searched right now!" Angelica hung up her phone, put it back in her jacket, and zipped the front up to cover the skin exposed from the torn pieces of her shirt.

"I want every one of you who isn't helping with Damian to come with me."

The available officers joined the ones that Baldwin sent from the guard booth. A large posse was now outside the garage with Angelica. "Search the perimeter from here all the way back through the forest and back to the guard shack. There is an opening in this wall somewhere, and I want to find it."

After giving the police officers her instructions, Angelica walked down to the guard booth, fetched her motorcycle, and rode up into the estate. She rode along the fence line in the direction that Shades had left out of the garage. Soon, a loud shout came from one of the officers. "Over here, Agent Brighten! I found the exit."

Angelica rode her bike to the opening. Shades hadn't taken the time to open the gates; he just rammed the Jeep through them. Angelica knew that it couldn't have been easy steering that old Jeep out of the compound through the brush that hid the exit.

Angelica maneuvered her bike through the broken fence, brush, and bushes until she was on the street. "Tell Baldwin about the escape route and that I've gone after Shades!" Angelica called out.

◊◊◊

When Angelica returned to her truck, she made fast work of loading her motorcycle. She unlocked the driver's side door, got in her truck, and turned it on. While it was airing up, she went to the sleeper area of her truck and reached for a clean shirt from the closet. As she went to pull a shirt from the hanger, she saw the blood all over her hands. She unzipped her jacket and saw Damian's dried blood on her stomach and all over what was left of the shirt she had been wearing. She slumped down onto the bed and held her hands out in front of her. "Damian is dead. Damian is dead because of me," Angelica moaned.

Her thoughts were suddenly interrupted by her cell phone—it was Cody.

"Yeah?"

"Angelica! You're there! It's Cody. Is everything okay?"

Angelica sobered to the reality of her surroundings. She stood to her feet and reached for a container of baby wipes. She began wiping at the blood on her hands and body. "Yeah, I'm here, Cody. Sorry."

"So, how did the bust go?" Cody asked excitedly.

"He got away, Cody, and Damian is dead. It didn't go well at all." She continued to wipe away the blood.

"I'm so sorry to hear about Damian, Angelica. I know he was a good friend."

Angelica wanted to cry, but she couldn't—not right now—she had a score to settle. "Yeah, but I have more pressing things to deal with. Shades is on his way to kill my family, and Shelby's, too. I need for you to get in touch with Rex and Jack. They have to get out of town, away from anywhere that Shades might be able to find them."

"Okay, I'll get on that right away."

"After I get myself cleaned up, I'm heading to Dallas. I want you to call Shelby. I need her to meet me at my place there. It's the closest place for Shades to go first, since he's intent on inflicting pain on me. Shelby and Jack live in Odessa, which is five hours further. I'm sure he will go to my house first, but if we don't take him out there, he'll probably try for Shelby's place. He's pretty stupid to think we won't pull our families out, but I'm thinking he'd prefer to have a confrontation with me and Shelby over our families."

"I'll pull her right away and send her to you," Cody agreed. "Wouldn't it just be easier to have the locals take him out when he gets there?"

"It might, but Shades is slick. But more importantly, I want to take him out myself."

"I got it, Angelica." Cody didn't want to argue with Angelica about the fact that she'd just outright threatened a subject.

"I'll be on the road in about thirty minutes after I fuel up. Make sure Shelby understands that I know she's got about 10 more hours of driving time over my eleven hours, but not to worry. I won't go in after Shades without her. I'll wait for her at our favorite truck stop."

"I don't mind telling Shelby all of that Angelica, but maybe we should just have a conference call?"

"Yeah, that might be a better idea. I would like to be the one to tell her about Damian."

"Got it. Call ya back in a few."

"Thanks."

◊◊◊

"It is our obligation to administer punishment upon the great infidels. Allah has commanded us, through his prophet Muhammad, that if the people do not conform to the doctrine of Islam by the prophet, then they must die," Omar declared in Arabic, via Skype to his fifty leading generals scattered across the United States.

"Praise be to Allah!" The fifty men responded.

"It is our destiny, and our prize, to bring the 'Great Infidel' America, and our arch-enemy, Israel, to their knees," Omar continued.

"Praise be to Allah!" His men shouted again.

Omar continued, "We have worked long, and in silence, to bring about the victory that will be ours just days from now. Remember, my brothers, we do this for our people, we do this for ourselves, and we do this for Allah!"

"Praise be to Allah!"

"Prepare the last of your weapons. Prepare your faithful men and women for war. In three days we descend upon the sleeping giant and her foul offspring in a rage of synchronized battles." Omar ended his address.

"Praise be to Allah!" the men cheered, and the video screen went black.

◊◊◊

Shelby was about to take the I-5 "grapevine" just outside the L.A. city limits and head north toward San Francisco when her phone rang. "Hi, Cody, what's happening?"

"Look, Shelby, I know you're not going to like what I'm about to say, but I have to pull you off your case. Angelica needs you to meet her in Dallas at her house. She wants to be the one to explain everything to you, so when you get turned around and headed toward Dallas give me a call. We'll have a conference call," Cody explained.

"Okay, I'll find a place right away to get turned around. However, if this is because I got out of my truck to spy on Shield Sheik, well, Cody, you were right there on my phone with me. You know I wasn't in any danger…"

"Shelby, chill, it has nothing whatsoever to do with the job you've been doing. It has everything to do with the fact that your partner needs you to back her up in Dallas. When we have the conference call, Angelica will explain everything. Now, please, just get your ass to Dallas as quickly as possible," Cody insisted.

"I'm turning around now. This must be really important."

◊◊◊

"Rex, this is Cody. I'm sorry to have to tell you this over the phone, but some stuff went wrong during the bust on Dante's mansion today."

"Is Angelica all right?" Rex said, panicked.

"Yes, she fine— just a little shaken up. That's not the reason for this call, Rex. Shades got away from Angelica again. You need to get Harley and go somewhere safe. Shades threatened to come for you and your daughter."

"That son-of-a-bitch thinks he's going to mess with my family? Does he have a death wish, trying to mess with two retired Marines and their kid? The man is a psychopath!"

"Exactly, and he's out for blood. I get that you can handle things on your own, Rex, but Angelica wants to deal with Shades herself. She wants you to take Harley someplace safe. She also wants you to contact Jack Mathews. Shades made threats against Shelby's family, too. Have them find some place outside of their everyday routine. She'll contact you once she and Shelby have apprehended Shades. Honestly, I think she's hoping she'll just have to take him out."

"Wow, he must have really pissed her off! I know there were times she thought a perp didn't deserve due process, but I don't think I've ever heard my wife ever threaten to go after someone without a trial," Rex explained.

171

"Well, he shot Damian Adams dead today right in front of her. I guess it's hit her pretty hard."

"No wonder Angelica is so upset."

"Yeah, from what the cops on the scene told me, when they filed their report, Damian died in her lap. Emotions are obviously running high."

"That's not good, Cody. If she's being driven by emotion rather than objectivity, things could go terribly wrong. Let me see if I can get my neighbor to take care of Harley. I can stay here and provide backup for Angelica and Shelby."

"Rex, you don't have authorization from the agency to backup other agency personnel."

"That's just bureaucratic bullshit and you know it."

"Angelica wants you out of harm's way. Besides, if it goes badly, I'll be held accountable. I don't really care what the DEA thinks, but it would devastate me if anything happened to Angelica, Shelby, or you—especially on my watch. No, Rex, take Harley, find some place safe, and stay out of this. That's an order."

"Sure. I'll call Jack and see what we can do about holing up somewhere while our wives defend us from the bad guy. That sounds really manly, doesn't it? Who are you to give me orders, anyway? I have seniority over you," Rex said.

"Manly or not, this is a dangerous situation, and I am in charge of this case. Angelica is the case leader, and you're not invited to participate. Please stop giving me flack on this and just comply with Angelica's wishes. She's got enough to worry about without having to be concerned with you and your daughter's safety."

"I get it, Cody. I don't like it, not one bit, but I get it. When Angelica gets a few free minutes, tell her to call me," Rex demanded.

"Thanks, Rex. I'll have her call you soon. She just got a call from Agent Baldwin. Unfortunately, before she can leave Atlanta, she has to go to the police station for a debriefing. She also has to claim Damian's body until the cops can find any living family members. Angelica made it clear before she left the scene that she didn't want anything to happen to him without her knowledge or consent."

"That sounds like Angelica, always taking care of her friends."

"She was hoping that they could wait on all that so she could catch up with Shades, but APD said it had to be done immediately. It will set her back a couple of hours behind Shades. It could all work out, though, because Shelby has an extra ten-hour ride from Cali, and you guys need time to get out of town."

"I suppose. I sure don't like this idea, Cody."

"I understand, but she's made up her mind. You'll need to argue with her later."

"I need to go, Harley's crying."

"I'll call you in a little while, Rex. Don't forget to talk to Jack."

"Okay, talk soon."

CHAPTER SEVENTEEN

Shelby got back on the I-10 and headed east. She thought about the conference call, Angelica's story about her pursuit of Shades, Damian being shot and dying in her lap, and the threat Shades had made to both families. At first, she was angry that Cody had pulled her off the Shield Sheik detail, but Angelica needed her and she would do anything for her partner. *Shades needs to pay for all the hell he's caused.*

When she first heard Angelica's voice, Shelby was worried about her mindset. She was in pure revenge mode. Shelby didn't know that Angelica could harbor such intense hatred. Shelby was able to distract her by offering a solution for Rex's and Harley's safety. Angelica's demeanor became more like that of a DEA agent and less of a renegade after.

Shelby told Angelica and Cody about the ranch in Brownwood, Texas that her parents had just bought. The purchase was just a few weeks old, and the ranch was pretty much off the grid. There was no way Shades could possibly know about it. And even if he did, her father had a personal arsenal large enough to outfit a small army. One man against that much gun power didn't stand a chance.

Soon after the conference call, Shelby called Jack and he agreed to make sure that Rex and Harley made it to Brownwood.

Shelby still had eighteen hours to reach Dallas, but she figured she should be in Dallas with Angelica by the following evening, which gave Angelica enough time to finish up with the Atlanta PD and claim Damian's body.

"If they can't track down any relatives, then I'm going to make sure he's buried next to Amber in Odessa…if Amber's parents don't mind," Angelica told Shelby.

"I think that's a great idea. I know her parents will agree. They loved Damian."

They agreed to meet at their truck stop off the I-45 and I-20 in Dallas.

"I'm going to do some surveillance on my house while I'm waiting for you," Angelica told Shelby. "I want to know every move that bastard is making before he makes it."

"Don't go in there without me, Angelica. I do not want to bury another one of my friends," Shelby pleaded.

"I won't, I promise. I want this asshole too much to allow myself to make any more mistakes."

"Good. I agree with what Cody said; we need to be thinking with clear heads—not broken hearts."

Shelby decided to check in with Jack to make sure their hideout plans were under way. "Did you speak with Daddy and Mama?"

"Yes, but I'm still not happy about this situation. You know I don't like when you put yourself in harm's way."

"I know, but I have to backup my partner."

"I get it, Shelby, but I don't have to like it." Jack scolded.

"It will be fun for y'all. My folks will love playing with the grand-babies—and little Harley will steal everyone's heart. Besides, you'll get to know Rex and Harley better. They're family now," Shelby pointed out.

"I already thought about your parent's place when Rex called. I called your dad, and of course, he was more than happy to accommodate all of us, including Rex and Harley," Jack said. "I love you, Shelby, but you always seem to get yourself into the damnedest shit. I try really hard to avoid problems, but they just seem to follow you."

"So, you're saying you still love me, even though I'm a stinky problem magnet?"

"Yes, Shelby, I still love you. I don't really have the time to be taking off work right now for all this bullshit, and I still don't like how you described Angelica's mood, but I still love you."

"I love you, too. It's going to be fine Jack, I promise. You just wait and see. Before you know it, Angelica and I will be rolling up in our white Petes with roses in our teeth, waiting to sweep you boys right off your feet." Shelby laughed.

"Mrs. Knight In Shining Armor," Jack laughed. "Seriously, though, there is nothing funny about this situation. Don't you think it would be smarter to get the local police involved, instead of the two of you trying to catch him on your own? I can't believe Cody is okay with this."

"The cops would blow it for us, Jack. They would unintentionally scare him away if they tried to apprehend him before we could get there. No, the element of surprise is the best way to catch Shades. He's too slick, and you have to play the game the way he plays it—dirty. Cody gets it."

"Oh, I feel so much better now. When I think about all the times you could have gotten yourself killed, it gives me a headache. And now you are purposefully putting yourself directly in the line of fire without backup, just to catch this freak. Do you really want to do this?" Jack asked.

"I don't want to do it, Jack. I have to do it."

Jack conceded. "Fine, just please be careful. We'll all be waiting for you and Angelica at your parents' place."

"I love you, Jack."

"I love you, too, Shelby."

◊◊◊

"I'm on my way to Dallas, Rex. There is nothing more to talk about. I'm going to get Shades."

"So, Harley and I don't have anything to say about this? You don't even care what we might want?"

"Of course I care what you both want. It's completely unfair to even ask such a thing. You've been in this business long enough, Rex, and we've both been Marines. When you have a job to do, you do it. If I don't take Shades out now, he's just going to come for us later."

"Angelica, I realize he'll just keep coming after us, but it doesn't make it any easier knowing that my beautiful wife, and mother our child, is out there looking for such an evil man. Drug enforcement is one thing, but now you're chasing down a killer."

"What the hell do you think I did in Iraq, Rex? At least here I know who my enemy is and I don't have to dodge mortars and land mines."

"True, but Shades is a snake. He will strike at you hard. Please, Angelica, take care of yourself. I know you're a great agent, but you're a great mother and wife, too."

"I've got this, Rex. I promise."

"You'd better, because I'm not raising Harley by myself. So, if you don't want some strange woman raising your little girl, you'd better bring your ass home to us safely," Rex warned.

"Just so you know, I've already made arrangements with Shelby. If anything happens to me, she would help you raise Harley. See, no need for a strange woman to step in," Angelica joked.

"Not funny, Angelica. I will go to one of those crazy ass mediums in Louisiana and have her call you out every day from the great beyond if you get yourself killed. You will never enjoy the afterlife in peace—I promise," Rex joked back.

"Now that's just wrong."

"I love you, Angelica; don't make me regret this."

"I love you, too, Rex; I'll come home safe. Give big kisses to my Harley. Tell her mommy and Auntie Shelby will see her soon in Brownwood. I promise, Rex, I'll be there."

"You'd better. I love you. Be careful." Rex pushed the end button on the Bluetooth. "Well, Harley, time for you to meet some horses."

◊◊◊

"Just a few hours, Angelica. Just a few more hours," Shades said to himself, as he drove to Dallas. Suddenly, the Jeep began to lose power. "Shit! What the fuck is wrong with this piece of junk?" Shades maneuvered the vehicle to the side of the highway.

Shades threw open the driver's side door and saw smoke billowing out from underneath the hood. When he opened it, the smoke blew into his face, making him cough. He couldn't see anything, and even if he could see where the smoke was coming from, he had no idea how to rectify the problem.

"Son-of-a-bitch," Shades kicked at the Jeep so hard that he put a dent in the driver's door. "Piece of crap!"

He looked around but everything along the highway was dark. Only a few eighteen-wheel trucks and a couple of cars were out on the road. *Now what?* Shades thought.

He tried flagging down a few of the vehicles that passed by, but there weren't any takers. He figured the fastest way to find a new ride was to start walking. He knew that there had to be a gas station, a store, or even a hotel close enough to the highway that he would eventually come across new wheels.

After walking several miles, Shades found what he was looking for, an exit with everything he needed—not only a store and a hotel—but a car dealership, too. Shades knew that he could simply use the gun that was secured in its holster under his jacket to get anything he wanted. However, that would draw attention, which was the last thing he wanted at the moment. He figured that Angelica was probably already on his trail.

She thinks she can rush home and save her family from the big bad man. The thought made him laugh. *What kind of sissy-ass husband is she married to anyway?* Shades formulated a plan: first, he'd get himself a hotel for the night. In the morning, he'd buy some fresh clothes and then get a car from that car lot. Then he'd head on to Dallas and surprise Angelica, who had no idea when he would be arriving or what he'd be driving. *I'll kill them all,* Shades thought as he walked across the road and into the hotel parking lot.

◊◊◊

An exhausted Angelica pushed the button on the door panel and opened the passenger side window of her big rig. A wave of cool air flowed into the truck. Determined to make Dallas before morning, Angelica kept her mind on how she planned to take Shades down. *What if he didn't even show up at her house? Will Shelby's and my family have to watch our backs constantly, wondering when that bastard will show his face again?* She shook her head defiantly. *No, that's not t going to happen.* Angelica knew that Shades was too self-absorbed and arrogant to allow himself to be out-smarted by a couple of female DEA agents.

The sight of an old Jeep parked along the side of the road caught Angelica's attention and jerked her from her thoughts. "No. It couldn't be," she said out loud. She tried to get a better look at the Jeep from her passenger side mirror, but the overcast night sky did not give off enough light to help her identify the vehicle. She thought about getting off at the next exit and making a U-turn to check out the Jeep, but she was already on a tight schedule. There were a lot of Jeeps out there, and if the one on the side of the road wasn't Shades', she'd just be wasting more time. *On the other hand, if it was his, it's possible I could have gained a small advantage of time over him.* In the end, she concluded that the evil Shades would secure transportation one way or another and she was best served by pressing on.

CHAPTER EIGHTEEN

The sun shined through the crack in Angelica's window covering. She had made it to Dallas, but she was too tired to go to her house. If Shades were there, that would be a fatal mistake in the condition she was in.

She had set her alarm for four hours of sleep, but the sun had awakened her instead of the alarm ten minutes earlier. "Oh, I don't want to get up." She dragged her body from her sleeper, gathered a few things, put them in her shower bag, and headed to the truck stop store. "A nice hot shower and a cup of black coffee and I'll be ready to defeat a dragon."

◊◊◊

Shelby had only taken a short nap when she stopped in El Paso, Texas for fuel. She had just made it to the I-20 and I-10 split. According to her GPS, she now had about seven and a half hours until she reached Dallas. She called Angelica.

With shampoo in her eyes, Angelica reached for her towel to wipe away the soap and the water from her hands before she pushed the accept button on her phone. She quickly transferred it to speaker and returned to her shower. "Hey, Shelby girl, where are you?"

"You sound like you're in a tunnel or something," Shelby remarked.

"No, I'm in the shower at our favorite truck stop. I put you on speaker." Angelica said, while rinsing her hair.

"Okay, well I can call you back if that would be better."

"No, I can talk. I'm almost finished. I got into Dallas early this morning, took a little nap, and now I'm clearing my head with a hot shower. Where are you?"

"I'm on I-20 headed toward Odessa. I really want to stop by my house, but I know you would rather I just come on through to Dallas," Shelby explained.

"I'm just not sure where Shades might be, that's why I didn't go to my house this morning. I think I saw a Jeep alongside the road last night. It looked a lot like the one he escaped in, but I didn't take the time to check it out for sure. If it was him, then we just got a break. You're what about six hours out?"

"Yeah, but I'm hauling ass, so once I clear Midland/Odessa, I'll be able to click off those miles pretty fast. I talked to my parents last night; everyone made it to the ranch. Daddy is loaded for bear, and Mama's having the time of her life with all the kids around."

"Rex and I talked last night, too. We're both glad they went down there. I think they will be safe," Angelica said as she put her wet hair up in a turban.

"You said you haven't gone by your house yet? Do you think Shades might be there? Do you think it's possible that Jeep you saw was his? Could he have had a breakdown or a flat?"

"No, I haven't gone by my house yet. I was beat when I got here. Yes, it's possible that Shades broke down in Louisiana last night. That would be great for us. In fact, when I finish getting dressed, I'm going to head home in my car to check things out. If he's there, then you'll miss all the fun, but if not, I'm going to secure a few things, like the garage and the gun cabinet to make things as difficult for him as I can. Then I'll come back to the truck stop and wait for you."

"Do you think he's figured out that we've moved our families?" Shelby asked.

"If he has, then I figure he's going to come looking for us, because we are the ones he really wants. If his arrogance has clouded his mind, which I'm pretty sure it has, he'll go to my house first. He's going to go ballistic when he figures out he's been outsmarted by a couple whores—his word, not mine. I predict I'll get a call for him right away."

"I take it you have a plan?"

"Of course! I don't know if it's going to work, but I have a plan."

"I knew you would."

"Hurry up and get your butt here so we can put it in motion."

"I'm running fast as I dare. We may be law enforcement officers, but I don't think the state police are going to let me slide if I'm speeding in an eighteen-wheeler."

"I know. Well, I'm done showering and my face is painted. I'm going to grab my hot coffee and head to my truck. I'll let you know what I find when I get to my house," Angelica said.

"Okay, be careful, Cover Girl."

"I always try to be. You drive safe, Barbie!" Angelica hung up her phone. She punched in the security code for the lock box on the back of her truck and removed the remote that controlled her trailer doors, the hydraulic lift, and ramp. It was time to check out her house.

◊◊◊

"Look, I don't know what your problems are over there at Homeland Security, but I've been asking you for weeks now to give me information on Shield Sheik. I had an agent who was tailing them for a while, and she has uncovered a lot of very suspicious activities. I have dozens of photos proving something is off about that trucking company," Cody insisted.

"Why was a DEA agent following a trucking company?" The DHS operative probed.

"Not that I really need to explain this to you, Agent Talbot, but Shield Sheik trucks were, and probably still are, hauling drugs for some of the criminals we've been tracking for years," Cody replied sternly.

"So, what's drug trafficking got to do with this department? You guys handle the drugs and we handle the terrorist threats."

Cody resented the agent's arrogance. "You are impossible. I want to talk to your supervisor," Cody demanded.

"Well, which divisional supervisor would you like to speak with, sir?" Talbot quipped. "We've got plenty of them. But I assure you, none of them are going to talk to some pisser handler from the DEA."

Cody ended the call without response and called his boss. "Deputy Director Homer, I have a serious issue out in the field, but I can't seem to get Homeland Security to listen to me. May I come to your office and fill you in?"

"Sure, Cody. As it happens, I have a dinner meeting with the DHS director tonight. I'll come down to your office in a few minutes to hear what you've got. If it is as serious as you contend, I'll bring it to the director's attention tonight."

"Thank you, sir. I've been so frustrated trying to make them understand the threat we face. They just don't want to listen, especially that Agent Talbot."

"No problem, I'll be down there soon."

◊◊◊

Angelica's house was so still and quiet when she entered through the back door it was almost scary. With her gun drawn, she scoped out each room, making sure that no unwanted visitor was present. Their newly built house held the aroma of baby powder and apple-cinnamon. The powder reminded her of her baby girl and the apple-cinnamon, her favorite scent, came from the plug-ins she placed in various rooms of the house.

Angelica touched some of her favorite things as she searched her home: the quilt on her king-size bed, Rex's bathrobe on the back of the door, and one of Harley's stuffed animals sitting on the dresser.

She sighed when she finished her extensive examination. Angelica couldn't imagine what her home was going to look like, or even how she was going to feel about it after tonight. She hoped she was doing the right thing luring Shades into her home. Although he wasn't there at the moment, she knew it was only a matter of time until the arrogant thug appeared.

Angelica quickly hid a few pictures and special mementos that were scattered throughout the house. She took the guns and bullets that Rex had left in the gun cabinet and loaded them in her Charger. She placed a broomstick handle across the sliding glass door rail that led to the pool area. Shades wouldn't be able to use that door as an escape. He would have to enter or leave from either the side door, by the garage, or the front door.

When she went into the garage, she noticed that her "mom SUV" was gone. Rex must have taken it for their trip to Brownwood, which made sense since it was more practical than the pickup. Angelica rummaged through some jars Rex had on one of his workbenches and grabbed a handful of long roofing nails. She reached for the hammer and a wrench, which hung from their designated spots on the organized pegboard on the wall. She also grabbed a flashlight and some other tools. Within a few moments, she had put the nails into the frame of the door that led into the house, thus preventing anyone from using it. She spotted the electrical power box next to the door, opened it, and flipped the breakers to everything except the refrigerator.

Angelica manually closed the garage door, but took the remote control with her and placed it in her Charger. She walked to the back alley and located her gas and water meters. She broke the seal on the gas meter and turned off the gas to the house. The gas company was probably going to fine her for that one, but she would deal with it later. She did the same to the water meter, using the wrench she'd grabbed from the garage. She located the shut-off valve not far from the water meter. She pried the metal plate off, exposed the turn valve, and turned it to the off position.

Once she eliminated the threats that she thought Shades might try to use to destroy her home, she walked back through the wooden alley gate, looked around the yard, and located a two-by-four propped up against the garage. Angelica wedged the board in between two posts near the back gate, which would prevent anyone from entering or leaving without a tremendous amount of effort.

It was starting to get dark. Angelica knew that Shelby would be at the truck stop soon. She also knew that Shades might arrive at her home at any moment. Her plan was to let the bastard make himself at home—for a short time. Angelica left her backyard and placed the padlock through the metal holes. She threw the tools she was carrying into the car's trunk and dashed to the side and front doors to make sure they were locked. Then she got into her Charger, revved the engine, and headed to the truck stop.

◊◊◊

"Well, well, what do we have here?" Shades said. "I guess Angelica forgot that I would be coming for a visit." Shades parked the car he had bought in

Louisiana a few houses away from Angelica's house. He decided to wait for the evening sky to become completely dark before going up to the house. From what he could see, things seemed fairly quiet. "It's going to be a piece of cake taking out Angelica's old man and her little girl."

◊◊◊

"Look, Robert, I know your man Talbot is a good agent, but he's been giving my agent a really hard time. All Cody is trying to do is share some important information."

Deputy Director Homer slid his DHS counterpart a stack of files across the dinner table. The files included pictures, GPS tracking reports, and transcriptions of the conversations that Shelby recorded at the barn and warehouses.

"What's all this?" Robert asked. "I thought this was supposed to be a casual dinner with friends tonight, Malcolm?"

"You need to see this," Homer said.

The director took the files and looked through them with growing interest. "Where did all of this come from, Malcolm?" The director was obviously concerned.

"That's what I've been trying to tell you, Robert. Our agents, Shelby Mathews and Angelica Brighten, stumbled upon all this while working a drug enforcement case out of Mexico. The best we can tell from all this evidence is that Shield Sheik is a sleeper cell. They're a terrorist group that is using a trucking company as a legitimate business to cover up what they are really doing. As you can tell, these people have been working on something for quite a while. From the transcripts, I think they are planning a massive terrorist attack here on American soil. And if my suspicions are correct, it could make 9/11 look insignificant."

"Why didn't you bring this to my attention before now, Malcolm? If this information is validated, the country is at great risk."

"My agent has been trying to tell your people for weeks now, but they just keep blowing him off. He went to them the first time he thought something was fishy." Malcolm pointed at the picture of the military Hummer. "He sent them that picture, along with the forged military paperwork. Their response was that it all looked legitimate to them. They never checked it out; they never even looked at it, I'm guessing."

"I'm sorry about that, Malcolm. There has been a lot of complacency and turmoil in my department lately. We hired several new young people who depend too much on computer reports. They are not seasoned analysts and don't yet understand how to look for nuances and inconsistencies. Budget cuts have really impacted our ability to train them properly."

Robert pulled out his phone. "I'm going to make a call right now. Please ask your agent Cody to send all of that information again. I want it to go directly to my deputy director. I am personally going to see to it that every Shield Sheik location across the country gets visits from my agents tomorrow."

As he waited for his deputy to answer his call, the director continued looking over the file. "Wow, they have as many as five different locations in each state. This isn't good, Malcolm. If we don't get a handle on this, it could all blow up in our faces—literally."

"I know, Robert." Homer took out his cell phone and placed a call to Cody.

◊◊◊

"You stay out here by the back door," Angelica told Shelby as they approached her house. "I'm not sure he's even here, but I'll go in through the front door. If he is here, you bring your ass in behind me. It's almost a promise that he's going to try and take me out the minute I open that door. I'll do my best to avoid getting hit, but you need to come in behind me and blow that bastard away."

Suddenly, Angelica's phone rang. Angelica looked at the caller ID; it was unknown. She pulled Shelby back toward her car that was parked a few houses down the street. "Wait, I think it's Shades," she whispered. She answered the phone, "Hello?"

"Nice to hear your voice, Agent Brighten," Shades mocked.

"What do you want Shades?" Angelica sniped.

Shades hesitated. "Well…what I wanted was to kill your family, but I see your house has been nicely secured, and you took me at my word that

I would kill them. No one is here. That's too bad. But I can still hunt them down—you; your partner, Shelby; your families; and Amber's family until I kill all of you!"

"So sorry to disappoint you, Shades," Angelica said confidently.

She pointed for Shelby to position herself next to the back door. Shelby used the neighbor's yard to sneak in beside the door without being detected. She withdrew her gun from its holster and held it in a ready to fire position.

"Where are you, Angelica? You have a beautiful home here with nice things in a nice little quiet, suburban neighborhood. Everything a perfect little mother could ask for. Except you're not much of mother, are you, Agent Brighten? You would rather be out chasing after people who are just trying to run a business," Shades rambled.

"Business my ass. You kill people for a living, Shades." Angelica replied.

"Well, regardless, why don't you come home. Just you and me, Angelica. You can turn the electricity back on and we can make a little dinner. You know, our last dinner was so rudely interrupted. The least you can do is make it up to me," Shades suggested. "If you sacrifice yourself, I'll leave the rest of your family and friends alone."

"So, if I give myself up to you and let you kill me, then you'll leave everyone else out of this? How do I know I can trust you to keep your word?" Angelica kept talking as she inched closer to her house.

Without warning, a neighbor came out of his house and walked to where Angelica was shielding herself from Shades' view. "What's going on out here?" The neighbor said loudly, surprising Angelica.

She put her phone to her chest, grabbed the man by the arm, and pulled him to the ground next to her. "Shut up! Go back to your house," she hissed. "This is police business."

The man quickly took off for his front door.

Angelica went back to her conversation with Shades, but he'd overheard and wasn't on the phone any longer. Angelica could hear the police sirens in the background—it was now or never. She sprinted across the lawn and drove herself through the front door with all of her might. After landing on her side in the front hall, she stayed low and crept into the living room using Rex's overstuffed recliner as a shield. Shelby came in from the back door with her gun drawn.

Shades tried to make an exit when he'd heard the neighbor's voice, but Angelica's booby traps did an excellent job of keeping him confined. He was attempting to flee through the kitchen, when Angelica and Shelby busted in from opposite ends of the house. He turned to the door, trying to use the kitchen wall for cover, and fired his first rounds at Angelica in the living room. One bullet hit the wall unit that held up the flat screen television; another hit the recliner; and the last zipped past Angelica's shoulder and slightly tore the cloth of her bulletproof vest.

Angelica fired back at Shades immediately. Several of her bullets hit the kitchen wall. One hit him in the bottom part of his leg. Shades screamed in pain and stepped out to fire again at Angelica. Shelby stepped forward from the back door and aimed her gun at Shades chest—she pulled the trigger twice. Angelica again fired at Shades' exposed body and hit him in the chest and shoulder. He spun around from the impact. Shelby once again took aim, and her shot hit Shades right between his eyes. Instantly, he dropped forward onto the floor, unable to get off any more rounds.

The sirens blared as they ascended on Angelica's house. Shelby helped her partner to her feet, and they walked out into the front yard. DPD cops had their weapons drawn on the two women as they approached them. "Drop your guns," a policeman shouted. Angelica and Shelby complied. They stood still in the doorway and allowed the officer to approach them and pat them down. When he was satisfied that they posed no threat, they identified themselves. He escorted them to the waiting ambulance.

Shelby gave a shoulder hug to her partner. "We did it, partner! The bastard is dead."

"It's over. Amber and Damian, I hope you are up there somewhere watching all of this. We did it for you guys," Angelica whispered as ambulance EMT attended to her.

CHAPTER NINETEEN

"Oh, wow! This coffee tastes so good," Angelica said over the breakfast table. I feel like a big weight has been lifted off my shoulders. Shades is dead. Now all we have to do is gather up all of his associates, and we have one less drug ring to deal with. Things are looking up." Angelica signaled to the waitress for more coffee. The woman topped off the mug, as Angelica and Shelby sat in the restaurant of their favorite truck stop.

Shelby dipped her toast into her fried eggs. "I don't mean to rain on your parade, Angelica, but we do need to talk about those associates, especially Shield Sheik." Shelby picked up the journal that was sitting next to her on the booth and placed it on the table next to Angelica.

Angelica took hold of the journal and started rummaging through the pages. "What's this?" She stopped at one of the pages and read every word. "You went into Mexico? Are you crazy or do you just have a death wish, Shelby?" Angelica put the journal down and stared at her best friend.

"I couldn't tell you and Cody what I was doing, so I wrote everything in a journal," Shelby confessed.

"That's all fine and good, Shelby, but I can't read this. If I do, I'll have to put you on report. You can't even give this to Cody, because then the DEA will have cause to fire you. Just how many operation rules did you break?" Angelica shook her head in disbelief. "Thanks for bringing down my day, it's definitely a good thing I had Cody pull you off that Shield Sheik detail when he did. God only knows what else you would have gotten yourself into. You could have been killed!" Angelica leaned back in the booth and crossed her arms.

"Oh, so it's perfectly fine if I get killed while I'm with you?" Shelby sassed her friend.

"I'm serious. Mexico?"

"That stuff in that journal isn't just about the things that I did that I wasn't supposed to do. The most important stuff in that book is about Shield Sheik. Cody and I talked about what they might be planning. Angelica, that trucking company and the people who are associated with it are dangerous. They are up to something really sinister. I wanted you to read it so you could know what I saw. My surveillance, along with the background information that Cody has come up with, leads us to believe that Shield Sheik is possibly a terrorist organization."

Angelica picked up the journal again and started reading it from the very beginning. "You really think they are planning an attack on the United States?"

"Yes, I honestly think they are planning something, and they've been using the Shield Sheik trucking company to carry it out."

The women sat in silence for a while as Angelica read through Shelby's journal. Their moment of peace was interrupted by a sudden call on Angelica's cell phone. Angelica reached for her phone and read the caller ID. "It's Cody. I told him I was taking a few days off to get my house cleaned up."

She answered the phone. "Yeah, Cody. What's up?"

"Is Shelby with you?" Cody asked.

Angelica could hear the anxiousness in his voice. "Yes, she's right here."

"Tell her to conference in on her phone; she needs to hear this, too."

When the three were connected, Cody continued. "I need both of you to come to Springfield, right away. The director of Homeland Security has requested that you both attend a briefing over Shield Sheik."

"Oh, come on, Cody. I told you I needed a few days to clean up my house before Rex and Harley can come home. Can't this wait?" Angelica pleaded.

"No, this is very serious. In fact, you are to park your trucks and use one of your cars to get to DFW. Get on the next flight to Virginia. There is no time to waste. Get it done, ladies." Cody hung up.

Angelica gave Shelby a roll of her eyes and then moved begrudgingly out of her seat. "Duty calls…again."

Shelby stood up, took one last drink of her coffee, threw twenty dollars on the table near the check, and the two women walked out of the restaurant together to their trucks.

"I have to grab a few things out of my truck, which vehicle do you want to take to the airport?" Shelby asked.

Angelica went to the passenger side of her truck and put her key in the door. "I don't care, let's…" Before Angelica could finish her sentence, the ground shook and a loud noise penetrated the morning air.

"OH, MY GOD!" Shelby dove underneath the sleeper part of her truck. She covered her head with her hands and put her face in the cement. Within a few seconds, the horrendous noise that had surrounded her seemed to give way to a deafening silence. Slowly, she lifted her face and peered through the space between the two front steer tires. Fire and smoke rose in the air. The mangled metal of several eighteen-wheel trucks and bodies—a lot of bodies— were strewn all over the parking lot. This was all that remained of their favorite truck stop in Dallas.

"Shelby! Shelby!" Angelica yelled, sliding out from under her truck where she had taken refuge. Angelica crawled toward Shelby. "Shelby, are you okay?"

Shelby turned her face in Angelica's direction. Because of the subtle ringing in her ears, Shelby could barely recognize her best friend's voice. "Angelica, it's Shield Sheik. They're attacking us; I know it's them."

Still in shock, Angelica stood up and helped her friend out from under her truck. "I agree with you that Shield Sheik has something to do with this." Angelica pointed toward the fire and carnage. "Two Shield Sheik trucks, or at least what's left of them, are parked right over there next to the store."

"I told you they were planning to do something awful! We just came out of that café…All those people in there…Oh, Angelica, this is worse than I could have ever imagined."

Angelica looked at the parking lot. "Right now, we have to go help as many of those people over there as we can." She looked at Shelby again. "Are you hurt?"

Shelby brushed at the dirt on her clothes. She was still in shock, which kept her from feeling any pain. As her head cleared, she surveyed the bodies, the store—now a pile of smoldering wood and broken bricks—and the fuel island. It was ablaze with flames that seemed to reach toward heaven. "I'm fine. Come on!"

Angelica and Shelby ran from the safety of their trucks toward the people who lay moaning in pain. Some were missing limbs, some tried to get to their feet, and others were wandering about the parking lot, dazed and confused as to what had just happened to them. Many lay motionless. Angelica pointed at what remained of the building. "I'm going to start up there. Shelby, flag down some of those truckers running in this direction to help you get a triage started over by our trucks, and send some of them to me."

Truck drivers who were staying at the truck stop or who had tried to pull in quickly joined to the women to help the wounded.

Angelica and Shelby's required training for all national emergencies kicked in. The sirens from inside the city could be heard in the distance. "I think we have help coming," Shelby stated.

"I hope so, but those don't sound like first responder sirens. Those sound more like civil defense warnings to me." Angelica said as she ran to the destroyed truck stop building.

Shelby didn't like the sound of that, but she quickly forgot it and began to bark orders at those who had arrived to help. "Gather all the blankets, sheets, water, and any first aid materials you can find, and bring everything over to those two trucks. Put some of the blankets on the ground and tear the sheets into strips for bandages." She pointed at her and Angelica's white Petes.

"The rest of you, come with me." Shelby and her group of helpers ran to one of the first victims. He was alive but held his arm in pain. Shelby knew from the looks of it that he had broken it. "Help this man over there to the blanket area. Make him comfortable; see that he doesn't move his arm much."

With each passing moment, Angelica and Shelby did their best to help those who were still alive, but soon, an hour had passed and there was still no sign of any first responders. Shelby used her phone to call 9-1-1, but all she could get was a busy signal.

Angelica soon returned from her side of the parking lot. "How's it going over here?"

Shelby was busy and frustrated. "Well, we've got at least five dead, several with broken bones, and a dozen without limbs that we are trying to keep from bleeding to death, not to mention the scores of cuts and bruises. Oh, and don't forget the three over there have lost it, because they are military vets with PTSD. Where the hell are the ambulances? How about you?"

"Not much better up there, worse really. There aren't too many alive, and those who are…well, they're just barely hanging on." Angelica said as she gathered a few strips of sheet and a couple of blankets. "I'm having the guys helping me bring those who can be moved over here."

Angelica whispered in Shelby's ear, trying not to worry those around, "I can't get anyone to respond to my 9-1-1 calls; it's busy."

"I know. I've tried, too. I haven't had time to call Cody," Shelby explained as she wrapped up another man's arm.

Angelica whispered again, "I called him. He's doing what he can, but Shelby, this isn't an isolated incident. I don't want to frighten these people or you, but our country is under attack."

Shelby stopped what she was doing. "Shield Sheik?"

"It looks like it."

"How bad?"

"It's happening in every state, in just about every major city, and a lot of the smaller towns have been hit, too."

Shelby reached for her phone. "I've got to call Jack."

"I've already call Rex. Everyone is fine. They don't have electricity right now, but your dad is working on that with his generators. A lot of the phone service is out, but they couldn't take out the satellites, and they couldn't get to all of the communication hubs. We lucked out on that one because we both have phone service, and we can talk to Cody," Angelica explained hoping to calm Shelby's anxiety.

Shelby looked around at the people on the ground. "What about them, Angelica? Is help coming for them?"

Angelica hugged her friend. "I don't know; we have to wait and see."

Shelby's face turned pale.

"Don't worry, Shelby, our country is strong, our people are strong, we'll endure. This is America."

194

The End

About the Author

Other Books in the Mother Trucker Book Series

Mother Trucker

Trucktress

Outlaws

Jumpers

Terror West